MAYHEM AT THE HAMPTON CLASSIC

MAYHEM AT THE HAMPTON CLASSIC

A Gabriel Fortuna Hamptons Adventure

GLEN BERKOWITZ

iUniverse, Inc.
New York   Bloomington

MAYHEM AT THE HAMPTON CLASSIC
A Gabriel Fortuna Hamptons Adventure

iUniverse books may be ordered through booksellers or by contacting:

iUniverse
1663 Liberty Drive
Bloomington, IN 47403
www.iuniverse.com
1-800-Authors (1-800-288-4677)

Because of the dynamic nature of the Internet, any Web addresses or links contained in this book may have changed since publication and may no longer be valid. The views expressed in this work are solely those of the author and do not necessarily reflect the views of the publisher, and the publisher hereby disclaims any responsibility for them.

ISBN: 978-1-4502-3714-7 (sc)
ISBN: 978-1-4502-3715-4 (ebk)

Printed in the United States of America

iUniverse rev. date: 06/07/2010

1

There may have been a national recession going on in the summer of 2009, but no one would have known it based on the night life in The Hamptons. Restaurants were packed, roads were crowded, and the lights from thousands of oceanfront mansions still burned brightly into the early morning hours. Most importantly, carloads, busloads and trainloads of pretty women from the city continued to come out every weekend looking for Mr. Right, even if Mr. Right was often only a one night stand. Many of those women could be found at a beach, or a stable or posing at a bar in any one of dozens of trendy Hamptons hot spots that came and went like dandelions on Agawam Park's lawn. That's the way it's always been on The East End and that's the way it was that late August night I pulled into the opulent Village of Easthampton, drove down high-end Newtown Lane and passed the long line of thrill seekers and social climbers outside a place old friend and army buddy, Oliver Dines, had suggested we invest some time. It was a new place in The Hamptons, a new place called, *Tatiana's*.

I passed the cavalcade of luxury retailers lining Main Street, turned into the village's municipal parking lot and trundled down one packed lane after another looking for a spot, finally finding one when two thirty-something guys in goatees flashed out of the night and hopped into a late model Mercedes Benz sedan. Speeding away like white rabbits late for an important date, they came straight at me but managed to veer away at the last moment and missed my vintage Caddy by a couple of inches, leaving me with an adrenaline rush and a muttered promise to give those guys some painful lessons in defensive driving should I ever see them again. After giving some citiot in a Porsche Carrera an evil eye for just thinking about squeezing past me and stealing my spot, I pulled between the yellow lines, left my car parked with its ragtop open to a perfect night sky and started out to meet my friend.

The short walk from the parking lot to the club cooled me down, but seeing *Tatiana's* line of over-excited party people pulsing down the street had me asking myself what the hell I was doing there after a three-month convalescence from the shootout at Saint Andrews. Noting the attendance of a great many attractive and presumably sexually active women, I quickly remembered my reasons and made my way up the block to try my luck with the bouncer at the head of the line, the one who looked like a refrigerator just delivered from a Gulag.

He had a bald head with enough craters in it to suggest an intimate acquaintance with a ball-peen hammer, a forehead that had to have been kissed by a sturdy two-by-four and a couple of cauliflower ears, the right one set over the tattooed red K inked into his short and brutish neck. I gave the respect someone who looked like this deserves and said, "Excuse me, Mr. Bouncer, but I recently got out of the hospital after being shot by a policeman who is now doing a life sentence for murdering three people. This is my first night out in a while and I'd like to spend some quality time with some quality women but I don't feel like waiting on line for two hours. How's about cutting me some slack and letting me in now?"

The guy looked at me like I was from another planet and said through an unfamiliar accent, using words of which I was quite familiar, "Get the fuck to the end of the line before I kick your ass. You ain't nobody and nobody gets in unless I say so."

Being my first night out in a while, I tried my best to avoid trouble and said, "Listen, Boris, you used a double negative. You ain't nobody means I am somebody, and if I am somebody, by your definition, I shouldn't have to wait on line. So, if you don't mind, why don't you just move your ass and let me in. All I want is a drink and a little time near some people who are softer and prettier than me." Flashing a winning smile and the fifty I was palming in my left hand, I added in my most friendly manner, "Come on, Boris. What do you say?"

Boris' fists balled into large knots, his carotid artery and jugular vein popped in monumental vascularity and the spark in his eyes told me he was gearing up to make a move. I tightened my core to meet his charge but his eyes flashed on something over my left shoulder, causing him to relax his fists, step back, and pull aside the maroon velvet rope that blocked my way. Glad that he was seeing things my way, I took a step towards the entrance and said, "Thanks, Boris," but before I took a second, the foreign hulk reached out and put his hand aggressively on my shoulder.

Big Mistake!

Instinct took over and I whirled and grabbed the bouncer at the wrist with my left hand, while with my right, I took hold of and bent back his three middle fingers, producing the audible *CRACKLE and POP!* that generally connotes dislocation. Keeping a firm grip, I was trying to figure out what to do with the guy when I felt a poke at my shoulder and turned my head to find a tall, thin and tan man, decked out in what anyone could tell were some very expensive threads. He wore his hair slicked back, Gordon Gecko style, sported a wide and toothy grin that screamed, *laminates!*, and had the same small red K tattooed on the right side of his neck as Boris had. There was an aura of smugness about the guy, and although I couldn't place him, there was something about him that was familiar and greasy. When he said, "Hi, Gabe. It's been a long time," I recognized the voice immediately.

"Holy shit, it's Danny Fisher."

My old acquaintance nodded toward the bouncer and said, "I'd appreciate it if you'd give Sergei back his fingers and let him off the floor. It might give people the wrong impression if our bouncers look incapable of handling the paying public."

Turning my head to check out the wobbling doorman, I asked Fisher, "You know this guy?"

"Sure I do. Sergei works for me and *Tatiana's* is my place. If you let go of him, I'll escort you inside and buy you a drink."

I released the bouncer's hand and offered mine to help him from the floor but he shrugged me off with an angry glare. Rising on his own, he rubbed his already swollen wrist, yanked out his disjointed fingers and threw me a cold warning stare but I couldn't have cared less. As far as I was concerned I'd kept the Hamptons' food chain intact, and satisfied, turned to Danny Fisher and said, "Shall we?"

Inside, *Tatiana's* proved to be what I expected: beautiful people milling about, looking for someone they might take home or from whom they could cop, loud music blaring from invisible speakers, sending drunks and druggies out to the already full dance floor where they might sweat out whatever was in their systems, a gigantic and crowded bar of mostly white, well-dressed and sweet-smelling customers waving hundred dollar bills as attention getting devices for booze and sexual partners, and the usual large round tables hugging the rear walls, where the big spenders sat in the shadows, reveling in their money and their honeys.

Fisher slithered through the pulsing throng with ease as I zigzagged my way left and right with frenzied clubbers bouncing off me like pinballs from a flipper. Coming to a halt at the end of the long bar at the rear of the place, he removed a key from his pocket, opened a thick wood-paneled door and we entered a large, well-appointed, sound-proofed room of soft fern walls and cream-colored carpeting. A well-stocked mirrored bar, a large mahogany desk and the rear of two dark brown leather chairs faced the entry. Between the leather chairs was a small glass cocktail table holding a pitcher of water, two glasses, two ashtrays and an unopened pack of Camels, unfiltered. The right side wall held the largest Sony plasma I'd ever seen, built-in speakers on either side, and a long four-cushioned couch of dark green velvet sat opposite the TV, three brown leather ottomans placed in front of that. Beyond the couch was a large open closet, its rear wall holding a tall gray wall safe, and fastened to the ceiling, in the left corner of the room, was a small camera I assumed recorded everything that went down in the place. Seeing it pointing directly at me, I smiled into its lens and waved hello.

Fisher walked past me and I recognized that same punky walk as when we were kids living in Queens. I grew uncomfortable at the mere sight of it, and it occurred to me that someone like Danny Fisher was not the kind of person with whom I wanted to spend this evening, or any evening, but I told myself that a lot of time had passed since I'd last seen the guy and that he'd stopped me from wiping the floor with his bouncer when he could have chosen to just stand by and watch, so I did something I rarely did with anyone; I gave him a second chance.

Reaching the wet bar behind the desk, my host shook his head with amusement and said, "Of all the places in the world to run into Gabriel Fortuna, my old buddy from Queens. What'll it be, Gabey-boy?"

I didn't like that Gabey-boy stuff and thought that after nearly twenty years of not seeing someone he was behaving in a manner that was a little too friendly. I gave him a never before heard of third chance and answered, "Jack Daniels on the rocks would be nice."

Fisher dropped a couple of cubes into a short glass, filled it with Jack Daniels and through a cocky smile, said, "You must be asking yourself, 'How did Danny Fisher manage to get all this'? Well, let me tell you, nobody gets this by just working hard. I've been lucky, made some money and gotten involved in some good things with the right people." Walking over to me and handing me my drink, he added, "I've kept my ears open and have heard some things about you, too. Too bad about all that trouble you had on the force a few years back. If we'd kept in touch, I might have been able to help you out with some of that. A few months ago, I read about all that crazy shit you had with the town police and some of the locals and the shootouts at The Castle and Saint Andrews Church." Laughing lightly, he finished, "You always did have a nose for trouble, Gabey-boy."

Strike Four!

Looking my host hard in his eyes, I said, "Okay, Fisher, that's enough of the Gabey-boy stuff. You don't know me well enough to call me Mr. Fortuna, let alone Gabey-boy, and another thing, while you were fixing my drink I started thinking back to the old neighborhood and some of my recollections of you are not of the fond type. You were in your early teens when you got busted for stealing cars, arrested for selling pot, beat up on kids who weren't tough enough to stand up to you and accused of trying to do some very bad things to Madeline Finkelstein when she was in the seventh grade." Chuckling at that memory, I added, "As I recall, the police were not summoned for that one because the next day Madeline came down to the schoolyard with her mother and the kid didn't need any help from anyone to kick your ass for all those cheap feels you thought were coming your way."

His wise-guy grin gone, Fisher responded, "You better watch your mouth, Fortuna. You were a tough guy when we were hanging around the schoolyard and I can tell from the way you handled Sergei you're still a tough guy, but I know plenty of tough guys. I thought we could have had a few laughs and that maybe I could have offered you a job, but I must have been crazy because now I remember you, too. You were always just a hardhead with a chip on his shoulder. Well, things have changed and I want you out of my place, now."

I wasn't looking for trouble; I was looking for Oliver and for women and not necessarily in that order, so after throwing Fisher a cold stare that told him my leaving his office was my decision and had nothing to do with what he wanted, I turned to go, but I'd taken only a couple of steps towards the door when it glided open from the outside, bringing with it the roar of the crowd, the blaring music of a Hip-Hop sound track, and a statuesque blonde I'd never before seen, except maybe in my dreams. She was quietly followed by a slight Asian woman dressed in black, who in the presence of the big blonde was nearly invisible. The diminutive one closed the door behind them and I stood still, admiring the bodacious blonde babe in silent appreciation.

In shimmering silver high heels and a tight, low-cut, silver-sequined minidress showing off every voluptuous curve of her body, she was six feet of drop-dead disco dynamite and immediately all I wanted was to become her fuse. She was in incredible physical condition: tanned long legs, muscular and chiseled at the knee where her quads formed perfect teardrops, lean and defined arms, especially in the rear where her triceps cut that cute little stirrup that spoke of hours in the gym, and a broad chest and full powerful shoulders, holding up a pair of the most magnificent and full breasts I'd ever seen. Her face was tanned to perfection, providing a perfect canvas for her pouty pink lips, pearly white teeth, high sculpted cheekbones, frosted blonde hair and icy cold big blue eyes. Not being into tattoos, the only imperfection on her body was the small red K, exactly like the ones Fisher and Sergei wore, inked into the right side of her neck, just below her ear and nearly hidden behind a dropped diamond earring.

She carried a little white dog in her arms. All perfumed fluff in a pink collar imbedded with a series of seven glimmering colorless stones, the tiny creature seemed to take an almost instant dislike to me, bared its teeth and cuddled deeply into her mistress' ample cleavage, an obvious attempt at showing me who was top dog with Blondie.

Stroking her pet with smooth and unusually long fingers, the bombshell asked Fisher through a husky voice and a cold accent that sounded exactly like Sergei's, "Is this man a friend of yours, Danny?"

Fisher took on a frightened expression, making him look like a little kid who'd just been caught by his mother doing something he'd been warned not to, but he collected himself quickly, smirked and answered, "Not quite. In fact, he was just about to leave. Weren't you, Gabey-boy?"

I'd warned him about the Gabey-boy stuff and one look at me turning towards him was all it took for his eyes to register the mistake he'd made. Taking two rapid steps to his desk, Fisher reached for a button beside the top drawer and pressed it.

I got to him a split second later, grabbed him by the wrist and said, "Now, why did you have to do that? All that means is that someone is probably going to get hurt." Squeezing his wrist tightly, I watched his eyes squint from pain, and then placing my free hand over his face, pushed him into his plush leather chair, pointed a stiff middle finger at him, and warned, "You stay there."

A moment later the door burst open and in stormed Sergei followed by some other refrigerator in a black muscle shirt. Remembering his disjointed fingers, the bouncer from the front door stopped in his tracks and looked a little concerned at seeing me again so soon, but the other guy, about six-foot four and three hundred pounds of Olympic wrestler from the super-heavyweight division of Iran, came at me like a dingo eyeing sirloin. I put everything I had into the short crisp punch I planted between his eyes, stamped a GF into his forehead with my gold-domed initial ring, and even though the guy was huge and had a skull made of concrete, he went down like a shot. Turning my attention to Sergei, who'd made the intelligent choice of remaining beside the door, I adjusted my ring and said, "I could just leave. This doesn't have to happen to you."

To my surprise, Fisher showed some personal growth and called from his chair, "Sergei, let him go! He isn't worth the trouble."

I turned, thanked my old neighborhood chum with a smile and an upraised middle finger, and after nodding a farewell to Sergei, gave the blonde bombshell a last serious top to bottom once over before leaving the office to the snarls and barks of that little white dog and the hard cold eyes of the lithe Asian woman.

Feeling a little deflated that the big blonde hadn't given me even the slightest of come-ons, I meandered through the throng at *Tatiana's* looking for Oliver Dines and wondering if nearing forty was making me a little too old for these kinds of places. Then, seated at the bar, a sexy little redhead with more curves than the Pacific Highway gave me a wink and a nod that put my fears to rest. I pushed Fisher, the big blonde, Oliver and that little white dog out of my head and thought that things were finally looking up. Just goes to show how wrong a person can be.

2

I was in my gym finishing my last set of three hundred pound bench presses on the Universal when I heard the sound of crushed gravel coming from my driveway. Throwing a towel over a pumped deltoid (I'd done a little rehab work on my shoulders that morning, too), I glided over to the front door, and not being in the habit of asking, 'Who is it?', opened it and found the big blonde from *Tatiana's* standing on my porch.

It's always nice to have a beautiful woman ring your doorbell, nicer if you haven't been with any woman in three months and absolutely nicest when it's unexpected, she's spectacular and sporting an outfit that just about screams, 'Take me!', but I didn't have too much time to enjoy my good fortune because a sharp pain suddenly shocked me at my ankle. Looking down, I saw the reason for my sudden discomfort; her little white dog was between my legs, working on me like I was a long lost Milk Bone.

Before I could shake it off and boot it from the porch, the big blonde swooped down, picked up her little pet, and kissing it on top of its puffy dome, purred without conviction in that same husky voice I'd heard at *Tatiana's*, "America. Bad girl." Turning to me, she smiled unconvincingly and added, "America doesn't like you."

I replied, "She's probably just afraid of some stiff competition."

Raising a sculpted eyebrow, my visitor asked, "Well, Gabriel, are you going to let us in?"

I stepped to the side, openly admired her luscious curves and answered, "Sure, come on in."

She glided past me, examined my simple but comfortable bachelor home and sat in the brown leather chair situated perpendicular to the fire place. Crossing her long sun-tanned legs, she settled her fawning pooch onto her lap and gazed out my picture window onto Noyac Bay.

I stood beside the small leather loveseat on the other side of the glass and chrome cocktail table that separated us. It was hard to take my eyes off my guest's alluring combination of long, long legs and firm full breasts, but after a few seconds of taking in her goods, I raised my vision to her icy cold blue eyes, felt their chill and asked, "Would you like something to drink, Ms....?"

"I will tell you my name at another time. And yes, I would love a little vodka and orange juice."

"Okay, Madame Mysterious, we'll play it your way as far as your name is concerned, but in terms of beverage, I was thinking more like an iced tea or an orange juice or a power shake. Sorry about the vodka, but I don't open the liquor cabinet until sundown."

The big blonde smiled and purred, "Alright, Gabriel, I will have only the orange juice." Kissing her pet's little black button of a nose, she added, "Perhaps you can prepare a bowl of water for America, as well? She must be thirsty."

After placing a bowl of cool water for the dog under the sink, I poured about five inches of orange juice into an eight ounce glass and dropped in two ice cubes. Handing it to Blondie, I made sure our fingertips touched, just to see if I would get that electricity I sometimes got when meeting someone new and beautiful, and was momentarily disheartened to discover I felt nothing except cold.

Placing her drink on my glass table without bothering to ask for a coaster, the lady removed one of those tiny airline bottles of vodka from her small silver clutch and poured its contents into the tumbler. Stirring provocatively with her middle finger, she lifted the glass towards me in a salute and took a refreshing sip.

I asked, "How do you know my name?"

"Danny Fisher told me who you were the other night at *Tatiana's*."

"What else did he tell you?"

"That you were, now these are his words, 'a son-of-a-bitch rat bastard who needs to get the shit kicked out of him once and for all'."

Smiling at the dubious compliment, I asked, "And what do you think?"

"I think that any man who can put fear into Danny and Sergei so badly as you is a man I want to know."

My guest's cellphone rang and she removed it from her bag in a leisurely fashion. With a cold and commanding voice, she said, "Yes, speak," and then looking at the diamond and gold watch adorning her wrist, added something in what I assumed was Russian, ending the call.

There came a sudden growl and a fresh bite at my ankle and I looked down to find her little white dog working on me again. Behind her wet white beard, she was gnawing away at my heel, making it abundantly clear that its thirst had been slaked and that it just didn't like me. I felt the same way towards it and might have knocked the pesty pup upside the head with my initial ring if Blondie hadn't quickly crossed the room, leaned over and picked it up.

Caressing her dog in a way that made me nervous and envious at the same time, she tossed me a cool smile and asked, "What were you and Danny speaking of at *Tatiana's* the other night?"

"Nothing much, old times mostly, and not much of that. Why?"

"Are you sure you aren't keeping something from me, Gabriel?"

I answered confidently, "Of course I'm keeping something from you, but we've only just met and I don't even know your name. I figured I would show you all you need to know some time during our first date, after a good meal and the requisite number of drinks."

Weighing my words, her disinterested reply was, "I have to leave but I would like to meet you again. Some time, perhaps, when we can discuss things that are important to me and lucrative for you."

I didn't want any part of her cash, having enough of that from my cop's pension, my personal savings and a few good land investments I'd made out here through Oliver's office, but my curiosity had been aroused, if not yet other things, and I said, "Let's not talk about money. We're just getting to know one another. Hey, I've got an idea. Why don't you give me your number and I'll give you a call?"

She answered much too quickly, "It would be better if I call you. Have you a card?"

Opening a sidetable drawer, I took out a card that read:

Gabriel Fortuna

Man of Action

631-555-7777

She took it and said, "You will be hearing from me, Gabriel."

I replied, "You still haven't told me your name. If I'm not home and you leave a message, how can I be sure it was you? After all, I get lots of calls from women with sexy foreign accents."

"Alright, Gabriel," she answered through a distorted smile. "I think the time for revealing my name is upon us. I am Ileana. Ileana Kutchakokov."

Taking a step back, I responded, "You're kidding, right?"

"Gabriel, should I allow you to get to know me, you will learn I never, how you say, kid."

With that, the blonde bombshell turned and left my house. I watched her sashay her spectacular ass to the powder blue Bentley convertible, where the lithe Asian woman I'd seen at *Tatiana's* stood at attention with the side passenger door open and waiting. Silently taking the dog from Ms. Kutchakokov, the diminutive chauffeur placed the animal in the back seat of the car and closed the door after her boss was seated. Walking around the rear of the Bentley, she threw me a sideways glance, locking our eyes for a very uncomfortable moment before she got behind the wheel, pulled out of my driveway and drove down Noyac Road.

Above the rear diplomatic license plate bearing the tag, DPL-IK, was that little white dog, America, standing on her hind legs in the back seat staring at me. Hamptons sunlight reflected brightly from the seven stones on her collar, creating something of a halo around her neck, and although I don't know much about canines, I could have sworn she was laughing at me.

Returning to my great room, as if the stinging in my ankle wasn't enough of a reminder, I was left another example of how that dog felt about me. Lying under the glass cocktail table, the little white bitch had left a perfectly spherical brown turd as her token of good-bye. Wrapping it in a tissue and throwing it into the toilet, it never occurred to me that America might actually have liked me and was leaving me a friendly message:

'*Fortuna! You don't need this shit! Stay The Fuck Away*'!

3

A couple of days later, I found myself sitting on the Sag Harbor Wharf catching early afternoon rays and eating lunch at B. Smith's, a scenic restaurant on the waterfront popular with tourists and locals alike. I had just finished a perfect omelet of four egg whites, peppers, mushrooms, and ham, when the curvaceous redhead I'd met at *Tatiana's* pulled out a chair at my small table and sat across from me.

With her hands folded rigidly in front of her, she eyed me with a deadly serious expression and I expected at any moment to hear the usual litany from a woman I'd spent some time with about not calling, feeling used and the rest of that guilt-tripping crap, when it suddenly occurred to me that nothing had gone down between us. As I recalled, we'd sat for a while at the bar, had a couple of drinks and shared a few good laughs. She told me her name was Samantha, and besides being really good looking, she was a lot of fun. I suggested we leave *Tatiana's* and go somewhere quiet where we could get to know one another better but she disregarded my suggestion, told me to slow down when I placed my hand on her thigh where her short skirt had ridden up to reveal some extremely superior leg and asked how I knew Danny Fisher. I explained that we were merely casual acquaintances from a wayward youth, and after a few more minutes of banter about my life in The Hamptons, she seemed to lose all interest in me and left me alone with nothing but the tab.

I never liked being used for free drinks, but remembering the feeling of my hand on that creamy thigh and the spark its touch brought, I decided to behave in a warm and welcoming fashion and said through a most charming smile, "Samantha the Pantha, nice to see you again."

My post-luncheon guest did not return my friendly attitude, recoiled at my amateurish attempt at rhyme and replied in a most businesslike and unappealing manner, "Good afternoon, Mr. Fortuna. There are some things we need to talk about."

It wasn't hard to see that Samantha was even better looking in the light of day than she'd been in the shadows of *Tatiana's*. Her short red hair, cut in a fashion that perfectly framed her pretty heart-shaped face, took on a fiery aspect in the bright sunlight, her lightly tanned skin held just the perfect amount of youthful summer freckles, and her ringless manicured hands were longer fingered than I remembered, always an admirable trait in a woman. Wearing tight blue designer jeans and a white cotton blouse with the three top buttons open to reveal the beginning of a deep cleavage and the trimmings of a very feminine and sexy lace bra, she was a total knockout, a perfect way to end a good meal and a reminder of what I had been missing for three months and counting.

Thinking she may like a tougher approach, I replied with just the right amount of manly snap, "Good, because there are some things I want to talk about with you, too, namely, what the hell happened the other night? I thought we were having a good time. Next thing I know, you get up and leave. And by the way, I don't remember telling you my last name. Where's this Mr. Fortuna stuff coming from?"

Flashing a badge in my face, she answered, "Okay, Mr. Fortuna, have it your way. I'm Agent Samantha Goodbody from Homeland Security. There are some questions I need to ask about people with whom you've recently been in contact. The faster you answer my questions, the faster this interview will be over and the faster you can leave."

I was stunned to hear that the lovely lady sitting opposite me was a cop but then remembered that times had changed and that I'd known more than my share of good-looking female police officers when I worked for New York City. My problem with Samantha was not that she was a cop; it was that she was a Federal cop. I didn't have any great fondness for that branch of our national security, having learned the hard way that its offices were often filled by a bunch of pencil-pushing assholes who usually found a way to screw things up. Shooting the pretty Fed a long hard stare, I hoped I would find something that would make her different from all the others I'd known and I did; she was really, really that good-looking.

Placing her attractiveness before her job description, I responded easily, "What makes you think I want to leave? We had a good time the other night and you can't make me believe it was all about your job."

"It was all about my job, Mr. Fortuna. I saw you leave Danny Fisher's office and needed to speak with you to find out what you were doing there. You were easy to corral. All I needed was to nod in your direction and raise my skirt an inch or two."

I responded coolly, "So, let me get this straight. What you're telling me is, if I hadn't been in Fisher's office you never would have come on to me?"

"That's right."

"I don't believe you. And let me tell you something else, Agent Goodbody. You need some help with measurements because that skirt of yours ran up your leg a good six inches."

Goodbody replied, "Fortuna, when it comes to my leg, you couldn't handle six inches."

I leaned across the table, brought my nose a mere half-inch from hers and responded, "Don't worry about me Agent Goodbody. I think the real question is, how well do you handle six?"

Game on!

The agent fell back in her chair, and looking at something or somebody behind me, said, "I guess you were right. There is something wrong with this guy. He's all yours."

I didn't need to turn around to see to whom she was speaking because a voice brought back bad memories and an instant itch at the gunshot wounds in my hip and shoulder.

"Some things never change, do they Fortuna? You're still the hound you were the last time I saw you in spite of everything that happened. What are we going to do with guys like you? You're a dying breed but you don't know it. One day your bones will be in a museum; *Homo Penis Erectus,* it will say on the plaque beneath your exhibit. Little kids will point at it and innocently ask, 'What's that'?, and their moms and dads will say, 'Don't look at it, son. You'll go blind'."

"Just so long as it says 'erectus'," was my terse reply.

"Big mouth," muttered the voice.

Turning to my unwanted intruder, I said, "Get this straight for the last time, Bedwetter; I'm a guy who knows who he is and I'm proud of it. I'm not ashamed to be a man, I'm not afraid to go after what I want and I don't need a stinking badge to help me feel like I've got some power. I treat everyone the way they deserve to be treated and beautiful women who are responsive to my particular charms make my world go round. I'm honest enough to recognize that and I behave in the way my nature calls. I don't waste time on internet porno like ninety percent of the men you hang with probably do, and I don't ogle at mens' magazines or the skanky women who pass as movie stars that dudes like you think are sexy. I go for the real things in life, things with a pulse and things with desire. If you can't handle that, well that's TFB for you. And if Agent Goodbody doesn't want to spend some time with me, that's her loss. Now, let's get this over. What brings you to The Hamptons? I thought I was done with you after The Al Shareef Affair."

Ledbetter barked, "Knock it off, Fortuna," and coming around my shoulder, pulled out the third chair of my little round table, sat stiffly and added through the familiar tight scowl to which I'd sadly become accustomed, "We've got to have a little talk and we're going to have it now."

Agent Ralph Ledbetter was dressed in the same kind of dark gray suit he was wearing the last time I saw him, which was when he was catching a bullet from Gasper at the Al Shareef Castle. His hair was still crew cut short, his shoes were the same black wingtips, and his sunglasses were still that dated Aviator style from the Sixties. About the only change I could see in the guy was that his sidekick was a beautiful woman instead of an uptight Fed from The FBI.

Sitting up straighter in my chair, I coldly eyed my would-be inquisitor and responded calmly, "We're not talking about anything unless I say so, or have you forgotten I don't take orders from you?"

Agent Goodbody sighed at my resolve, looked me hard in the eyes and said, "Ralph, you were right. This guy is a definite asshole."

My chances of getting anywhere with the sexy Agent Goodbody seemed to be diminishing with every passing moment, so I smiled brightly for her and said, "Alright, Ledbetter. You came up big for me when things got tight and I owe you for that. What can I do for you?"

"As much as I hate to say this, Fortuna, we could use your help."

"You're kidding. You want my help? You must be desperate."

"No, Fortuna, I'm not kidding, but we very well may be desperate. Turns out, your old friend, Danny Fisher, was mixed up with a very dangerous group of thugs from Russia belonging to an organization called *TRASH*, an acronym for Terrorism, Revenge, Anarchy, Subversion and Humiliation. They are murderers, kidnappers, drug-runners, pimps and thieves in their home country and are guilty of terrorist activity inside and outside of it. Sometimes they work for their government, disposing of whomever the powers that be want gone, and sometimes as independent contractors, doing heinous jobs for bad people strictly for cash, but there is no doubt that someone with governmental power in their home country shields them from our scrutiny and they often carry diplomatic immunity. Now they're in The Hamptons. Their leader, a monster from the Moscow slums named Ilya Kutchakokov and his twin sister, Ileana, have moved into a Southampton estate off Gin Lane. Our sources have informed us this group has recently met with certain North Korean higher-ups as well as some Fundamentalist maniacs but our sources have ceased to exist. We haven't heard a thing from them in weeks and we suspect the worst. Fortuna, we need to know what The Kutchakokovs are up to."

I chuckled at the implausibility of what the Fed told me and said, "You're telling me the Russian Mafia is expanding to The Hamptons?"

"You can call them Mafia if you want. I just call them dangers to America."

Shaking my head, I asked, "Why? Why would the Russian mob come here? This is a resort community. The only time there's big money in The Hamptons is during the summer season and most of that money is looking for a great restaurant, an oceanfront rental or a prime tee time."

Through a tight grimace telling me I might have caused his acid reflux to act up, he responded, "We don't know why they're here but the fact is they are here. Finding the reason is why we need you."

"Why me? Haven't you got anyone else to sacrifice? For all you know, the Russians are here to enjoy the end of a warm Hamptons' summer instead of a frigid September in Siberia. I advise you do the same. As for me, I'm a private citizen and intend to keep it that way."

Agent Goodbody listed in my direction, revealed an impressive cleavage and said seductively, "I thought more of you, Gabriel. I thought you were the kind of man who did things for his country."

Having had this particular, 'I-thought-more-of-you', ruse applied to me a few thousand times before, I ogled her delectable breasts for a few glorious seconds before raising my eyes to hers and replied easily, "Listen, Goodbody, I've done more for my country than you'll probably ever do and I have the scars to prove it. One day, if you're a good girl, I may show them to you. I think you'll find some of them very impressive."

Her icy demeanor returning, she coolly replied, "Don't hold your breath."

I smiled at her tough response, but something the top cop said earlier was eating at me, so turning my attention to Ledbetter, I said, "Before, when you were talking about Danny Fisher, you said he was my old friend. What did you mean, 'was'?"

"Oh, did I forget to tell you? Danny Fisher's body washed up on the beach at Montauk this morning. He was neatly wrapped in a large plastic bag… all six pieces of him."

Gulping down some bile that had climbed its way into my throat, I stood and threw a twenty and a ten onto the table and said, "Don't take that Bedwetter; it's for, Darlene, the waitress." Turning to the foxy Fed, I added, "And as for you, Agent Goodbody, if you'd like to discuss my patriotism, your friend over here has my address and phone number. Have a nice day. The weather in The Hamptons is great this time of year. And now, good-bye."

I left the two Feds at the table, satisfied that I'd made it clear I wasn't about to do their work for them, but if Ledbetter had wanted to plant a seed saying I was somehow responsible for Danny Fisher's death, he had been successful. What he didn't know was that I could live with that. Fisher had always been a bad guy and as far as I was concerned he'd finally reaped what he'd sown over his short and sour lifetime, but then there was that visit from Ileana Kutchakokov to think about. She'd made it clear when she visited me that it wasn't necessarily about sex, so what the hell was her story? Formulating one idea after another about what might be going on, I couldn't directly connect the Russian Mafia or *TRASH* with anything or anybody I knew in The Hamptons, but what I did know was that if there was big trouble about to go down on The East End, it was probably about one thing, the same thing it was almost always about, and that was property.

Crossing the street for *Choppin' Charlie's,* where January Pulaski, my barber ever since that day ten years ago when I first saw her in long blonde pigtails and a short barber's skirt working her father's shop, I hoped that Agent Samantha Goodbody was as hardheaded as me and wouldn't take no for an answer. If that was true, and I had a pretty good feeling it was, I knew I'd be hearing from her within a couple of days. My only other concern was wondering what the two guys in goatees from the Easthampton parking lot were doing trailing me. I spotted them across the way, standing in front of The Sag Harbor Launderette tugging hard on their cigarettes, but not wanting to be late for my appointment, I decided I would give them a chance to explain their careless driving behavior right after my haircut and made my way into the shop.

January had put a few pounds in all the right places since I'd last seen her, and her bright smile, coupled with the rather luxurious sweep of her barber's cloth across her full body when I entered her establishment, proved very enticing. Hoping that the guys following me would wait patiently if my haircut ran a little longer than usual, I sat in the chair and said charmingly, "Good afternoon, January. I'll have the usual, please."

4

I gave January a fifty and walked out of her place with a smile on my face and one of her Dad's, *Hamptons Golf,* board games under my arm. Hitting the sidewalk, I was disappointed that my two friends across the street had disappeared, but turning the corner to the town parking lot, my disappointment was assuaged because there were the two amigos from Siberia leaning against my car, smoking fresh cigarettes.

At my approach, they threw their butts onto the gravel, ground them down with their thick black military shoes and went on to display a high degree of thug professionalism by separating themselves far enough so that they could easily squeeze me between their brutish hulks. Each was about six feet and carried around two hundred pounds and I noted the shapes of their heads were unusually square, something like the Frankenstein monster's, only without the bolts running through their necks. What was on their necks, I noticed, was that little red K I'd been seeing a bit too much of lately.

Reaching an arm's distance from them, I pointed at The Caddy and said, "I hope you guys haven't messed up the paint by leaning against the finish. You both look young and strong. Why don't you use your legs?"

They gave each other a quizzical look but remained where they were, so I lackadaisically threw the board game into the backseat of the open car, and after a sarcastic smile at first one and then the other, barked, "What the hell is wrong with you guys!!? Get your asses off my car!!"

The two goons jumped away from The Caddy, either because they were used to taking harsh orders and reacting quickly or because they were totally surprised at my intrepid response, but these guys were pros and recovered quickly. The battle shine in their eyes told me they were prepared for anything, except maybe me, and the one on my right took a quick step towards me. The other grabbed his shoulder fast, stopping his partner before we could become intimate, and after shaking his head, 'No', the goon I assumed was in charge, turned to me and said, "Mr. Fortuna, we would like for you to come with us."

I pointed my finger from one to the other and said, "Say, don't I know you guys from somewhere?"

The one who had taken the step at me showed his impatience and barked, "Just do as we say!"

I laughed lightly and said, "Hey, now I remember. I saw you guys in the parking lot in Easthampton a few days ago. You pulled out of a spot without looking and just missed hitting me. You know, we have rules of the road out here in The Hamptons. You guys should familiarize yourselves with them if you intend to stay. Rule Number One says, anyone who comes close to hitting my car because of extreme carelessness gets to have the shit kicked out of him."

The thug on the right snorted at my recitation of Rule Number One and came at me again but this time his partner did not stop him. Extending his arm to collar me, he said, "Enough of this! You come with us."

Road Rule Number One!

I grabbed the Ruskie's arm at the wrist and twisted it three times until I felt and heard a sharp snap. My Russian friend yelled in the universal language of pain, and having only about a split second to drop him before his partner got into the act, I took full advantage of the time allotted and landed a tight hard fist into his exposed armpit, dropping him to the floor.

The other was on me before I got my fist fully out of his partners pit, and striking me with his fist above my left eye, I reeled backwards a few steps before falling squarely onto my butt. Shaking the cobwebs from my head, I saw my adversary go to his back pants pocket to pull something from it. With a flick of his hand a blade appeared and I watched the glint of sunlight play off the sharp metal of an open switchblade knife. He came at me quickly and I dizzily jumped to my feet but was a split second late at defending myself. His knife cut through the air and slashed at my right arm, slicing through the fabric of one of my favorite shirts but miraculously missing my skin.

Circling the knife ominously in front of him like some punk from Hell's Kitchen, he said, "You should not hit Ivan. We want only you come with us. We don't want hurt you."

I replied, "Fuck you, Raskolnikov. I go where I want when I want." Taking a look at my sleeve, I added, "And you just tore one of my favorite shirts. You now owe me two hundred bucks. You can pay me in cash or I can take it out of your hide, but you know what, I think there's room for both."

Through a vicious and twisted smile, my attacker said, "I change mind. I think you need pain. Maybe I do hurt you."

Bracing myself for his attack, a black stick suddenly flashed through the air and cracked the Russian explosively across the back of his head. His eyes spun crazily in their sockets, he dropped his knife, and moments later he followed it and lay splayed out on the ground in an Eastern European heap of out cold.

Agent Samantha Goodbody stood over her victim with a small suitcase at her side and a disintegrated riot stick in her hand. She dropped what was left of her weapon onto the Russian's body, and glaring at me with her hands on her hips, said, "You're a real tough guy, Fortuna. Real tough. Maybe I should have stayed out of it and let you handle this alone."

Brushing off the seat of my pants, I replied, "Agent Goodbody, how nice it is to see you again." Pointing at the Russian lying at her feet, I added, "As for this guy, I was just building up our young immigrant's confidence in his knife-fighting ability before giving him my personal introduction to a good old American roundhouse. Now you've gone and taken away all our fun."

Goodbody snapped, "Sure, right. Listen, Fortuna, let's move. We should get out of here before these two get up."

I coolly responded, "Who said they're getting up?"

Walking over to the first goon whose arm I'd nearly twisted off, I found him sitting with his back against The Caddy, squinting with pain and trying to return his shoulder to its socket. Raising him to his knees, I looked into his eyes and asked, "Are you okay?"

Hate filled black circles stared back at me and when he opened his mouth to tell me just what he was thinking, I smoked him over his left eye with my hard right fist, imprinting a deep GF just above his brow, and down he went for a good afternoon's nap.

Smiling at Goodbody, I walked over to the guy she'd clubbed and who had somehow managed to rise to his knees. Getting as low as I could for maximum leverage, I said, "Rule Number Two,

Igor…Don't fuck with me," and delivering a solid right uppercut to the guy's chin, sent him reeling head over heels before he came to a dusty halt, flat on his back, and like his fallen comrade, out cold.

"Nice going, Fortuna. Are you finished yet?"

"I think so, Agent Goodbody."

"Great. Then, let's get out of here."

I opened my car door for the fabulous Fed, but closed it behind her unable to shake the feeling I'd forgotten something. Glancing at the two bodies lying on the parking lot gravel, I diagnosed the problem and said, "Hold on a second, Goodbody. This is my town and I don't leave litter on the streets. I've got some cleaning up to do."

In the far corner of the parking lot was the garbage dumpster Hop Sing's Chinese Kitchen kept behind the restaurant. After taking two hundred dollars from each of their wallets to pay for my shirt plus a little interest, I dropped Goon Number One and then Goon Number Two into an oozing sea of oxidizing watercress, bok choy and bamboo shoots and closed the lid over them with a resounding clang.

Hopping into the car, I turned to Agent Goodbody and said cheerfully, "My place or yours."

My federal agent rolled her eyes and sighed, "Yours, you big meat."

Oooh, Baby!

5
___

She didn't talk as we went over the Lance Corporal Jordan Haerter Memorial Bridge and she didn't talk as we drove down The Lost-At-Sea Pike. She remained tight lipped when we passed Foster Memorial Beach and stayed that way when we drove down my driveway and stopped in front of my house on Noyac Road. Unwilling to take any more of the silent treatment, after shutting down the engine, I said enthusiastically, "Alright, Goodbody, what's the problem? What did I do?"

She answered dully, "You didn't do anything, Fortuna. I'm just not interested in anything you have to say. Agent Ledbetter told me to stick close to you and here I am. I don't think there's any reason to be secretive about it any longer, but that doesn't mean I have to speak with you. That's all."

I asked, "Hey, what do you mean by 'secretive' and 'any longer'?" A moment later, I added, "Say, how long have you been watching me?"

"Fortuna, for an ex-detective, you are thick. What do you think, it's an accident we met at lunch today? We've had our eyes on you ever since you left Danny Fisher's office. If Ileana

Kutchakokov and her bodyguard hadn't paid you a visit the other day, we might have packed it in and we wouldn't be having this conversation. For some reason, she's got an interest in you and we want to find out what that interest is."

"Isn't it obvious? She saw me in action in Fisher's office and liked what she saw. Is that too hard for you to understand?"

"My God," came Goodbody's succinct reply, "you are a caveman."

I knew she had a point, but past experience told me I still could have been right about Ileana. Tired of all the verbal jousting, I said simply, "I'm going in. You coming?"

Her tight answer was, "Get used to me, Fortuna. From now on, where you go, I go."

I entered my place and Goodbody followed, suitcase in hand. After an indiscreet look around for whatever Feds look for, she dropped her bag on the floor by the door, sat on the loveseat in my great room and eyed Reggie's picture approvingly.

I asked, "Would you like something to drink?"

"No, thanks, but I am interested in this painting. Who's the artist?"

"That was done by my ex-neighbor, Reggie Rosenberg."

"It's very lovely. I adore her brushwork. The story feels sad, but it's beautiful. Where's the artist now?"

I answered dully, "She's dead. The same goes for her life-partner, Carla. They were my friends and neighbors and I loved them. It's a long story. If you want to know about it, ask your boss. I'm sure he'll be glad to fill you in on all the sordid details."

Agent Goodbody took on a somber expression and rose from her chair. Stopping at the mantel, she examined some of the photographs from my life: pictures of my parents, my brother, David, award ceremonies of me as a cop and the one of me on horseback at The Deep Hollow Ranch out in Montauk, the oldest cattle ranch in the United States.

Laughing at the picture of me in cowboy gear under a huge brimmed sombrero, she finally let down her guard and in the friendly manner I'd heard at *Tatiana's*, asked, "What's this one about, Tex?"

I answered through a soft smile, "I'm no one trick pony, Agent Goodbody. I've been riding horses since I was a kid. First at a couple of stables in Forest Hills with my father and brother, and then out here once in a while with horses belonging to some friends and sometimes out at the ranch. It's a fun thing to do but I don't get out as much as I'd like."

Just when I thought I might actually be getting somewhere with my fine Fed, there came five solid raps, a pause, and then five more solid raps at my door and I said, "Excuse me, Goodbody. Someone I know requests a meeting."

From the waistband at the rear of her jeans, the agent pulled a snub-nosed revolver and simultaneously placed a finger to her lips. Scurrying to the side of the door, she got into position, and moving her head anxiously to signal she was ready, encouraged me to open it.

It took all I had not to laugh at the agent's unnecessary zeal at protecting me, but I went along with Goodbody's game and opened the door slowly and suspiciously.

"Muthafuck!!!! I got it!!!!"

Enrique Santiago, my new neighbor and friend, was standing on my porch in his ill-fitting and odd-looking business suit, smacking an envelope with the embossed seal of the Town of Southampton into his empty hand.

Pointing to the envelope, I asked, "What have you got, Enrique?"

"The contracts, man, the fuckeeng contracts. Shit, the town gave me the landscaping and painting contracts for all the parks and town buildings in fuckeeng Southampton. They told me my bids were so low compared to the others they had no fuckeeng choice but to hire The Latin Zombies as their fuckeeng contractor. These are tough times, Muthafuck, but those other guys are so stubborn, they won't lower their fees a dime. Muthafuck, I am going to be one fuckeeng reech Zombie. Me and my boys have finally made it, man. Thanks for everything, Muthafuck."

Shrugging, I replied, "Thanks for what, Enrique? I didn't do anything."

"Cut the shit, man. You know whats I mean. I knows you helped to gets my feets in the door and that you spokes for me. All I wants is to say thanks and to invites you to my party this Saturday nights to celebrates. Brings a lady if you wants, but I knows Esmie still has it for you if you wants her. I know she's my seester, but hey, do what you want. I owes you, man."

Recalling my short affair with the magnificent Latina and my dire sexual circumstances of more than three months without a woman, I considered his generous offer and answered, "Thank you, Enrique. I'll try to make it."

"Great, Muthafuck. It's at the Polish Hall on Pine Street at eight o'clock. Don't eat nothing before, man. There's going to be so much food, you're going to fuckeeng explode."

"Thanks for the warning, Enrique. I'll see you then."

Closing the door, I smiled at my erstwhile protector, wiped my hand across my brow and said, "Whew, that was a close one."

Goodbody rose from her shooter's crouch, and returning her pistol to her waistband, asked, "Who was that?"

"That, my good lady, is the future of Southampton and possibly the future of The United States. You know the phrase, 'Give me your huddled masses yearning to breathe free'. Well, there was a small but growing part of that huddle. His name is Enrique Santiago. He's the leader of a gang in The Hamptons called The Latin Zombies and now appears to be on the verge of being one of the most successful local capitalists on The East End."

"You're kidding, right?"

I answered, "Not this time," and then my phone rang.

"May I answer that, Agent Goodbody?"

"Of course. You're not in prison, you know. Just don't tell anyone I'm here."

I said, "I'll take it in my room. I still have a private life, even if you and Ledbetter don't want me to."

I went into my bedroom and had an interesting conversation with my caller, telling her I was happy to hear from her and made arrangements to meet at a time and place convenient for both of us. Returning to the great room, I whistled merrily, opened the fridge and rattled things around pretending to look for something.

Agent Goodbody, seated on the sofa with her legs crossed, asked nervously, "Well?"

"Well what?"

"Who was that?"

I replied hotly, "Hold on, Goodbody. I thought I was allowed to have a private life. You can tail me and camp out with me but you can't stop me from seeing other women. I just won't have it."

The Fed hollered, "Listen, Fortuna, I'm responsible for you and I've got to know where you're going and with whom you're spending time. Personally, I couldn't care less about anything or anyone you do, but this is my job."

"Well, when you put it like that, I guess I have to comply. That was Ileana Kutchakokov. She's invited me over to her place for breakfast tomorrow and, now these are her words, 'some recreational activities'. Nine o'clock, I believe was her suggestion."

"What?"

"You heard me."

"Well, you aren't going. It's too dangerous."

Walking up to Agent Goodbody, I placed my lips so close to hers we were practically kissing and said, "Listen, Samantha. Listen and get this straight. Nobody tells me what to do. I'm going to Gin Lane to have breakfast tomorrow morning with Ileana Kutchakokov and there's nothing that you or Ledbetter can do to stop me. I've got a couple of scores to settle over there: one, the murder of a citizen of the United States, and two, the tearing of a damned fine linen shirt, and that's just the way it goes. Also, and this is not a small matter by any means, I'm dying to find out just what Ileana's definition of 'recreation' is."

With her two hands against my chest, Goodbody pushed me away and said, "You're my responsibility, Fortuna. You're not going anywhere without me."

I replied easily, "Don't worry, Goodbody. I always had every intention of bringing you along. I just wanted to see how badly you wanted to be near me. Now, let's you and I take a little rest and later we'll shower and change. I'm taking you out for dinner tonight."

"I don't think that's a good idea. Kutchakokov's people may be watching you."

"Then they can watch me having a good time because I've got weekly Wednesday night dinner reservations over at Romey D's Barbecue Inn on Town Line Road in Sagaponack and I'm not about to give them up because some gang of rich Russians just discovered Hamptons' real estate. Now, are you coming with me or not?"

Samantha answered unenthusiastically, "I have no choice. If you're going, then I guess I'm going."

"Good. Your bedroom is the first one down the hall and to the left. Mine's the door past that. I'm going to relax a while before dinner. Want to join me?"

"Not on your life, Fortuna."

"Fine. Have it your way. See you at 7:30."

Turning away from my bodyguard, I headed towards my bedroom and was halfway down the narrow hallway when I stopped and called, "And Goodbody, when we leave tonight, try and make yourself look a little less like a cop and more like something desirable. It may mean nothing to you, but I live out here and have a reputation to consider."

Samantha Goodbody shook her head and asked, "Fortuna, what is your problem?"

I wanted to tell her I wasn't Picasso and I didn't paint; I wasn't Sinatra and I didn't sing; I wasn't Balanchine and I didn't dance. I wanted to tell her I was Gabriel Fortuna and making love was the way I best expressed myself, but I knew there wasn't much sense in telling her that because some people just don't get it and some people never will. Leaving Agent Goodbody standing perplexed in the center of the great room, I closed my bedroom door behind me and made a phone call.

6

"When I told you to look desirable I didn't mean you had to look like a movie star. Forget about dinner at Romey's. I'm going to Cromer's and getting a bucket of fried chicken, some cole slaw and a six-pack of Diet Coke. You and I are going to spend the rest of the evening at home. I'm not going to share you with anyone."

Samantha's blush faded quickly and in a moment she responded to my compliments in the choppy federal cadence that's the required parlance taught in Fed School, "Take it easy, Fortuna. We all know about your reputation and I guess that if I'm going to be with you I'm going to have to play the part of being one of your bimbos. Just remember, I'm only playing a part. I won't drink with you, I certainly won't kiss you and there is absolutely no chance of me having sex with you. Do I make myself clear?"

I answered stoically, "As clear as a bottle of Peconic Water, Agent Goodbody, but don't worry, lots of people say things they don't mean. I won't hold you to it."

She left the house ahead of me, moving so quickly I felt like a dinghy following in the wake of a sixty-footer leaving Shelter Island. We got into my car, she still playing the role of a hot and bothered federal agent instead of a sexy and alluring woman, and we took the back-roads scenic route to Romey's to avoid traffic. I made my final right, passed the magnificent Wolffers's Estate, its vineyards and corrals glowing in a purple dusk, and finally arrived at Romey D's Barbecue Inn on the northwest corner of Route 27 and Sagg Road.

The gravel parking lot was jammed with late model Mercedes, Infiniti and Lexus SUVs, along with the occasional eight and twelve cylinder sports cars, Bentleys, Aston Martins and Jaguars (not much worrying about the price of gas out here except for the Greenies driving luxury equipped Priuses), but I pulled the big Caddy in, stopped it in the middle of the tight lot and tossed the key to one of the two valet parkers working the place.

"Hey, Cornell, how's it going?" I called.

Slapping me a high-five, Cornell answered, "Pretty good, Mr. Fortuna. Maybe a little too busy if anything, but business is business and I can't complain. Tips sure are good. Diddy dropped me fi' hundred the other day after coming by for just two minutes to say hello to Romey. Then Simmons and The Rev dropped by for some take-out and a hello and tipped me handsomely as well. I wish some of you rich white folk was a bit looser wit the green, but yeah, all in all, things are going fine for Romey and his crew."

"Is he in?"

"It's Wednesday, ain't it? That's the night you come by. Course he's in. He's probly at the bar waiting for you."

"Thanks, Cornell." Nodding at The Caddy, I added, "Take good care of her."

"Don't I always?"

Samantha came around the rear of the car, her knockout

figure and beautiful face provoking Cornell to jump a full step backwards before snapping to attention. With eyes bulging like ripe white mushroom caps, he emitted a mellow wolf's whistle and exclaimed, "Ooooweee! Who's the new fox with you, Mr. Fortuna?"

Pointing nonchalantly over my shoulder, I said, "Who? Her? She's just a federal agent whose job it is to tail me."

"Shit man, I could use some of that tail myself."

"Watch it, Cornell."

"Sorry, Mr. Fortuna. Go on in. I'll take care of The Caddy."

Taking Samantha by the elbow, I directed her out of the gravel parking lot and towards the large wood plank entry door of the log cabin serving as Romey D's Barbecue Inn. Music, noise and a general good-time feeling filled the air along with the aromas of sweet roasted pork, braised beef, corn bread and collard greens, but stopping short at the door, Samantha surprised me with her strength, spun me around, and having gotten my attention, asked, "Did you have to tell the parking valet I was an agent? Does everyone have to know our business?"

"Sorry about that, Agent Goodbody. From now on, if your prefer, I will refer to you as Samantha, my dinner date for the evening. This change of identity allows me to put my arm around your waist, hold your hand and maybe even snatch a kiss or two from you as the night progresses. Otherwise, you will remain Federal Agent Goodbody to everyone we meet. Are we clear on that?"

"Yes, quite clear." After a moment's thought, she added petulantly, "You may continue to call me Agent Goodbody."

"Just as I thought."

Escorting Samantha to the greeter's desk, I introduced her as Federal Agent Samantha Goodbody to a perplexed but curvaceous

Shaquanetta Love, Romey's statuesque and comely cousin from the South Bronx serving as summer hostess. Ms. Love giggled and hugged me joyfully before nodding towards the bar where Romey D sat sipping on a Diet Coke, watching the floor. Our eyes met, his face lit up like a charcoal briquette under a bellows, and he used his big paw to throw a wave telling us to come over. Taking Samantha by her hand, that's what we did.

"Yo, Mo'fo', what's happening?"

Romey and I grabbed hands, shook in a soul-brotherly fashion and I introduced my evening's escort, saying, "Romey, I'd like you to meet Agent Samantha Goodbody. Agent Goodbody, may I introduce Romey D: capitalist, bodyguard, HipHop enthusiast, most excellent friend and seller of the finest barbecue this side of South Carolina."

He said, "Thanks, Mo'fo,'" and turning to Samantha, added through a brilliant grin, "Pleased to meet you, Miss Goodbody. Hopes you don't mind if I refuse to call you by your agent name, but I think a pretty lady like you is allowed some down time, especially in my place, which is about as down as you can get." Positioning his massive arm for Samantha to take, he continued, "May I escort you to your table, Miss Goodbody? You probly need a little private time away from Fortuna, here, just so's you can figure out a good way to get rid of him without causing yo'self too much embarrassment. Best way to do that is to duck out through the ladies room after having some of my delicious pork ribs, black eyed peas, corn bread and gravy. There'll be a cab waiting for you outside should you decide to make a run for it."

I said, "Thank you, Romey, for the kind endorsement."

"Ain't no thing, Mo'fo. Right this way, Miss Goodbody."

Romey guided us to my usual table in the corner of the room, far away from the smoky barbecue pit, most of the dining noise, and the Zydeco Band that was just tuning up off the edge of the small central dance floor. Two complimentary bottles of house red were on our table, along with two glasses and the usual set up of plastic knives and forks. Two rolls of paper toweling on a wooden stand were to the right of each chair, and due to the unusually generous portions of food and barbecue sauce Romey served, they were never enough.

Our host had to leave to check something out in the kitchen, and pulling out my personal Fed's chair, I asked, "Could I interest you in a glass of Romey's house red, Agent Goodbody? Its from an old family recipe and quite good."

She answered flatly, "Fortuna, I told you I wouldn't drink," but then, smiling at the good time surrounding us, added, "but I guess one glass to be sociable couldn't hurt. You may pour, Fortuna, but only one glass. And don't get any ideas."

"Ideas? What ideas? Who said I had any ideas? I think you'll find me completely spontaneous." Holding up a just-arrived-at-our-table steaming basket of dinner rolls, I asked, "Cornbread, Agent Goodbody?"

Samantha looked like she might actually be relaxing a bit and took a piece of the delectable southern staple from the basket, but then her eyes got tight as she squinted at something over my shoulder. I got the feeling that someone was coming up behind me and the sound of a voice that always made me feel like a happy kid proved I was right.

"Hiya, Gabe. How are you doing this fine night?"

Turning in my seat, I smiled broadly at the sight of my old friend, newly appointed Captain of the Southampton Town Police, Melanie Dines, and replied, "I was doing fine until a second ago, and now I'm doing great. Hi, Melanie. How are you?"

I rose and gave my old friend a kiss on her cheek, and then, holding both her hands in mine, took a step back to check her out, just as I'd done ever since she became my first Hamptons' summer girlfriend back in the summer of '85, when we were both just fourteen years old and trying to figure out what our bodies were about.

She was still tall and lovely, filling out a pair of blue jeans and a pullover cotton sweater better than any police captain had a right to. Her long and wavy dark brown hair hung loosely past her shoulders, showing some recent gray, and there were some smile lines at the corners of her big brown eyes and laugh lines around the sides of her lovely mouth. As beautiful as ever, she was living proof that the passage of years don't have to be a bad thing.

Turning to Samantha, I said, "Agent Goodbody, I'd like to introduce you to Southampton Police Captain, Melanie Dines."

Samantha answered flatly, "Yes, I know. The Captain and I have already met."

Feeling the sudden chill at my table, I tapped my fingers on its top and asked, "Is that so?"

Captain Dines broke in and answered, "That's right, Gabe. Agent Goodbody and her federal boyfriend, some stick-up-his-butt named Ledbetter, came to my office yesterday morning."

I said, "I know the man well, Melanie, and you are correct; he does have a stick up his butt. And just what did our federal agents ask of you?"

"They told me to keep out of the Fisher Murder, that it was strictly a federal issue and that I wasn't needed or wanted to be a part of the investigation."

Delving into Samantha's eyes, which had become even more spectacular with a touch of real anger in them rather than the fake anger I was sure she had been flashing at me since our rendezvous at B. Smith's, I asked, "And what did you tell them, Captain Dines?"

"What do you think I told them? I told them they could take a deep dive off Sag Harbor's Long Wharf. There was a murder on The East End and it's for us to find out who did it. If they didn't like it, they could take it up with the Obamas."

Smiling at my old friend, I kissed her cheek a second time and said, "That's my girl." Pulling out a chair for her fine backside, I asked, "Would you care to join us?"

"Sorry, Gabe, not tonight. Oliver and I are hosting a little gathering in the garden for some of his lawyer friends. Romey told me you were here and I just came by to say hello. I do need to speak with you, though. You were one of the last people seen with Fisher and I've got to ask you some questions. Tomorrow in my office okay?"

"Could we make that late in the afternoon, Melanie? I've got a breakfast date in the morning."

Melanie smiled at Samantha and said, "Oh, I see. Well, just make sure you don't catch anything."

Fuming, Samantha contributed, "You don't have to worry about that, Captain Dines. The only thing Fortuna is going to catch this evening is a good night's sleep."

Melanie laughed, gave me a dig in the ribs with her elbow and said, "How many times have we heard that one? I may have even said it a few times myself. Well, good night, Gabe." With a wink at a suddenly wine-pouring federal agent, she added, "Sleep tight, Agent Goodbody."

Placing my arm around the police chief's waist, I said, "Mind if I escort you to your table, Melanie? I wouldn't mind saying hello to Oliver. It's been a while since I've seen him." Turning to Samantha, I added, "Excuse me for a moment, Agent Goodbody. I've got to say hello to an old friend."

I walked away with Captain Dines, my arm around her

waist, the two of us looking like lovers who couldn't wait to finish dinner and get home to get it on. After thanking her for taking my afternoon phone call and agreeing to meet me at Romey's place (I hadn't wanted to talk about police business over the phone-I had the feeling someone was tapping it-if not the Feds, then The Kutchakokovs), she told me she had nothing on the Russians except that they were in the US with diplomatic passports and that she would keep searching and get back to me should anything turn up. After I told her about what went down during my meeting in Fisher's office, she went on to tell me there was no need for me to come and see her the next day, unless I wanted to use that as an excuse to lose the Federal heat. I told her that heat with Miss Samantha Goodbody was what I was looking for, adding that all I needed to find was the right kindling and I was sure there would be flame enough to get me through the coldest winter night.

Reaching her rounded table of eight, I walked over to and shook hands with a tight-lipped Oliver. He seemed unusually tense and I figured that might be because of the presence of two men at the table whom I didn't recognize. Seated on either side of Oliver, they silently sipped their straight-up vodkas while eyeing me suspiciously.

Nobody introduced them and I wanted to ask what the fuck they were looking at with those uptight Eastern European leers of theirs, but that wasn't necessary because I knew who they were from the small red K's tattooed on their necks. I noted that Oliver wasn't tan the way I knew this old beach bum buddy of mine always liked to be in summer and asked him how he felt. He answered that he was fine, just working hard on the purchase of some acreage he'd recently bought for a new home in Hampton Park and was finishing up a summer cold.

I asked, "Is that why you didn't show up at *Tatiana's* last week?"

Oliver looked at Melanie with the guiltiest expression I'd seen in a long time and then turned back to me and said weakly, "Sorry, Gabe, you must be mistaken. I don't remember having set up a meeting with you."

Watching Melanie glower at her husband and not wanting to cause any more trouble than I was sure I already had, I said, "You know, you're right. That was something I set up with a different buddy." Poking Oliver in the ribs, I added with a laugh, "I would never go to a club with you, anyway; a puss like yours would scare away most of the women and that couldn't be good for anyone."

I chided Oliver to get some color, said good-bye to the table of lawyers, ignored the K-men and placed a last loving kiss on my police captain's turned-cold cheek as my final act of farewell. Crossing the restaurant, I was wondering how much trouble I'd just gotten Oliver into, but was more concerned about why he seemed so uptight around me, why he felt he had to lie about our planned evening at *Tatiana's* and what those two guys with the tattooed Ks were doing seated on either side of him. I put those thoughts behind me when I reached my table and found Samantha in her chair, wearing that silly expression I'd often seen on other women, the one that told me she was half-way into the bag.

Downing the remnants of a glass of wine in one rapid chug, she stared at me cross-eyed and said, "The nerve of her." Pouring another glass of Romey D's Down Home Red, she chugged that one as well and went on to release the cutest little burp I'd ever heard.

I said, "Hey, take it easy, Agent Goodbody. On top of everything else your boss wants to pile on me, I don't want to be accused of corrupting a federal agent."

After burping again, this time not so adorably, she said, "Shut up, already, Fortuna. I swear, I've never heard anyone talk as much as you…and all of it is just plain bullshit."

I took a sip of red and replied with a wry smile, "Thanks for the compliment, Agent Goodbody." Another sip and I asked, "And how do you like my good friend, Captain Dines?"

Samantha threw me a dirty look and chose not to answer, polishing off what I counted as at least her sixth glass before Romey sent over a third complimentary bottle. That one I was determined not to open…at least not until we got home.

7

I awoke at six the next morning with a smile on my face and a pretty federal agent's head on my shoulder. Samantha was still out cold, with just the tiniest stream of drool leaking out of her half open mouth and down her chin, that trickle ending its short journey as a milky pool of saliva on my left deltoid. Her tousled hair covered most of her face and her naked body was hidden from view, completely protected from sight by my king-sized down comforter, except for her left arm, which she had draped haphazardly across my chest, using that appendage to cling to me much like a drowning man clings to a Sag Harbor buoy.

Gently holding her wrist, I delicately removed Samantha's arm from my body and slowly deposited it on the blanket between us. Nudging my shoulder from beneath her chin, her drool served as an excellent lubricant enabling me to slide out from under her and I left the bed with her head on my pillow, snoring away like the little engine that could.

I put up a pot of coffee and hit the gym in my smallest bedroom, working my usual Thursday routine of back, triceps and abdominals. Three hundred concentration crunches and three hundred leglifts in the Roman Chair brought out my six-pack and three sets of lat pull downs, two-armed rows and dead lifts using two hundred pound weights proved enough to accentuate that V-shape I liked in my back. Tricep pulldowns with a one hundred pound weight on the pulley and six sets of tricep kickbacks with a fifty pound dumbbell was all I needed for my arms to feel like they were going to explode and by seven I hit the outdoor shower, put on my short robe and was back in my kitchen preparing breakfast.

Standing at the kitchen counter, I heard a weakly whispered, "Where am I?" Turning to the distressed sound, I found Samantha leaning against the far wall, one hand to her forehead and the other tightly clutching the comforter to her naked body.

I chirped, "Good morning, Agent Goodbody," and watching her grimace at my spirited hello, added with appropriate gusto, "Coffee, tea or me?"

A trace of bad memory must have attacked her because that cute little river of drool meandering down her chin suddenly morphed into something hanging from a mad dog's mouth and she barked, "What the hell happened last night?" Wincing at her own voice, Samantha added painfully, "I swear, Fortuna, if you took advantage of me, I will kill you."

"Take advantage of you?" I protested. "If anything, Agent Goodbody, last night you took extreme advantage of me, my car, my friend's restaurant and my good nature. The way you heaved all over the ladies room in Romey's place, I'll be lucky if he lets me eat there again without first paying a sanitary surcharge. Then, after carrying you out of the place, you take a puke in my car, depositing a couple of rather large chunks down my window slats so that I'll probably have to have the door panels removed just to clean out the black-eyed peas and get the mechanism working again. It took everything I had to undress you and shower you down, not that you put up any kind of fight. You were dead weight, and I've got to tell you, I never knew a hundred and fifteen pounds could feel so heavy. Worst part was, as drunk as you were you insisted on sleeping with me, crying that you weren't going to let me out of your sight and that watching me was your job and you weren't going to blow it, a poor choice of words if I ever heard one. Hell, you couldn't even open your eyes, let alone watch me. Just to shut you up, I agreed to sleep with you, and if it means anything to you at all," (this was when I gave her the BIG SMILE) "you've got one hell of a spectacular ass." Noting an increased level of discomfort at my lofty grade, I casually added, "By the way, I think you ruined your skirt, blouse and bra. I rinsed them thoroughly and they're hanging out back over the deck railing to air out, but I've got to tell you, I never smelled anything so rank in my life. When was the last time you saw an internist? You may need a colonoscopy."

Gathering her strength, she attacked me about the one thing that seemed paramount to her well-being. "You slept with me?"

"Yes, I did," I answered, taking a relaxed sip of coffee.

"You undressed and showered me?"

"Yes, and yes, again."

A worried expression crossed Samantha's face. Clutching the comforter closer to her chest, she asked, "What else did you do?"

Her uptight attitude had finally taken all the fun from our jousting and I answered, "I don't know what you think I am, Agent Goodbody, but I don't have sex with women who have passed out cold from Romey D's Down Home Red. I may not have been with a woman for a while because of a few bullet wounds suffered in the defense of my home town, but I am not so horny that I would poke a federal agent who is too plastered to even move. I like my women to participate at least a little bit when we make love, you know, at least do something, even if it's only to summon a quiver when they reach their special moment. You were nothing more than a clammy lox lying in my bed and I do not copulate with fish. Now, coffee or tea? I don't like your attitude and am declaring myself no longer on the breakfast menu."

Samantha did not answer my question, choosing instead to turn and run down the short hallway to her bedroom. I heard a few gags, gurgles and galoomphs from the powder room and forty minutes later she returned, freshly showered and dressed, hair combed out and make-up applied, all remnants of drool gone.

She said, "May I have a cup of coffee, please?"

"Of course," I answered and poured.

Sitting calmly at one of the bar stools at my island, she interlocked her fingers like a schoolgirl and said, "You saw me naked."

"Yes, Agent Goodbody, I saw you naked. By the way, did you know the little beauty mark at the top of your left butt cheek looks a lot like George Washington's profile?" Placing her mug of hot coffee in front of her, I asked, "Milk and sugar?"

She whispered, "Yes, please." Then, after a sip of hot java, she asked, "Was I much of a fool last night?"

I answered gently, "No, Samantha. You were not that much of a fool, just foolish. You let the pressure of things get to you, but that's something I can understand. It's bad enough having to earn a living dealing with murderers and terrorists; I guess the thought of having to share me with Melanie Dines just pushed you over the edge."

Her immediate reply to my psychiatric diagnosis was short and succinct. "Fortuna, you are such an asshole."

I answered agreeably, "Thank you, Samantha, for that kind and generous appraisal of my character." Grinning, I added, "More coffee?"

I excused myself and left her alone at the island, returning to my bedroom where I dressed in a tan linen shirt and a pair of clean but faded old jeans for my morning meeting at The Kutchakokovs. Back in the great room, I found Samantha at the sink, rinsing the coffee mugs in a detached fashion before placing them into into my dishwasher.

I called, "I'll see you later. I'll try and phone if it looks like I'm going to be late."

She shot back, "Hold on. I told you before, you don't go anywhere without me."

"Well, I'm going to The Kutchakokovs."

"Then, so am I."

"You're not planning to ruin things between me and Ileana, are you?"

"Would you just shut up already, Fortuna? I'll get my things and join you. Just give me a minute."

I said, "Alright, Samantha, you may come with me, but let's get some things straight. Once we're at The Kutchakokov Estate, you will do whatever I tell you to do and not speak unless I ask you a direct question. Then, answer as simply as you can. If I go off with Ileana, and I'm hoping to do just that, you wait patiently for me to return and do not go looking for me. Are we together on this? If not, I'm tying you to that chair and going there alone."

Samantha bit at her lip for a few seconds and then replied, "Alright, but you get something straight, too. I am a federal agent and your safety is my job and my concern. If I think you're in danger I will act. Otherwise, I will assume the role of bimbo. Satisfied?"

"No," I answered, "but I'm hoping Ileana will cure me of that problem. Let's go."

*   *   *

We headed south on Snake Hollow Road and passed the large pastures where The Hampton Classic, an event that had grown from an end of summer plaything created for the children of a few Hamptons' millionaires to become the richest horseshow in America, had just begun its weeklong, annual celebration and competition. Hundreds of horse trailers, corrals, large and small vendors tents, grandstands and temporary stables had been assembled on the vast open fields, and jumping fences, moats and other obstacles had been erected in different stations throughout the open pastures. Many thousands of people were expected to attend the events throughout the week and I explained to Goodbody that many of those were millionaires and billionaires eager to see how their horses, or their neighbor's horses, were going to fare against some of the greatest equestrian champions in the world.

Leaving the flatlands of Watermill, we crossed Route 27 and headed south. A cooler ocean breeze picked up on Flying Point Road and in another mile we reached Gin Lane, home to oceanfront mansions built at the turn of the twentieth century by robber barons who never could have dreamed of the money they would have made if only they'd scrapped their factories and invested all their cash in oceanfront real estate. A mile of driving past twelve-foot tall hedgerows brought us to the beginning of a ten-foot tall, red brick wall that ran for half-a-mile. The top of the wall was covered with thick green ivy, serving as both decoration and camouflage for the razor wire that looped ubiquitously in and out of the greenery. The wired brick wall ended with the start of an equally tall and twenty-foot wide filigreed iron gate with the initials IK swirling conspicuously in its center. Small placards were stuck into the grass surrounding the gate, advertising the names of the contractors who worked at maintaining the integrity of the mansion and its land: Atlas Painters, Tesoro Construction, Zombie Irrigation, Tanfastic Pools. On the other side of the gate, the brick wall continued down Gin Lane and then out of sight, as it turned the corner onto Meadow Lane.

On either side of the closed gate were two small brick and concrete guardhouses that looked as if they had been shipped to Southampton from France immediately after the Battle of Verdun. Multiple gunslots had been carved from the brick façade of each and the nicks and dings of bullets or shrapnel or both decorated the outside walls with a sense of fatality. Stopping the Caddy at the closed gate, I waited for the person or persons manning the small gatehouses to greet us, and to my surprise, it was not a square-headed mercenary who came out to say hello, but a lovely, long legged, blue eyed blonde in her mid-twenties. Wearing tight white shorts and a matching white blouse of a modern material that showed her superb fitness level, she had a small red K tattooed onto the right side of her neck and carried a clipboard in her left hand with all the authority of a top flight secretary in a Wall Street boardroom. Unlike any Girl Friday I ever knew, she also wore a white patent leather gun belt strapped across her narrow waist, a pearl-handled revolver tucked neatly inside its holster.

Through the bars of the closed gate, she asked in a monotonous Eastern European accent, "What want you here?"

Samantha grabbed my leg at the knee and squeezed hard, her way, I assumed, of telling me to cool it and just go along with the woman at the gate. I respected Samantha's wishes, and her grip, as well as the guard packing the Colt and answered good naturedly, "Good morning, my fine and curvaceous Transylvanian friend. I am Gabriel Fortuna, here to see Ileana Kutchakokov by her request."

Pointing at Samantha, the guard asked bad-naturedly, "And who she?"

I wondered what the hell was wrong with these people that no matter what their sex or whatever the weather or whomever they were talking to they all sounded like they were headed for their last meal on a frozen tundra. Letting it go, I replied jovially, "She, newcomer to my homeland, is my friend, Samantha. Now, why don't you call Ileana Kutchakokov, get the okay, and let us in."

The guard looked puzzled and then shook her head, replying, "You enter. Her, no."

I smiled broadly and responded, "We come as a team, my little nutcracker. Now, go call your boss and tell her that Gabriel Fortuna is here with a friend and will not attend breakfast without her."

Frowning at my insubordination, the pretty lady at the gate retreated to her lair, hit the phone and a moment later the gates glided open. Reappearing, she said, "Go to big stone house. Stop. Someone take car. Now, go."

I said, "Thank you," and drove off, and sadly, Samantha removed her hand from my knee.

The driveways of many of these great estates in The Hamptons often run for a half-mile or longer and this one belonging to The Kutchakokovs proved to be one of those great interior roads. Lined on either side by alternating fully-leafed cherry trees and massive white pines, the graveled thoroughfare meandered through acre after acre of perfect open lawn. The great green carpet was interspersed with large sculptures of glass, bronze and aluminum, showing themselves whenever there was an architecturally planned break in the line of trees, and it was through one of those breaks, in the distance and on the right side of the compound, sitting before a set of high beach dunes that sheltered the property from the mighty Atlantic Ocean, that I spotted the largest horse stable I had ever seen outside of Belmont Racetrack. To the right of the stable, in a dip in the land and set behind a dune so that it was nearly hidden from view, were the oversized blades of what had to be a military helicopter, and in front of the stable, a large open field of ankle high grass, naked of statuary of any kind except for a tall blue pole stuck into the ground at the far end of the field and a shorter red one at its center. A stand of white pines suddenly blocked my view, and after a long and lazy S-Turn, we came to the end of the driveway and found one of the largest private residences I'd ever seen.

Of limestone construction and not the cedar shingle of most Hamptons' mansions, the imposing edifice was four stories tall and at least two hundred feet long. Its multi-colored slate tile roof, shimmering and glowing in the early morning sun, held four large masonry chimneys separated by equal distances at the roof's peak with each the owner of four ceramic flues. Copper flashing, piping and gutters ran down and under the roof, transporting rainwater underground and then to the sea, where it would not disturb the gardens surrounding the foundation of the manse, and what looked like a hundred sets of French Doors, each with a lovely Juliet **B**alcony, served as windows, allowing enough sunlight and ocean breeze into the mansion to power a small city. There was ample parking in front of the house for scores of cars, should a May Day celebration or a visit from Taras Bulba ever occur, but none were in sight when I pulled up to the massive oak double-door entry and stopped The Caddy.

Opening one of those doors and walking toward us before I'd even shut the engine was a near clone of the woman at the gate. She went around the nose of my car to my driver's side door, opened it and said, "Car."

I did not hear the word, 'please', and was about to discourse on proper American etiquette to the rather attractive, if robotic, valet, when the sound of crunching gravel again turned my head towards the house.

A tall dark-haired bear of a man had just walked through the open doorway of the mansion and was taking loping and confident strides towards us. At least six-foot four and two hundred-eighty pounds of what once might have been hard muscle but was now loose flesh jiggling under a black turtle neck shirt, he wore a pencil thin mustache that ran precisely above his jagged thin lips and below a long hooked nose whose nostrils proved too thin for ample breathing, causing every breath to sound like a wheeze. His face, the color of sharkskin, was heavily pock-marked and held a pair of slits-for-eyes that looked like a couple of stab wounds. A wiry Breznevian monobrow was spread above those dead orbs, the exact color of the long and straight jet black oily hair that topped his head. His hand raked through his wet mop and I saw that they were thick and huge and dangerous, tapering to fingers ending with long and sharpened nails.

Extending one of those hands towards me, he said, "Good morning, Mr. Fortuna. I am Ilya Kutchakokov. How nice of you to accept our invitation for breakfast and a bit of recreation."

I took my host's hand to be cordial but was more concerned in discovering how much strength it held. Impressed with the size of his mitt but not so much with its power, I answered, "My pleasure, Kutchakokov. Anyway, how could anyone turn down an offer from your sister." Wiping my hand on my pants, I gave the keys to the valet and added, "Ileana is a very beautiful and engaging woman."

Kutchakokov's smile broadened, revealing a set of yellow stained teeth which looked eerily sinister next to his gray skin, and he said, "Yes, Ileana. I am afraid she has taken all the beauty from our family and left me with none. Still, I consider myself fortunate to have been blessed with brains. Beauty fades, does it not, Mr. Fortuna, but an insatiable curiosity and the ability to process information quickly and expertly is something that can last a lifetime." Through a sly grin, he asked, "Tell me, Mr. Fortuna, which would you prefer, brains or beauty?"

"Me? I'll take good looks every time. I've known too many smart guys and women who turned out to be more trouble than they were worth, but then, I've never been accused by anyone of being too smart, so what the hell do I know?"

Chortling at my remark, he removed a pack of Camels unfiltered from his shirt pocket, took out a stick and lit up. Turning to Samantha, he released a cloud of blue smoke and said, "And whom have we here?"

With a wide wet smile on his gray mug, he took her left hand in his right, lowered his lips to deliver a continental kiss, and finished his old-world fishing expedition by raising a malevolent eyebrow towards me and asking, "Mr. Fortuna, are you not going to introduce me to your lovely companion?" Grinning like a hungry cat, he added, "I am not so sure Ileana will like the presence of your friend at our table. She always insists on being the most beautiful and desirable woman seated when dining with a man that interests her. The presence of this enchanting beauty may confuse things and provoke Ileana to irritability."

Reaching in and freeing Samantha's hand, which had become captive to Kutchakokov's big fin, I said, "You don't have to worry about that. This is an old family friend, Samantha Goodbody. Being quiet by nature, she doesn't like to speak and lets me do all our talking. You won't even know she's here and she won't be a distraction to anyone. Anyway, we've already had breakfast. This is more of a social call than an outing for a free meal. Your sister invited me and I don't like saying no to beautiful women. It's as simple as that. Now, where is our hostess? I'd like to say, hello."

Kutchakokov laughed, coughed and said, "You have, what is it you Americans like to say, some pair, Mr. Fortuna."

I replied, "That's no secret, Kutchakokov. You could have learned that from half the women in The Hamptons."

He laughed and coughed again, and guiding us into his palace with a glad hand to my back, said, "Come in, come in, please. Ileana is waiting for us in the garden, where you simply must have something to eat. I know you said you have already had breakfast, but with what we have planned for the day, I am sure you will have need for more energy than you thought."

We entered the building and were greeted by a massive hallway floored by large squares of white and black marble set on the diamond. Walls covered by thick hand-painted paper of gold and cream surrounded us and four large crystal and gilt chandeliers, hanging like brilliant suns from a sky blue ceiling, illuminated the place like it was Apollo's castle on Mount Olympus. Antique furniture and mirrors that had to have been appropriated from The Hermitage in Saint Petersburg filled the room elegantly and tastefully, and at the end of the entry foyer, beyond the arteries leading to the east and west ground floor wings of the manse, was a marble radial staircase with gracefully curved walnut railings and balusters leading to the master and guest bedrooms. Beyond the staircase, the ground floor opened into a vestibule of amber covered walls leading to a garden, where Ileana Kutchakokov sat in the near distance, beyond a set of open French doors at a square white-cloth covered table topped by two large vases of blue hydrangeas.

Walking through the amber room and approaching the French doors, I said, "Quite a place you have, Kutchakokov."

He replied, "Thank you, Mr. Fortuna. Yes, I am quite proud of what we have done with our new home in our short period of ownership. It took a lot of work to get things as we desired. Did you know that this estate is composed of four old Hamptons' parcels whose family ownerships date back to the early 1900's?"

"No. I didn't."

"Well, after the Madoff scandal and the problems with your economy, some owners of large properties decided to rid themselves of land rarely used so as to be able to continue living in their other homes in the manner to which they had become accustomed. After all, what is one less estate when you possess five or six others? It is merely what you Americans so perfectly call, an ego trip. Ileana and I were able to buy this and the three adjoining estates, converting all the properties into one of eighty acres running continuously along the ocean and Gin Lane for three-quarters of a mile. We now own the largest Hamptons estate property on the ocean, except for the Rennert Mansion in Easthampton, and are in negotiations for a possible purchase there."

I said, "Sounds like you're already a success in the real estate business, Kutchakokov. Pretty impressive."

"If we so wish it, it is only the beginning." Smiling radiantly through those yellow teeth, he added, "It's amazing what one can do these days with a mere hundred and twenty million dollars."

Money generally didn't impress me, not even the big money Kutchakokov was throwing around, but I wondered why I hadn't read about the purchase of these properties in any of the town papers and then realized that it was not something anyone, especially the town government, would want publicized. Sure, the transactions would have to be listed in the town management office, that was the law, but you'd have to know about them to look for them, and these days most people were worried enough about their own pocketbooks and didn't really care to go looking into other peoples' business.

I said, "A hundred-twenty million, eh? That's a hell of a lot of money but not so much for what you got for it. I think you did pretty well for yourself. I'd like to meet your real estate agent."

"You make me laugh, Mr. Fortuna. What do you Americans say…does Target tell Walmart? I am sorry, but our agent is exclusive to us. Perhaps, we can find someone else to help you." Breezing through the French doors, we reached the table where his sister sullenly sat and he added, "Some people have to sell, Mr. Fortuna. Neither time nor good fortune is on their side. We were lucky to be here to pick up their pieces."

I checked out his slits-for-eyes, gray skin, yellow teeth and turkey neck, and said, "Yeah, Kutchakokov, you strike me as one lucky guy." Turning to his sister, I changed the subject and added, "Good morning, Ileana. You seem lost in thought. I hope it's me your thinking about." Checking out the snarling little animal she held in her lap, I concluded, "And good morning, America. It's nice to see you again, too."

A cold smile replaced Ileana's wayward stare and she said, "Good morning, Gabriel. I am glad you could come. And how nice for you to remember my little America." Sending a cold eye to Ilya, she added, "My brother must be boring you with his talk of property and money. I cannot bear to speak of such things with strangers. I was sure he felt the same. I hope you do not find anything he said of interest."

I replied, "I always find it interesting to see how our country grows in strength from the inclusion of others. It's just unusual to see our latest batch of newcomers starting at the top. Unfortunately, that leaves only one direction for them to go."

Samantha gave my right butt cheek a tweek and I gave a small hop. Reaching behind me and grabbing her pinching hand firmly in mine, I pulled her forward so that we stood shoulder to shoulder and said, "I'd like to introduce my friend, Samantha Goodbody. I sometimes work with Stony Brook University and she's a visiting graduate student from Cornhole, Georgia, out here to examine the flora and fauna of The Hamptons for a paper she's doing. She'll be with me for a week or so and I thought she'd like to see how the super-rich live. I hope you don't mind."

"Of course I mind, Gabriel," was Ileana's tight answer. "I wanted your attention for myself. I did not wish to share you with another beautiful woman, but seeing as she is here, we will behave in a civilized fashion and welcome you both to our table. Please, be seated."

Ileana was at the right side of the table and Samantha and I took seats on either side of her, but when her brother went to sit at the open end, she said, "Why don't you check on the horses and the riders, Ilya? You have already eaten and I would like for Gabriel, his friend and I to have some privacy. We will join you at the stables in a short while."

Ilya growled a bit before throwing his cloth napkin onto the table. Plastering a phony smile on his face, he looked in my direction and said, "If you will excuse me. Unfortunately, my sister still lacks manners and there is not the time to teach them now. Good-bye, Mr. Fortuna. Miss Goodbody."

Her brother left the table with that same loping stride I'd

noticed when we'd met and Ileana said breathily, "Idiot." Turning to me, she added, "Now, Gabriel, are you ready for breakfast?"

"Like I told your brother, Samantha and I have already had our breakfast. We're here out of respect to your kind invitation." Knowing that there isn't a woman alive who doesn't like a compliment, I added, "Of course, I am also here to see you. I couldn't believe how good-looking you were the last time we met and I wanted to see if my eyes were playing games with me or if I needed glasses."

Placing America on her seat, Ileana rose from the table, showed off her perfect hour glass figure and spectacular sexuality, and asked, "And what do your eyes tell you now, Gabriel?"

I gulped and answered, "They tell me I wasn't wrong, that I don't need corrective lenses and that you are easily one of the finest looking women I've ever seen."

"Thank you, Gabriel, for your sincere compliment. And may I say in return that you are a fine looking man. I wonder what our future holds."

I responded, "I don't think we need a gypsy to tell us the answer to that one, Ileana. You and I have some unfinished business. The only questions to be answered are when and where we'll take care of it."

Stroking her pet in a most provocative fashion, she replied, "You are an unusual man, Gabriel, but even the strongest and most carnal of men need to eat. I have prepared for you some exotic treats from my homeland. Each delicacy has been prepared with a special herb that provides superior strength and vitality." Turning to Samantha, she said icily, "You, too, must have to eat Miss Goodbody. You may need more strength, as well."

Ileana clapped her hands and from behind a tall hedge the lithe Asian woman I'd seen at my house and at *Tatiana's* appeared, carrying a large circular tray topped by dishes of varying sizes. Setting the tray on the huge server behind Samantha, she removed from it a small stack of empty chargers and placed one in front of each of us before filling our water goblets with cold sparkling water. With a pair of tongs, she served Samantha and me from each of the different dishes until our oversized plates had been supersized with what Ileana had called Russian delicacies, but what to me looked and smelled more like puddles of ferment from the Major's Path Transfer Station. Finished with serving, the Asian retreated behind Ileana, where she stood rigidly at attention, looking at me through dagger eyes that warned I might be the next thing she'd be serving on a plate.

Trying my best to ignore her gaze and to maintain a good relationship with my beautiful and buxom hostess, I behaved in a gentlemanly fashion and lied, saying, "Looks delicious Ileana. Want to tell us what we're eating?"

Waving her hand over the table, she pointed to each plate in its turn and described the elements of our questionable feast: studen-large pieces of boiled meat served in a cold jellied stock, two pots of offal-liver and tripe baked in a pot with cereal, zharkoye-an entire fowl flash baked on a tray in a hot oven, shaslyk-the Steppes version of shish kabob, a wide selection of zakuski-various cold fish hors d'oeuvres, and syrniki-fried curd fritters. For dessert, vatrushka-a cake filled with raisins and tvorog, what Americans call cottage cheese, and to drink, imported cold Caspian water or Diet Coke.

Checking out the studen, its calves feet and pork snouts floating languidly in purple gelatin, I gulped and said, "I think I'll pass. Like I told you before, I already had breakfast."

Samantha stifled a gag and said painfully, "I'll just have a Diet Coke, please."

Ileana responded flatly, "You Americans, so loathe to try the exotic tastes of central Asia. I would think you'd prefer one of your Big Macs to a blini filled with our most expensive Beluga caviar."

I countered with sincere jingoism, "Make that a Double Whopper with Cheese and there's no contest."

A look of disgust washed Ileana's face, and turning to her aide, she said, "Thank you, Miss Yu, but our guests appear to be neither hungry nor interested in our food. You may clear the table." Remembering that she was living in the USA and no longer on a Siberian tract of ice, she added, "Oh, excuse me. I seem to have forgotten the quaint American custom of treating servants as equals. May I introduce Wo To Yu. Miss Yu has been with me for many years and will, I am sure, be with me for many more. I trust her with my life."

I put out my hand to Ileana's Jackie-of-all-trades and said, "Nice to make your acquaintance, Miss Yu. Any friend of Ileana's is a friend of mine."

Scowling at my American pleasantry, as I expected she would, she ignored my friendly gesture and silently went about her work.

With the table cleared, Ileana said, "Miss Yu. Go and prepare my mount for *Buzkashi*. I will join you at the stables shortly."

Difficult as it was to raise my eyes from Ileana's magnificent cleavage, I managed to tear them away, and hoping her answer would be some kind of exotic aphrodisiac or magical elixir, asked, "What's Buzkashi?"

"We are people of The Steppes, Gabriel, not so fine as those who spend their time on your Bridgehampton polo fields hitting a tiny ball with a harmless mallet and singing, 'Score! Score', whenever their insignificant orb passes through two posts. We of The Steppes are made of sterner stuff and play Buzkashi. Our riders drive their mounts hard, whipping and kicking and tearing at each other until one member of either team grabs the tars tarkus from the central stake and makes a complete tour of the playing field. If strong enough, the bearer of the tarkus will pass the blue pole at the far end of the field and once again race to the other to throw the tarkus into 'The Circle of Justice'. A game may last ten minutes or it may last ten days. It all depends on how determined the riders are for victory." Raising a curious eyebrow, she asked huskily, "Tell me, Gabriel, do you think you have the strength to play Buzkashi with people from The Steppes?"

I wasn't afraid of playing any game that had a 'Circle of Justice' as its goal, but I hedged my bets and answered, "It all depends, Ileana. What does the winner get?"

"We do not play for money, as seems to be the only thing for which Americans challenge themselves. Our prize is greater. The player who throws the tars tarkus into the 'Circle of Justice' may claim as his reward any object belonging to an opponent or the services of any player on the opposing team for a period of twelve hours. That person is a virtual slave, something money cannot buy, and the services demanded can be anything of which the victor desires."

This talk of making an opposing player a willing slave for twelve hours suddenly made the game sound a lot more interesting and I asked with renewed enthusiasm, "And you're a participant in this Buzkashi thing?"

With a hint of desire that I couldn't have missed if I was ninety-four, living in a nursing home and my hearing aid batteries had just died, Ileana answered, "I have never missed a game of Buzkashi since having twelve years. Of course, I play."

"Then, count me in." Injecting a demand of my own, I added, "Naturally, there is one thing upon which I insist."

"And that is?"

"You cannot be on my team."

Ileana responded through an icy smile, "Of course you will not ride with me, Gabriel. I have every hope of winning and making you my slave. You will oppose me until the game is decided, and then, if you prove deserving, you will be opposed to me again."

I figured I was going to finally break free and have the night of my life with a woman of my dreams, that was, so long as she honestly answered my questions about Danny Fisher. Knowing that if she had something to hide, answering truthfully was something I could not expect, I turned to more mundane matters and said, "Good, but just one more thing before we play. What the hell is a tars tarkus?"

"You Americans, so ignorant of our ways and yet expect us to know of your baseball and your football and all the rest of your silly pastimes. A tars tarkus is the carcass of a dead goat, Gabriel. The animal is beheaded, its limbs are cut off at the knees and it is disemboweled. After soaking in cold water and salt for twenty-four hours, the goat's skin toughens so that it will not disintegrate even after many hours of hard play. We would prefer to play with a calf's skin but many of you Americans have this thing about veal so we are forced to use goat while on your shores. That is our polo ball Gabriel. Now, follow me. We go to play Buzkashi."

Ileana turned, and with little America leashed by her side, began her slow walk towards the stable at the far end of the field. I wondered what the hell I had gotten myself into but somehow became transfixed by the firmness of Ileana's magnificent body and was wondering just what a slave of hers would be forced to do after a hard game of Buzkashi, or quite possibly, what I would have her do for me. Feeling a tap on my shoulder, I put my fantasies to rest and turned to find Samantha Goodbody staring angrily at me.

With hands set defiantly at her hips, she said, "I want you to know I am not taking part in any of this."

I replied nonchalantly, "I never said you had to."

We left the garden table with Samantha one pace behind, crossed the open field and were almost at the stable when she stepped in front of me, looked me dead in the eye and said with complete confidence, "You know, Fortuna, you are an absolute idiot."

I didn't say anything to argue the point, because judging from what I was about to do, for the first time since I'd known her, Agent Samantha Goodbody had said something with which I might have completely agreed.

8

The teams had already assembled by the time we reached the stable. On the left side of the open doors, I counted ten men in thick black leather shirts, pants and boots standing beside massive horses, quietly checking out the secure placement of the flat leather strips atop the thick Afghan blankets serving as saddles. Not one of the rugged and muscular men was smiling or wearing the look of excitement that competition prints on the faces of most athletes. Their faces were stern and battle ready, visages appearing more likely to charge into Tennyson's Valley of Death than onto a large open Hamptons' playfield. The silence of the rugged group was punctuated only by the occasional snorts and whinnies of the horses, all of which appeared as strong and thick as Bradley Armored Vehicles and as fierce and ready as the men who were to ride them.

Six of the men in black I recognized from past meetings. The two I had deposited into the dumpster in the parking lot in Sag Harbor were staring at me in a fashion that did not insinuate teammate, looking instead like a pair of thugs who couldn't wait to knock me off my mount and trample me into dust, and the two I had taken care of at Tatiana's the night I met Danny Fisher didn't look too happy at seeing me either. Sergei eyed me malevolently, and the guy I'd stamped between the eyes with my ring was actually salivating and grinding his teeth in a failed attempt at staring me down. The other two guys I recognized kept turned from me as much as they could, but I saw enough of their profiles to know they were the fellows whom I saw with Oliver Dines the night before at Romey D's. I wondered again what the hell they were doing having dinner with my old friend and a bunch of Hamptons' lawyers out at Romey's place, but put it in the vault for later.

The opposing team gathered quietly on the other side of the stable and was composed of twelve women, two of which were Ileana and the ubiquitous, Miss Yu. Dressed in white leather, they were every bit as protected as the men in black. The women's demeanor was as dour as the men's, but wearing carefully applied make-up and their hair pulled back tightly from their faces to form tight round buns at the back of their heads, there was something exceedingly attractive, if not quietly dangerous about them, and I thought that this must be how lady spiders appear to their mates just before chomping off their heads.

Four foot long bamboo sticks protruded from cloth bags fixed to either side of the women's flat saddles and each rider placed a two foot leather whip with ball bearing tails in her teeth before mounting. The women's horses, all white and clean and marvelous, waited patiently with their riders for Ileana and her mount to move to the front of the phalanx and lead them to the open field. Seated atop a handsome and magnificent beast that had to have had Pegasus in its lineage, she did this at a gentle gallop, and when she did, the women dutifully followed.

No one wore helmets.

"It is good to see you, Mr. Fortuna. Some of my men did not think you had the courage to play."

Turning to find Ilya Kutchakokov seated atop a large and well brushed palomino, I replied, "Courage is something I never lacked, Kutchakokov. If your men had said they thought I had enough horse sense to sit this one out, that may have been true, but, as you can see, here I am."

Parrying my clever retort with a lascivious smile, he looked down at Samantha and asked, "Will you be joining us on the field, Miss Goodbody?"

I spoke for Samantha and said, "Sorry, Kutchakokov, but like I told you, Ms. Goodbody is here strictly as an observer. She'll watch the match and wait for me from a safe place off the playing field."

Through a pout of disappointment, Kutchakokov replied, "That is too bad. I would have liked to share my victory with a beautiful American woman. It has been my experience that they are difficult at first, but then, when they surrender, they surrender completely."

I didn't have to tell my host to go fuck himself because I was sure he saw those words in Samantha's eyes. Instead I said, "You must be hanging around with the wrong American girls, Kutchakokov. The ones I know would have your nuts in a vice and have you hoisting a white flag before you hit the sheets."

Kutchakokov murmured, "Insolent beast," and then tossing me a stack of my own black leather: pants, shirt, boots and a short nine-tailed whip, said, "Change into this, Mr. Fortuna. You will find the leather will protect you from most of the lashings and the sticks. Of course, you will feel the pain of a solid blow, but in most cases your skin will not be cut. However, you must be careful of your eyes. These women of ours, they are like wildcats and ruthlessly go for them should you allow one to get too close. I warn you now, many a good man has been lost because they underestimated the power and ferocity of one of Ileana's riders. Be wary of them."

I replied, "Thanks for the tip, Kutchakokov, but I can't remember ever being afraid of a woman with a whip. On the contrary, it's something to which I've often looked forward."

Smirking at my bravado, he pulled tightly on his horse's reins and reared his mount twelve feet into the air, exposing a scarred and massive underbelly and a set of thrashing hooves. Settling his animal with only a light tug, he glared at me through hard and bloodshot eyes, and said, "That could be a fatal mistake, Mr. Fortuna, but I suspected you to be a man of danger and so am not surprised by your reckless manner. However, I would be a poor host if I did not give you one last warning. Of all players on the field, be most wary of me. You see, in Buzkashi, as in life, you may trust no one. I want to win as badly now as when I was riding The Steppes with my father beside me, fiercely driving me forward and teaching me how to whip a man so that he will fear me and turn from the tarkus rather than again feel the wrath of my lash. The last time I earned the prize was three years ago and Ileana has never forgiven me my victory. And why should she? That night, I chose her as my slave and it was a glorious evening… at least for me. Now, change your clothes quickly, Mr. Fortuna. The players are eager to begin."

Turning his mount to the field, Kutchakokov galloped away to join his men. Their ancient battle cries filled the air and I took that as opportunity to order Samantha to the outdoor dining room where she could watch the contest without becoming a distraction, explaining to my frazzled Fed that this Buzkashi didn't seem as much a game as it was a war and that I didn't need to worry about her while trying to save my neck. She protested, telling me it was her ass that was on the line should anything happen to me, but her dissent fell on deaf ears. Throwing her hands up in surrender, she turned and scurried away with only one concerned look over her shoulder.

Entering the cavernous stable, I found my mount standing at the front of an empty stall, western saddle set and waiting for me. White, with large brown markings and a nearly jet black tail, he was the thickest horse I'd ever sat, and although I thought his size would make him slow, when I moved him toward the playing field he took off like a jet flying out of MacArthur Airport. I had to pull hard on the reins with both hands to get him to slow down to a pace where I felt at least somewhat in control and patted his neck gratefully when he listened. Hoping to further communication with my animal, I called him, Kimosabee, a name I remembered from back when I was a kid watching Saturday afternoon television with my brother. Reaching the line of eager men and horses, Kutchakokov pointed me to my position and I wordlessly fit into place about twenty feet to his right and twenty feet to the left of the next player, a scowling Sergei.

Kutchakokov called, "Are you ready, Mr. Fortuna?"

"As ready as I'll ever be."

"Do you see the tars tarkus impaled on the pole in the center of the field?"

"I see it."

"That is what we must control and take around the blue pole to our left. Then it is onward to the 'Circle of Justice' on the other end of the field to our right. Do you understand?"

"I understand."

"Good. Then let us begin."

Kutchakokov raised his hand high over his head and from

across the field a half-mile away I saw Ileana raise hers. A moment later, a horn blared and a wild cry rose along my line, echoed from the line of women opposing us. The next thing I knew, Kimosabee reared and off we went, all of us, galloping across an open field that might easily have been called, No-Man's Land.

A good horse can do the quarter mile in thirty seconds and I was surrounded by good horses converging on each other to form a point around Kutchakokov. Whipping his mount like a maddened Cossack, shouting Russian expletives to his valiant men, he turned his head only to exhort them onward. From the other end of the open field, a spearhead of ululating women raced towards us, Ileana leading her crew as fiercely as Ilya led his men. Closing in upon one another at incredibly high speed, I clearly saw the savage snarl of a Siberian wolf form on her lips and simultaneously felt the thrill of attack come to life within me. Screaming like a banshee, I found myself in the middle of the crazed pack of racing men and thundering horses, and when we reached the tarkus, like tsunamis crashing into each other from opposing ends of the ocean, the two teams smashed into each other- man, woman and horse- with a deafening roar.

A beautiful woman in white, staring at me with the most amazingly gorgeous hate-filled blue eyes I'd ever seen, had chosen me as her target and had charged into my horse at a full gallop. The thud our animals made as they crashed their massive chests was symphonic and both horses stumbled before going to their knees. After a strong pull at the reins, mine rose from the ground a moment before hers and I took advantage of my superior leverage to lean towards her and push her from her mount. She had other ideas, however, and pulling a bamboo cane from her saddle, struck me hard across my forearm, rending a tear in my leather shirtsleeve and producing a sharp sting that radiated up my limb and into my neck. I took that strong blow as permission to become a little more physical with my opponent, and grabbing her cane with my left hand before she could whack me with it again, used it to pull her closer to me and tapped her lightly on her chin with my closed fist. Her eyes rolled back in her head and as she slid from her horse, I deposited her as gently as I could onto the grassy field.

The red veil that had filled my eyes when I'd charged into the white line of Russian women lifted and I found myself surrounded by the fallen bodies of five men and four women, including the one I had dropped with that short crisp right to the jaw. Horses lay on the field as well, struggling to get up or laying still as death. Looking to my left, my eyes followed the sound of hooves pounding at turf and I saw Ilya Kutchakokov racing towards the blue pole, holding the tars tarkus high over his head with his left hand as he insanely lashed at his horse with his right. Trailing him by mere inches was Ileana. Whipping at her brother's legs with her left hand while caning his torso with her right, she, too, rode without the use of hands, turning only to spur her fellow riders to catch up and steal the tarkus from her brother. Miss Yu followed the siblings closely, and then came the mass of black and white horses galloping at high speed, riders whipping, caning and kicking at each other as they raced to catch, protect or attack Ilya Kutchakokov.

I kicked Kimosabee in his ribs with the heels of my heavy boots and that was all that was needed to set him galloping. Closing in on that tangled mass of black and white, I saw one of the guys who'd sat with Oliver at Romey's catch a female rider across the bridge of her nose with his bamboo cane. She toppled from her horse, and cradling her head in her hands and arms, scrambled and rolled to her left and then to her right but could not elude the danger surrounding her. Trampled by the horde of charging horses, she was tossed aside like a crumbled piece of paper destined for a Buzkashi waste bin.

Kutchakokov circled the blue pole and began his crazed dash back across the field towards the 'Circle of Justice', Ileana and Miss Yu on either side of him, still only inches behind. Spurring their horses madly to pass him, they did that and turned abruptly, coming to a skidding halt so close in front of his charging mount that Ilya had no time and nowhere to turn. Holding the tarkus high over his head with his left hand, he skidded to a halt and used his right to whip at Ileana, who had brought her horse directly astride his and was brutally punishing his legs, torso and face with stiff lashes from her cat-o-nine-tails.

A sharp pain in the small of my back told me I had not been forgotten, and turning to my left, I found the maddened face of the Russian whose shoulder I'd dislocated just days earlier outside Choppin' Charlie's. He was driving his horse hard and hacking at me mercilessly with his bamboo cane, as his cohort, the guy I'd clipped on his chin outside the very same tonsorial parlor, suddenly came up on my right and began swatting me across my legs. Letting go of the reins, I fought back, but their frantic pursuit of me and not the tarkus proved to me that winning at Buzkashi was not nearly so important to these guys as kicking my ass and maybe killing me was.

Urging Kimosabee forward, I broke away from my would be assassins and thundered ahead. Peering over my shoulder, I saw the guy on my left pull a short spear from his saddle, its sharp metal point gleaming when it caught the Atlantic coast sunlight. Standing tall in his stirrups, he took aim and appeared ready to hurl it, when a black cat-o-nine-tails came from out of nowhere and whipped across his face. Ball bearings tore across his cheeks and eyes, blood spurted from a spider web of cuts and divots, and as he toppled from his saddle, the small white figure of Wo To Yu raced away. My other attacker wore a suddenly shocked expression and I took his loss of concentration as the opportunity to smash my bamboo cane hard across his forehead. He fell from his mount like an anvil falling through water and I let loose a bloodcurdling howl. Inciting Kimosabee onward, I felt the bloodlust coursing through his veins as heartily as it pounded through mine.

Halfway across the field and closing in on the 'Circle of Justice', I trailed the pack but was pressing in, waiting for an opportunity. Ileana lashed a hard charging Sergei across his open throat, embedding a ball bearing so deeply into his skin that as he turned from her and fell, her whip was torn from her grasp. Without losing a beat, she took instead to caning her brother, smacking her stiff bamboo shaft across his legs and ribs, one blow following another in a steady rhythm of pain. A solid blow caught Ilya across his chest, causing him to momentarily dip lower in his saddle. It took only that instant of weakness for Miss Yu to swoop in from his other side, and using her cane, smack Kutchakokov at his unprotected wrist, setting the tarkus into the air where it was captured in mid-flight by the diminutive bodyguard.

On a dime, the horses reversed course and began heading back towards the blue pole, this time with Miss Yu holding the tarkus aloft and Ilya and Ileana Kutchakokov charging close behind her. This sudden change in direction gave opportunity for the remaining warriors to close in and do battle and when the dust cleared from the ensuing conflagration only four riders remained: Ileana, Ilya, Miss Yu and me. Galloping as hard and as fast as our foaming horses could carry us, we again circled the blue pole and this time it was Ilya's turn to whip at Miss Yu in his fierce attempt at getting her to relinquish the tarkus, but with every stride towards the 'Circle of Justice', Miss Yu and Ileana pulled away from Ilya and I knew that if I was going to win the contest, my time had come.

Kicking at my horse, I released my hands from his reins and begged him to give me everything he had. I cried out a hearty, "Hiyo, Kimosabee," and my brave stallion accepted my entreaty, shifted into another gear and with every massive stride, we closed on the trio ahead of us.

Catching up to a laboring Ilya, I viewed a savage snarl form on his jagged lips as he swung his left whip-holding arm at me. Being a lot fresher and quicker than he was, I ducked below the lash, grabbed his boot at the left heel and lifted with all my strength, throwing him from his mount. Taking a quick peek over my shoulder, I watched him topple over the rear of his horse and land squarely on the top of his head, where he remained balanced and still for a few moments before toppling to lie face down in the grass.

The two female riders continued dashing towards the circle. I gave Kimosabee his lead, leaned into the wind and closed on them until we were all just mere yards from the goal. That was when Ileana and Miss Yu chose to slow their horses. The little Asian woman tossed the tarkus towards her employer, and Ileana, waiting patiently as the carcass floated through the air, never expected me to come charging between them to snatch it just before it was in her grasp, but with a loud "Thank you, Miss Yu. I'll take that," that was just what I did.

Once again, it was time to circle the field, but by keeping my mount from much of the caning and beating the other horses had been subjected to, Kimosabee was fresher and stronger than the two remaining and no matter how hard Ileana or Miss Yu drove their charges they simply could not catch us. I circled the blue pole filled with confidence but wondered why the sounds of horses' hooves had turned silent behind me. Starting my return, I discovered the reason; instead of chasing me, the women had changed their tactics and were sitting astride their mounts, waiting for me in the center of the field. Not wanting to do combat with either of them, Ileana for my own rather selfish reasons and Miss Yu because of her still unexplained saving of my solid American ass, I decided that instead of crashing through them I would guide my still strong horse around them. Expecting a Buzkashi collision, they had dug their horses' hooves into the grassy turf and by the time they realized I wasn't going to challenge them and chose instead to circumnavigate their little blockade, it was too late for their tired mounts to give adequate chase.

I turned one last time to survey the battlefield and saw Ileana, holding her bamboo cane with both hands as one would a baseball bat, twist her body into a corkscrew before uncoiling to deliver a severe blow to the rear of her brother's head as he knelt helplessly in the grass. As much as I disliked Ilya, I winced with the shot she gave him, the loud *thwack* of bamboo on skull crossing the field as clearly as a Southampton church bell tolling on Easter Sunday. Ilya fell face first into the grass, his heels flying into the air from the force of his short quick drop, and I couldn't help but wonder if he was ever going to get up after the smoking he'd just received. Gliding to the 'Circle of Justice', I held the tars tarkus above my head and waited at its perimeter for Ileana and Miss Yu to reach me.

Riding gently towards me, Ileana called, "Well played, Gabriel. It appears you are to be the victor."

I said, "Not yet, I'm not," and throwing the carcass to her, added, "I'm a guest in your house and you'll find that in our country we show proper respect to our hosts. In spite of what

Vince Lombardi said, winning isn't everything nor is it the only thing. You earned this as much as I did, and anyway, I'm sure you'll find a way to repay me."

Ileana whispered, "You are quite a man, Gabriel Fortuna." Then, tossing the carcass in a high arc into the middle of the 'Circle of Justice', she called to the defeated contestants, many of whom had gotten to their feet and were hobbling towards the goal, "I take as my trophy, Gabriel Fortuna. He is to be my slave from sundown to sunrise." Smiling coolly, Ileana asked, "Does this meet with your approval, Gabriel?"

Patting my valiant pinto on its neck, I answered, "Kimosabee and I wouldn't have had it any other way."

9

"Well, just what am I supposed to do?"

It was four in the afternoon and Samantha Goodbody and I were in a bedroom suite in the Kutchakokov Mansion that looked like it may have once been inhabited by Tsar Nicholas. I was in the bathroom, having just taken a hot shower, and was applying house supplied ointments and salves to some of the cuts and bruises I'd received during the Buzkashi contest. Samantha was standing in the bedroom, staring at the closed bathroom door and shouting questions and demands into it that were more irritating than any of the minor wounds I'd received.

Wrapping myself in a cashmere robe bearing the IK crest on its left breast pocket, I left the bathroom and passed Samantha without a wink or a nod and fell into the oversized armchair sitting on the diagonal beside the king-sized bed. I made myself comfortable in its billowy pillows, adjusted my robe to prevent any possible leakage of the Fortuna jewels, and checking out the complimentary IPhone laying on the nightstand, said matter-of-factly, "You, Agent Goodbody, are going back to my place. I am spending the night with Ileana Kutchakokov. There's nothing you can do or say to make me change my mind. I'll find out what I can about Danny Fisher and the Kutchakokov's reasons for being in The Hamptons, but anything beyond that is my business and not yours."

Samantha dropped her jaw into her chest and frustratingly replied, "I told you that you were my responsibility and that I was going wherever you were going. That was our deal."

"Deal? Deal? What deal? I didn't make any deal. Did you hear me say I was making a deal? I didn't think we had a deal. Besides, I don't think Ileana is in the mood for a threesome."

Samantha snapped, "I don't like this one bit, Fortuna. I'm a federal agent and you'll do as I say."

I snapped back, "Not in this lifetime. Now, go to my place and wait for me there. I'll be back in the morning and let you in on all I get out of Ileana, at least all I get concerning her motives for being in the States. I doubt you'd want to hear *all* I get out of her. That may include some sounds you've probably never heard and some bodily fluids that may prove to be a bit too personal and sticky for your provincial Federal tastes."

Turning as red as a Bridgehampton beet, she exclaimed, "Asshole!"

I countered calmly, "Be that as it may, you're out of here. Tell the valet you want the keys to The Caddy and leave. Try and get some sleep and I'll see you in the morning. If things go the way I plan, I guarantee you'll find me much more agreeable to speak with when I return home."

"You just be careful," she ordered. "Remember, it's my ass that's on the line."

I replied somewhat truthfully, "If that were actually the case, Agent Goodbody, I'm sure I would not be allowing you to leave."

Samantha's eyes blazed, her chest heaved and I was sure she

was about to give me another harangue about the basic anal quality of my character when at that exact moment there came a strong rapping at the hallway door. I rose from my chair, adjusted my robe teasingly for Samantha's displeasure and opened the door to find the diminutive Miss Yu. On her left was a double-tiered metal cart bearing a stack of thick white towels, several open jars of exotic oils and a few sticks of aromatic candles. On her right, a massage table.

"Ah, what have we here?" I asked.

Miss Yu leered her way past me, ignored Samantha, and began setting up shop in the middle of the room. After covering the opened massage table with luxuriously thick and pristine white towels, she lighted a few scented candles and closed the chamber's shades. Finished with her preparation, she stood at attention beside the table and waited.

I looked at Samantha and said, "It appears that it's time for you to go."

With a particularly loathsome expression, but not a word of protest, Samantha left the suite, slamming the door so hard behind her that several of the candles supplied by Miss Yu flickered and went out.

I shrugged, and sidling over to the massage table, said, "Sorry about that, Miss Yu, but Miss Goodbody doesn't like to share me with other women." Changing the subject to what I hoped would have a more happy ending, I added, "I assume you were sent here by Ileana to relax me before the evening's festivities. I've got to tell you, I'm plenty relaxed already, but a good massage is something I never pass up, especially after a hard game of Buzkashi. Now, would you prefer to do me with or without the robe? I don't get embarrassed by nudity as many other guys do, my body being my temple and all, and I certainly don't mind being naked with a professional. You are a pro, I assume. I mean, why else would Ileana have sent you?"

To my stupefying surprise, Miss Yu replied in perfect English, "Fortuna, would you please just shut the fuck up? I haven't been alone with you for five minutes and already I've got a headache. Just lie face down on the table, put your head in the hole, chill out and let me do my job. And one more thing, don't you dare remove that robe. The last thing I want to see is your package. Do I make myself clear?"

I answered, "Perfectly," and proceeded to drop my robe to the floor, giving my soon-to-be masseuse a dramatic full-frontal of that which she would soon be rubbing down. Her flat eyes widened in either appreciation or shock, satisfying me that I'd successfully shown her who was in charge despite her tough talk.

Lying on the table, I placed my head in the aperture and said, "I'm glad I have the chance to thank you for helping me out today. Those so-called teammates of mine may have done me some harm if you hadn't and I just want you to know I appreciate it. Now, feel like telling me why you did it?"

Miss Yu answered, "I take my orders from Ileana. She told me to make sure you didn't get hurt. Having seen what happens to people who let her down, I try not to disappoint her. Believe me, when I came to your aid I was more interested in saving my own ass than in saving yours."

I said, "You certainly are one charming masseuse, Miss Yu," and after a couple of seconds of listening to her puttering around in preparation of anointing me with oil, added, "Whatever. Thanks just the same. I owe you."

She said crisply, "No more questions," and began kneading away at my muscles, her fists digging into them so deeply I thought she was about to go in and pull out a lung.

"Hey, take it easy, lady. This is supposed to be a massage, not an hour on the rack. And you know what I said before about owing you; after this you can consider us even."

Miss Yu exclaimed, "Don't tell me how to do my job!" and smacking me vigorously with an open palm to the small of my back, barked, "It was already hard enough without you coming into the picture. Gabriel this and Gabriel that...Ileana hasn't stopped talking about you since that first night at *Tatiana's*. How the hell am I supposed to learn anything with you always in the way?"

I took my head out of the hole, turned it towards my sadistic masseuse and said, "What are you talking about, and say, who the hell are you anyway and where did you learn to speak English like that?"

Miss Yu vigorously pushed my head back into the hole, and obviously forgetting what she'd earlier said about observing my boys, grabbed them firmly from behind and said, "Fortuna, just shut the fuck up and listen. My real name is Linda Wu. I work for the CIA and have been with the Kutchakokov's for eight years. In that time, I haven't seen my family, had a date, made love, enjoyed a sip of alcohol or seen even one episode of *America's Got Talent*. I am one tightly wound little bitch so don't fuck with me. You're the first American I've actually spoken with in all that time and judging from the experience I'm almost glad to be working undercover in Russia. Now, remember this and remember it good; Ileana is no one to mess with. I've seen many men go into her bedchamber and none of them has ever came out the same. I've even heard that more than a few have committed suicide soon after the experience. I don't know what the lady does with them, but whatever it is, it's lethal. And another thing, as far as I'm concerned, you keep your mouth shut. To you, I'm just Ileana's servant and bodyguard, no more and no less. If I find out you said anything to anyone about me," she emphasized with a sudden twist, *"these boys are mine."*

Finding myself in the most compromising of positions, I replied, "Miss Yu, your secret is my secret. Now, if you'd kindly let some blood flow to my nads, I think you'll find them up to anything Ileana can throw at me."

"Good," she said, releasing her grip. "I think we understand each other. Now, let me finish. Ileana wants you oiled, glowing and fragrantly prepared for your big night."

I said, "A few questions first, Miss Yu, or is it Wu?"

She answered harshly, "It's Miss Yu, you muscle-bound idiot." *SMACK!!!!!*

"Alright, alright, Miss Yu! Now, tell me what The Kutchakokovs are about. I've already entered the lion's den and I think I've got a right to know."

Pouring what felt like a pint of scented hot oil at the base of my neck and then working it deeply into my traps and lats, she answered, "That's easy enough. In Russia and its surrounding environs, I've seen them kill men, women and children, commit high and low level government assassinations, extort from the rich, steal from the poor, dismember the handicapped, burn whole villages, rape, pillage and commit tortures beyond anything you might see on *Sixty Minutes.*"

I said, "Woof, that's a whole lot of bad, but it's all in Russia or The Third World and none of it is our business. I want to know what they've been up to here in The States."

Miss Yu's surprise response was, "The answer to that is nothing. We've been here since early May and the boldest thing I've witnessed Ileana do was fire her landscaper and hire some excitable Latino to take care of her roses. The only thing she makes sure to do every day is practice jumping her horse, Rasputin, from six to eight in the morning. She drives the Bentley to The Topping Ranch out in Sagaponack by herself, taking only her dog with her. She never misses a day, including today before you arrived, and she's determined to win the Jumping Competition at The Hampton Classic this Sunday. Other than that, she catches rays at the pool, plays some tennis at the Easthampton Tennis Club, golfs at National Golf Links, beaches at Flying Point and spends the rest of her time taking care of America or shopping on Jobs Lane or Newtown Road. Once in a while I drive her into Manhattan and check out Bergdoff's and Bendel's, but other than that... nothing. It's almost like she became one of the *Real Housewives of the Hamptons* without the husband."

Contemplating that ugly little picture, I asked, "What about her nightlife? I saw her clubbing at *Tatiana's*. The way she was dressed tells me she spends a lot of time on the prowl."

Smacking my left butt cheek with more than a moderate degree of rancor, Miss Yu said, "You've got that wrong, hardass. As far as *Tatiana's* is concerned, The Kutchakokovs own that place and she goes there once in a while to pass some time. I'll tell you one thing though, neither she nor Ilya trusted that Danny Fisher with anything. He was a good front, but they knew he was skimming and they let it go only because they were still making a ton of cash and had a legitimate business going in The Hamptons in case they wanted to stick around. As for the way she dresses, that's just the way the lady likes to do things. She knows she's got the goods and likes to show them off, but as far as I know, she hasn't bedded a man since she got here. That's good and bad news for you. Ileana is probably a little out of condition for a marathon night in the hay but she must be horny as hell." Slapping me on my other cheek with a bit more relish than was necessary, Miss Yu added, "Alright, I'm finished with your back, now turn over."

I was loathe to give her the opportunity to work her sadistic magic on my really important side and said, "I still feel a little tight in the hamstrings. Would you mind working on me a little back there?"

Miss Yu laughed and answered, "No problem, Romeo."

Smack!!!!

Wincing, I asked, "What about Ilya? What's his story?"

"Now, that's more interesting. He's the third Ilya I've known in my eight years with this crew but he's no different than any of the others."

Stunned by this information, I interrupted the wee one and said, "Wait a minute. You mean there's been two others."

"That's what I said."

"So, Ilya's not really her brother?"

"Unless he's one of a trio of Ilya's that popped out with Ileana, he's as much a twin brother of hers as I am."

I put this into the vault and said, "What else can you tell me about the guy?"

"Just what you'd expect. Whenever there's a murder or an arson or some torture doled out, he's always there supervising. Since we've gotten here, though, he rarely leaves the house, spending most of his time at home on the phone or cavorting with any number of hookers the gang has recruited from the mother country to provide these thugs with recreation. He spent a lot more time with Danny Fisher than Ileana, though, and the last time I saw those two together it seemed like Fisher couldn't get to his car fast enough. His murder had all the hallmarks of an Ilya Kutchakokov rubout, plastic bag and all, but when it comes to making business decisions, I've never seen him at a meeting with any of the Ruskies who run their backwards country. It's always Ileana."

After a couple of elbows pressed deeply into my calves, I raised my hand in surrender, sat up and placed a white towel across my lap and vitals. Satisfied that there was nothing more I would get from Miss Yu, I said, "I think we're done. Thanks for all the intel. I'll give the good word to Ileana about the great workout you gave me."

The little Asian silently got her things together, placed them on the cart and already had one foot out the door when she turned to deliver one last bit of news, "Fortuna, the only reason I'm helping you out is because I got a message from my gatekeeper telling me you were working with Homeland Security. Other than that, you're nothing to me. I will not compromise myself and if you get into trouble, you're on your own. Now, Ileana expects you at her suite at six-thirty. Someone will pick you up at six-twenty-five. Don't be late. And remember what I said before. Ileana is a man eater. Be careful."

I went to the window, opened it wide and hit the sack for some pre-coital relaxation. Sitting up against its purple damask headboard, I looked out upon the slate blue ocean and cloudless blue sky and watched The Kutchakokov helicopter rise and head out to sea. The craft was about a mile out when an object fell from it and dropped a couple of hundred feet to make a small and silent splash and I turned on my side and thought about my chat with Miss Yu. Except for confirming them, nothing she'd said about Ilya had changed my initial feelings about him. He'd given me the creeps when I met him and he still did. And as far as the lovely and leggy Miss Kutchakokov was concerned, not much had changed there, either. Contrary to what Miss Yu thought, after three months of going it alone, man-eater was a term that sounded pretty darn good.

10

At six o'clock I rose from bed, showered, sprayed myself with some of the Zaporoshtie Cologne sitting on the bathroom vanity and dressed in the set of casual clothing laid out atop my dresser. The soft black pullover and matching relaxed slacks were a weave of fine cashmere and silk, the smoothness of the ensemble on my recently lubricated skin making me feel like a six-foot-two erogenous zone, and of course, the initials IK were embedded into the garments, at the breast pocket and the right hip, but I didn't care; there wasn't a red K on my neck, I knew I wasn't anyone's property and everything was going just the way I wanted.

At six-twenty-five, just as Miss Yu said, a knock came at my door and I opened it to find two new white vinyl perfectos. They didn't say anything but motioned to me with a gracious wave of their arms, and positioning themselves at either of my shoulders, escorted me down the long hallway to a small gilt elevator. A door slid quietly open, the three of us got into the tight compartment and the lovely escort to my left pressed the top button on the control panel, the one labeled IK, and up we went.

Moving tantalizingly slowly, the car came to a sensuous stop and its door glided open with a soft *swoosh*. A pair of delicate hands at the small of my back urged me forward and I gladly stepped into a large chamber of cloud white walls and deep-pile white wool carpeting. Some crappy French jazz was playing softly through a set of hidden speakers, the room was scented with lavender, giving the place the sensual illusion of a Provencal paradise, and a king-sized bed covered by a shimmering white duvet and two large white satin pillows sat against the far wall, the ceiling above it decorated with a large mirror. There were no windows or doors, and aside from the elevator, I assumed, no escape. In the center of the room, lying languorously on a floating large red chaise providing the only color in the room, lay a voluptuous Ileana and a docile America.

Dressed in layers of soft white fur and looking more like a gauzy dream than a real person, Ileana revealed only seductive patches of her perfect legs, a glimpse of her ample breasts and a tantalizing view of her siren's face. Placing her pet delicately onto the floor, she moistened her lips with the tip of her tongue and whispered seductively, "Come to the chaise, Gabriel. I think it is time we become better acquainted."

I approached Ileana and bent down to kiss her, but seeing a Calypson smile form on her pouty lips forced me to hold back. My head said, 'Go, man, go', but my body said, 'Keep it in your pants', the problem being I felt nothing but strong senses of danger and revulsion and I lurched away.

Behind an expression of profound puzzlement, Ileana gasped, "What is wrong, Gabriel? Is there something wrong with my kiss?"

I didn't know what was wrong but felt like everything was, and trying to figure out what was preventing me from getting down to business, I changed the subject and answered, "Before we make love, Ileana, there are a few things I'd like to know."

"Don't be silly, Gabriel. The only thing you need to know is how to satisfy me and that knowledge I am sure you possess." Patting the empty space on the chaise she had reserved for me, she added, "Come. You are my slave for twelve hours. You must do as I say. It is our way."

"That may be your way, Ileana, but it's not Fortuna's Way. I let you win because I wanted to be alone with you, but you and I aren't only about sex. I want more than that."

"More? What more can there be between a man and a woman? I know how you feel. It is your nature. Now, give me your hand and take me to bed. It is time for us to make love."

I couldn't believe how reluctant I was to make it with this spectacular piece who was really just begging for it, but with a shake of my head, I again rejected her offer and said, "Sorry, Ileana, no can do. Before we get down to pleasure, there's some questions I want answered."

Ileana raised an eyebrow, gave a quick glance to that private place below my waist and asked, "Is there something wrong with you, Gabriel? Are you not the man I thought?"

I didn't like what she was inferring and wanted to show her I was more man than she could have imagined. I wanted to scoop her up in my arms, throw her onto the bed and teach her the meaning of the word, woman, Fortuna style, but Ileana was right: something was wrong, something that had never happened before and something I could not explain. At a loss in more ways than one, I chose to skirt the issue of my puzzling predicament and asked, "Just what are you doing in The Hamptons, Ileana? I know your reputation. You and your brother are feared wherever you go. So, again I ask, why are you in The Hamptons, and why now?"

The sexual fire in her eyes was extinguished faster than The Jay Leno Show playing prime time and she answered flatly, "So, it has finally happened. You and this place are like all the others. Here in The Hamptons, I thought all that was needed was money for one to be welcome, but it appears I was wrong."

I felt no sympathy for Ileana's plight and broke in, saying, "It takes more than money to make a home, Ileana. That goes for wherever you are. Murdering the local populace doesn't get you any favors either."

A different kind of flame than what she'd shown earlier appeared in her eyes and she shot back, "Murder? What do you mean, murder? I have hurt no one."

I said, "Maybe not. The jury's still out on that one, but you still haven't answered my questions. Why are you in The Hamptons and why now?"

Releasing a world weary sigh, she retreated into the chaise, reached down to stroke deeply into America's fur and answered, "Gabriel, I am tired of life in Russia. I want to be as nearly everyone else in the world wants to be...I want to be American. With your failing economy, there was great opportunity and I bought this land to make my home. I do not want to return to Russia. There is nothing there for me. I have all I need to be happy except for a safe home and a man to love. In spite of what you may have heard, I am not a monster; I am a person. I want to have those things and I want to have them here...in The Hamptons. I want that more than anything."

Slowly rising, she stood before me more like a magnificent blonde phoenix about to give her own personal rendition of *God Bless America* than the terrorist of which Miss Yu had warned, and shrugging gently, she allowed her soft robes to fall from her sumptuous body in a cascade of silent fur. Dressed only in her burgeoning lace bra and white silk panties, she took the few steps needed to stand before me, took my hands in hers and whispered,

"I am not a monster." Moving her succulent lips closer to mine, she added in an erotic rush that sent my pulse soaring, "Kiss me, Gabriel. Kiss me and make me your woman."

I wanted to say, 'No, never gonna happen, no way, Jose', but Ileana was too alluring to resist. Battling waves of anxiety, I wrapped my arms around her waist, pulled her close and brought my mouth roughly to hers.

The kiss we shared was long and deep and hard, leaving both of us gasping for air when our quivering lips parted. Pressing her body into mine, all the while moaning my name over and over like a madwoman with nothing inside her save an all-consuming lust, she brought her long and lovely neck to my mouth, where I savaged it, covering it with a thousand deep and longing kisses before working my tongue in hard circles over her fiery red K.

Ileana shuddered violently for several seconds and then fell limply into my arms. It took a while, but her breathing finally calmed, and as she looked up and stared into my eyes, her intense expression told me that what she had experienced was something new, something exciting and perhaps something a bit overwhelming.

Unable to keep her mouth from mine, our lips met again, this time in a frenzied collision. Her roving hands reached under my shirt, where she raked her long fingernails down my back and along my chest. Spiraling their way down towards their ultimate goal, lower and lower her marvelous fingers traveled: to my waist, beneath my pants, searching, searching, reaching, deeper and deeper and then... both of us gasped.

Breaking free from her grasp, I panted, "Did you kill Danny Fisher?"

Through heavy breathing, she answered, "No. What is wrong?"

"Did you have him killed?"

"No, why would I? He meant nothing to me. Let me help you. I can make it better."

"Why are you here?"

"I told you; I want to be an American. What is wrong with you? Take me. I'm yours. Whatever you want. Just take me."

There was nothing more to ask, nothing more to do and certainly nothing for me to take. Neither Ileana nor I had gotten what we'd wanted, but I knew that was just the way life worked: one rarely gets what one wants; one can only hope to get what one needs, and for some reason I didn't comprehend, my body told me I didn't need this. Turning my back on Ileana and our mutual night of passion, I walked dejectedly to the elevator and pressed the gilded button.

Ileana called, "Gabriel, please, don't go. No other man has ever done for me what you did with only a kiss. Come back. I will help you. Whatever you want I will give. Say it and it is yours."

I looked over my shoulder and replied half-heartedly, "I don't need anything from you, Ileana. What I want, you don't have, and what you want is obviously something I can't deliver."

No longer pleading, Ileana fired into my back, "You must stay. You are my slave. I have you for the next twelve hours."

"Forget it, Ileana. This is the USA and we fought a Civil War to end slavery, but don't worry, there's someone for everyone. If you stick around long enough, I'm sure you'll get what you deserve."

I rode the elevator down, got out and was escorted to my room by the same two guards as had picked me up, but instead of gleaning over their fabulous bodies and beautiful faces as I had earlier, I hardly knew they were there. I got dressed, left the cashmere outfit I'd been loaned neatly folded on the bed, and called Hometown Taxi from the nightstand I-Phone, telling the dispatcher to have the cab meet me at the front gate in ten minutes.

Leaving the mansion, I walked to the gate and found the cab waiting. Strong feelings of upset and failure lingered within me, but for some reason I could not fathom, I also felt a strong sense of relief, as if I had just escaped from some evil I was unable to feel or see or hear. Giving the driver my address, I got into the back of the car, reclined deeply into its worn seat and wondered what the hell might be wrong with me. Remembering how things were often not as they seemed to be, I hoped that the answer to that was a simple one: nothing that a good woman couldn't cure. Now, I just had to find one.

11

In the distance, whirring blue and red lights lit the early evening around Noyac Road like a scene from one of those god-awful Halloween movies. With colors bouncing eerily off moving leaves of the surrounding oaks, hickories and maples, a macabre dance was produced that only insinuated trouble. I told the cabbie to get me home fast but before he'd driven much farther we were stopped by the white-gloved big right mitt of Southampton Town cop, Jon Levitsky, standing in the middle of the two-lane blacktop, turning cars back to Millstone Road.

Tossing two twenties into the front seat and telling the driver to keep the change, I jumped out of the cab, raced to the officer and asked anxiously, "What's going on down there, Jon?"

His folksy return was, "Hello, Gabe. It's been a while. Nice to see you, too."

Not in the mood for any of his small town, power-trip cop games, I got into his face and hollered, "Cut the shit, Jon! What's going on?"

Levitsky, looking like he'd put on twenty soft pounds since I'd last seen him, hiked up his pants and answered, "Take it easy,

Gabe. I haven't been down there myself, but there are reports of an explosion and now there's fire. From what I got over the radio, a couple of cars and maybe a house or two are either going up or have already gone up. I've been notified that everything's under control and that traffic will be allowed to pass in a few hours. They've just got to make sure there are no flare-ups. Must be a real mess down there, though. I hear the blast broke windows in homes a half-mile away. I know I felt it all the way in Sag Harbor."

With this new bit of bad news, the hairs on my neck stiffened and I barked, "I've got to get down there, Jon. My place is down the road and I've got a bad feeling."

Officer Levitsky replied, "Listen Gabe, like I said, it's a mess down there and you'll just have to wait until things cool down. I've got orders not to let anyone pass and that includes you."

"Then, you'd better take out your pistol and shoot me, Jon, because there's nothing else you can do to stop me. Now, get out of my way before you lose your head."

After two and a half miles of a hot run, I reached my place and was devastated by what I found. Charred hulks of The Caddy and Enrique's once white painting van were nothing more than burned litter in the driveway of what had been my lovely Hamptons' home. With its windows blown out, cedar shingles scorched, front porch turned to charcoal, foundation shrubs blackened, and water everywhere, soaking anything that might have survived the flames into waterlogged pieces of crap, my home as I knew it no longer existed, but I didn't dwell too long on my loss because it was just stuff and all stuff could always be replaced with money and hard work and the proper insurance. Instead, my thoughts were of Samantha Goodbody and Enrique Santiago. Searching to find the largest crowd of firemen, I saw a huddle of them near a large red and white SUV and raced to it, whipping Fire Chief Peter Glennon around by his shoulders when I reached him.

Thirty years on the force and receiver of hundreds of commendations, Chief Glennon was not the kind of guy who was used to being manhandled. His eyes glowed like burning embers and he appeared ready to give me the back of his meaty hand, but recognizing who it was who'd spun him and seeing the pain in my face, he checked his instincts and said gently, "Oh, hi, Gabe. Sorry about all of this. There was nothing we could do."

I cried, "What the hell happened here, Pete? What the fuck is going on?"

Placing a well-meaning hand on my shoulder, Chief Glennon answered smoothly, "Take it easy, Gabe. We don't have all the answers and probably won't for a while, but judging from the crater, it appears that a pretty good sized bomb exploded in your driveway. It looks like the van's tire went over and detonated it, causing all the damage you see and some you don't."

I wailed, "A bomb!!?? A bomb went off in my driveway!!?? Are you telling me someone planted a landmine or some kind of IED on my property!!?? Where the hell are we: Afghanistan, Iraq, The South Bronx? This is the Town of Southampton, Suffolk County, East End of Long Island, State of New York, United States of America, damn it. People living here don't go planting land mines around other people's homes. Not here!! Not ever!! And not my home!!"

"Well, Gabe, there's a first time for everything and I guess the world is just getting smaller because that looks like what happened here. We'll know better once the official report is in, but in my humble opinion, you got bombed."

I asked anxiously, "Did anyone get hurt? Is everyone okay?"

The Chief answered, "Nothing as big as this must have been

is going to explode and not hurt people. We've sent a few of the injured from surrounding houses to the hospital and still have to check out some homes where the glass was blown out to see if there are people in them for whom the hospital might be too late. The guy in the van, well, he didn't make it and neither did the woman sitting beside him. That was one ugly sight, but you don't need to know about that. We pulled a woman out of your place, too. Pretty little thing, she was in the back of the house and probably just relaxing on your deck. She caught some flying glass, giving her a few nasty lacerations, but mostly she got some water in her lungs when she was blown into Noyac Bay. Must have swallowed half of it by the look of her. She's one tough cookie, though, and somehow had the strength to get out of the water and passed out on the shore. She's at the hospital now."

That was all I needed to hear. Running from the Chief I jumped into the nearest police car, where Tom Pontani sat behind the wheel filling out a report, and screamed, "Get me to Southampton Hospital now, Tom, and make it fast before I clock you one and get behind the wheel myself."

Peace Officer Pontani watched me huffing and puffing like a steam locomotive about to blow and knew that if he wanted to actually keep the peace he'd better do as I asked. Nodding to Chief Glennon that he should tell his boss where he was going, he pulled away from my smoldering home and charged up Noyac Road. Only once did I have to tell him to put on his siren and step on it, and ten minutes later we turned onto Meeting House Lane and neared the entrance of Southampton Hospital.

* * *

There was no getting all the way to the emergency room by car, not even with a police car because three ambulances and a multitude of police and civilian vehicles blocked the side streets and the entrance. I jumped out while Tom was still slowing down, ran the rest of the way to the emergency room doors and forced my way into a jammed waiting room of cops, firemen, doctors, nurses, medical technicians, volunteers, crying family members and the usual assortment of people with broken appendages waiting for care.

Racing to the information counter, through some fast and heavy breathing I asked the elderly female volunteer behind the desk, "Lady, can you tell me where Samantha Goodbody is? She was brought in a short time ago. I need to see her."

The old woman didn't answer, but looked over my shoulder and nodded, indicating someone was coming up behind me. I turned quickly and again found myself face to face with Federal Agent Ralph Ledbetter.

The arrogant federal twerp placed his face about an inch from mine and said, "You're a little late for a friendly visit, aren't you, Fortuna? Hospital hours end at eight PM."

I wanted to pop him a good one but held back and said, "Listen to me, Ledbetter. All I want to know is how Samantha's doing and where she is. I don't need to hear any of your bullshit and if you insist on giving it you ought to consider yourself lucky to be in a hospital surrounded by doctors. You got that?"

"Tough guy," Ledbetter began, but taking a quick look down at my balled fists wised him up fast and he said, "She's okay. She's in a room on the second floor getting a few cuts stitched up. You know, Fortuna, maybe if you'd been with her as you were supposed to be and not chasing after some Russian tail this never would have happened. But you, you've always got to try and make time, even when time might be running out for someone else. You've got a real problem, and the worst part of it is, you don't know it."

He was wrong. I had a couple of problems. One of them was named Ledbetter and the other was certainly none of his freaking business. Eyeballing him hard, I said, "I want to see her."

"I told you, they're treating her. And anyway, what makes you think she wants to see you?"

"Right now, it doesn't matter what she wants. All I know is I want to see her now. And I want to see her without you."

"Why's that, Fortuna? Feeling guilty?"

"You've got the wrong guy, Ledbetter. I didn't do anything to feel guilty about. If there's any guilt to be meted out, you can be first on line to get your share. You had no business placing her with me knowing the kind of trouble I might be headed for. If anyone is guilty, it's you. Now, tell me where she is."

He bit at the inside of his cheek and finally said, "Alright, I'll tell you, but first we play by my rules. I need some information. You spent quite a bit of time with The Kutchakokovs. What do you think they're up to?"

"I'm not getting into it now, but like I've told you a thousand times, if there's something going down in The Hamptons it's got to be about land." Taking a step forward to pit my chest against his, I concluded with a question of my own, "Now, where is she?"

He responded coolly, "We'll continue this conversation later. Samantha's in Room 204. I hope for her sake she tells you to get lost."

I found an empty stairwell, raced upstairs and then down the second floor hallway, finally reaching Room 204. Barging in without a knock, I found Samantha lying on a bed, eyes closed and surrounded by a doctor and two nurses. The doctor was carefully working a needle and thread in and out of her right arm and there was an IV set up beside her, its tube planted in her left forearm delivering the mix of juice she needed to get her strong and yet sedate her. There were already a few bandages on her right arm and one large gauze pad on her right cheek. I couldn't see if she was bandaged anywhere below her waist because that part of her was neatly parked beneath a hospital blanket. Aside from giving the doc a dose of silent confidence, neither of the nurses appeared to be doing much of anything.

Racing the few steps to her bedside, I nudged aside one of those nurses, took Sam's warm hand in mine and said, "I'm so sorry, Samantha. I had no idea it was unsafe at my place. I would never have let you go back there if I had any clue what might happen."

Opening her eyes at the sound of my voice, Samantha smiled and said weakly, "Gabe, it's you. I should never have left you. What will Ledbetter say?" Drowsily, she added, "You really ought to be nicer to me. You're so handsome. Why haven't you even tried to kiss me?"

That little speech must have taken a lot out of her because a second later she was asleep. With a nod, the doctor led me from the bed to the far side of the room and said, "Look, I'm new here and don't know who you are, but you seem important to the patient so I'm not going to give you a hard time about breaking into her room and pushing aside my nurse. The drugs are taking over and she's sleeping. She doesn't seem to have suffered too much damage, just some minor cuts and bruises, nothing too serious. We pumped her stomach and removed the seawater so there's nothing to worry about there, either. All she needs is a good night's rest, so, if you don't mind, I'd like you to kindly leave. I'm sure she'll be allowed visitors tomorrow, or more than likely, get released to go home. In either case, you may speak with her then."

Walking over to a sleeping Samantha, I kissed her cheek and left her room. No longer feeling the need to rush, I took the elevator to the first floor, entered the mob scene that was the Emergency Room and recognized an exotic high-pitched wail sail high above the common disorderliness of the space. I followed the sound to its source and spotted Enrique Santiago leaning against a wall, banging his head solidly against it and crying.

Concentrating on Samantha, I'd forgotten about Enrique and the two bodies in his van, but watching him use his head as a demolition ball and remembering how hardheaded he could be, I quickly zigzagged my way across the room and placed an empathetic hand on his shoulder and said, "I'm glad to see you're still with us, Enrique. What happened?"

Turning his bloodshot eyes and already black-and-blue forehead my way, the Latin Zombie fell into my arms and cried, "Muthafuck!!!! I sent Esmie and her new boyfriend to your place to tell you that you were welcome at the party and that there would be no hard feelings. Now, there's no Esmie, no boyfriend and no party. Oy mio, Gabe, what the fuck is going on? I have lost my seester. I have lost my fucking seester and it is all my fault. What kind of place is this? Who would kill for losing a bid on a lousy two-coat paint job on the Agawam Park Comfort Stations?"

Stroking Enrique's back, I told him he was not to blame, that it wasn't the result of the commercial contracts he'd won and that it was alright for a man to cry. He shuddered violently at my acceptance, broke down further and wept grievously for his lost sister, and as he did, my heart hardened. I now had more than

Danny Fisher's death to think about; someone was out to kill me, had come close to killing Samantha and had murdered Esmie and her new boyfriend. With a grieving Zombie in my arms, I swore that vengeance would be mine. No longer was I to be a mere gopher for Homeland Security; it had become personal.

In the buzz of the emergency room, it seemed like only a few seconds passed before a horde of Enrique's friends arrived. I left him in their company amid the hard stares of the Townies waiting their turns for doctors, and not having much of a home to return to, figured I would catch a cab, check in at The American Hotel and try to get a decent night's sleep in a dry bed. Tomorrow morning held the promise of being a long one and I'd start it by seeing what was left of my place. Afterwards, I'd return to the hospital to look in on Samantha and finish it by going to Southampton Town Hall to check the Records Department for some things that were bothering me. After that, if my hunches were right, it wouldn't be long before some bad stuff would have to go down.

Taking a step into the fresh night air, I raised a finger for the cab that was waiting at the curb and a familiar voice said, "Gabe, don't make this harder than it has to be." A second later, it added, "Gabriel Fortuna, you are under arrest for threatening an officer of the law and commandeering a police vehicle without proper authorization. Now, place your hands behind your back."

12

"You gotta be shitting me!"

Southampton Town Police Chief Melanie Dines took a sip of coffee from her *Moms Make the Best Cops* mug and replied, "Not this time, I'm not. And please refrain from that kind of street talk. You're being detained in the Southampton Police Station on Peacekeeper's Lane, not in a precinct mired somewhere in Brooklyn. Watch your language."

I answered my old friend and once upon a time lover directly, as I was sure she knew I would, "And fuck you, too, Melanie. What the hell goes on here? I didn't commandeer anything. Officer Pontani was nice enough to give me a lift from my burning home to the hospital, or have we forgotten that my house was in flames and that I was the victim of an assassination attempt?"

"You? I don't see anything wrong with you. Your Hispanic neighbors are the ones who got torched. You're still walking around and making trouble, only I'm not going to let you make trouble for me. Everyone knows we have history and I'm not going to let people say I let you get away with your tough guy stuff because of it."

"Get away with what? Are you forgetting that bomb was in my driveway? It was meant for me. Agent Goodbody was in my house and I was worried about her. All I did was get Pontani to drive me to the hospital so I could see her. What's the big deal with that?"

"There's plenty of a big deal, Gabe. It's one thing if an officer drives you to the hospital with the advice and consent of a superior officer or because the person in need of transportation is injured or facing an emergency; it's another if the officer takes that ride because he's afraid of having his head handed to him. Officers Pontani and Levitsky felt threatened, and because of that you are spending the night here in the lockup."

"This is all bullshit, Melanie. I don't know why you're holding me, but it's not because Tom Pontani or Jon Levitsky thought I was going to kick their asses, although I may have to reconsider those possibilities for opening their big traps."

"Be careful, Gabe. Overt threats directed at police officers may cost you more time. Don't make me throw away the key."

I was looking at Melanie through new eyes, and glancing around the office where she'd sequestered me so that we could be alone, I saw pictures of herself, her daughter and her husband. In all of the shots, she was happy and spirited, but the most obvious emotion was love. It was always there: in her eyes, in her smile, in the way she stood. It was in every picture, love for her husband and especially for her child. There wasn't one photo of the many on her desk and walls that didn't show a woman proud of her accomplishments and her life. She had a lot to fight for, and knowing Melanie as I did, I knew that's just what she would do if it came down to it.

I asked, "How long do I have to stay here?"

Melanie answered, "Judge Shapiro should be in court tomorrow morning. You'll be arraigned then and a trial date will be set. Bail will be set or not, depending on the judge's opinion."

The mere mention of Judge Shapiro's name made me want to hit something. That guy had a hard-on for me for the past five years because his daughter had a very different kind of thing for me and she and I had spent some ultra-fine conjugal time together. She'd been a great-looking twenty-two year old fresh out of college and I showed her a few things her college chums didn't know, things that made her feel like a woman and things that gave her the crazy notion she was in love with me. You can't make love with someone a couple of hundred times without developing some strong feelings for that person, but the affair came way too soon after my break-up with my ex-wife, and still licking my wounds from that disaster, I told her and myself it was only sex and tried to let her down easily.

After I dropped her, she moped around a lot at home, finally crying to her father and mother about me and her unrequited love. Being a man of some power out here, Judge Shapiro freaked out, came to my place and warned me that if I ever went near his daughter again he'd see to it I'd get locked up and never again see the light of day. Naturally, I told him to fuck himself and that his daughter needed to grow up. He must have known what I'd told him about his daughter was true, but she was still his little girl and insisted on showing his displeasure by spitting on my porch and leaving in a dither. The dither was caused by my bringing my initial ring down on his way too big head in my hope that such a surprising shot would make him remember he was a servant of the people and not my boss, and further cause him to cease and desist from ever again dropping a lungee on my porch. Now, he was going to be my judge.

I barked, "Judge Shapiro?"

Knowing my history with the Judge, Captain Dines replied through a way too obvious smile, "Have you got a problem with that?"

I answered, "Up yours, Melanie. I'll call my lawyer in the morning and get this shit straightened out."

"Oliver's out of town for a few days, Gabe. You'll have to wait for him to get back if you want his services."

"That's something I won't need. Oliver's history. Just like you. Now, where am I sleeping tonight? It's been a long day and I need some rest."

Melanie picked up her phone, hit a button and a couple of seconds later, two burly young cops came in and escorted me out of the captain's office and down the hall to the small cellblock of six, two cot, one sink and one toilet barred rooms. Two of the cells had a couple of sleeping drunks in it and one had a tattooed Latino, bruised and dazed, laid out on the floor. I was led to the last cell on the left. The cop on my right took a key and opened the door as the one on my left removed my cuffs. Without a word to either of them, I entered the cell, walked to the cot and flopped down. The door clanged shut behind me and I closed my eyes. Melanie Dines didn't know it, but she had done me a favor: I was safe from danger, had a roof over my head, looked forward to a free all-you-can-eat town breakfast coming my way in the morning and didn't have to shell out the hundreds of dollars it would have cost me for a room at The American Hotel. The only thing that gave me a shiver was the thought of facing Judge Shapiro, but a call to my new lawyer would take care of that. At least I hoped it would.

13

I had already left a message for my lawyer, eaten a breakfast of bacon, eggs and coffee and completed using my aluminum toilet when I heard the metal door to the cellblock swing open at nine the next morning. Sitting on the cot in wrinkled clothes, my thumbs busily twiddling away between my folded hands, I gazed at the bars waiting for my attorney to appear and was not disappointed by what I saw.

Five-feet-six inches tall with long black hair cascading down her shoulders to frame her lovely and youthful face, she wore a light gray woolen business suit that accentuated her full bosom, tiny waist and long and shapely legs. Carrying an expensive leather briefcase in one hand and a silver Montblanc pen in the other, she looked at me and smiled in a way I knew no attorney should at her client. Placing the tip of that pen to her lips and taking a quick nip at the end of it, she dispensed with legal formality and said, "Hello, Gabe. It's been a long time."

I replied, "Five years, three months and seventeen days."

Her eyes gleamed at my response and in a few seconds she smiled in a relaxed manner and asked, "What took you so long to get in touch? I've been in town for over a year. I've been waiting for you to call."

Watching her eyes measuring me, I said, "Just waiting for the right time, Beth. I'd been busy with things, then got pretty badly banged up and decided to completely recuperate before getting back to you. I remember what you were like and wanted to be at full strength before making my call."

My attorney folded her arms over her truly magnificent set and said, "Same old bullshit. Same old Gabe."

Drinking her in with my eyes from the top of her head to her four-inch heels, I responded, "And I can see you're the same old Beth."

A few silent seconds passed before she said, "Well, let's first get you out of here. I see you've been scheduled for a ten o'clock arraignment at Town Hall with Judge Shapiro."

"Your daddy," I piped.

"Yes," she responded. Then, with hands on hips and her head tilted to the side, she added, "Isn't that just so convenient for you."

"That's a yes and a no. Look, Beth, I need a lawyer. I know that everything you do you do right, so I called you. The fact that you're gorgeous, great in bed, and your father is my judge and hates my guts had nothing to do with my reaching out to reconnect." Smiling mischievously, I added, "How am I doing?"

Beth answered much too rapidly, "Poorly," and then quickly added, "Now listen to me, Gabe. I don't care about our past. All that stuff happened more than five years ago and I've gone on with my life. I've been with plenty of guys since then and some of them were even better lovers than you. So don't get any ideas about me wanting to get back with you or my father helping me out because my perfect law record is at stake and he wants to keep it that way.

To both of us, you're just another inmate who needs to be dealt with fairly in the eyes of the law." Her eyes sparkling, she added with a hint of larceny, "Now, how am I doing?"

"Better than me, so far as the legal stuff is concerned, but when you say you've had better lovers than me, well, counselor, I have to object and demand to see some kind of material proof to back up that statement. Perhaps a video of some sort?"

Beth fought back a smile and said, "Okay, Gabe. I'll get the paperwork done and pick you up at nine forty-five. We'll go to court together, get this behind us and then head to Barrister's for lunch. We've got a lot of catching up to do and this time my father can't stop us."

Beth Shapiro, attorney-at-law, left the cellblock in a rush of jiggles and jasmine. Falling onto my cot, I sent the springs to jangling, got lost thinking about some of our torrid times together and wondered why simply thinking of those intense love-making sessions failed to arouse me in body as well as in soul. I recalled what the doctors told me about my post-gunshot condition, that there would be no permanent damage and I would be the same as ever in no time, but I couldn't help but wonder if those wounds I received at Saint Andrews had done some irreparable harm to me, something that neither doctors nor untrained eyes could see. Neither Ileana nor Beth had provoked the desired and never before unattained Fortuna response. Nothing was working out the way it should, at least nothing that mattered.

14

Being noonish and the Thursday before Labor Day Weekend, Barrister's was hopping with long-weekenders, seasonals and locals and getting a table promised to be a difficult thing, but upon entering Beth winked at young Tyler Levitsky, (yeah, this is a small town and it was the same threatened cop's son) and the summer-job lunchtime host quickly got us a table in the lattice-ringed outdoor garden. Surrounded by women in tennis whites, men in golf clothes and teenagers and twenty-somethings in shorts, sandals and t-shirts we sat and checked out the menu. Beth ordered a cheeseburger de-luxe and a regular coke from an attractive Czech waitress I'd somehow missed, and I got a large health salad, some grilled chicken and a bottle of Peconic Water.

The kitchen must have hired some extra help for the Labor Day Weekend crush because in a few minutes our food came. I frowned at Beth's luncheon choice, saying, "I see you're still chowing down the same way you did before we met. I would have liked to have thought I taught you something about proper diet in our short time together. Do you know how many empty calories there are in that stuff you're about to eat?"

Leaning towards me, Beth whispered, "You taught me plenty, Gabe. I haven't forgotten those predawn trysts on Flying Point Beach." Taking a bite of her burger, she chewed lasciviously and added, "But, don't worry. All this means is that there'll just be more of me to love. Got a problem with that?"

I pictured my full-bodied beauty, gulped down some Peconic Water and answered, "Nope, no problem whatsoever."

I should have continued pondering Beth's nude body, but as enticing as that was, I couldn't stop myself from thinking about Samantha lying on a hospital bed surrounded by strangers. Losing my appetite, I pushed the food around my plate, managed to down a couple of strips of chicken just to get some protein into me, and in a lackluster fashion, pushed the rest of my lunch to the center of the table.

"Something wrong with your salad?" Beth asked, dabbing delicately at a tiny dollop of ketchup resting at the corner of her mouth. Through a salacious smile, she added, "Why don't you get something else? After all, a man like you never knows when he'll need his strength."

I was in no mood for flirting, not even with a class piece like Beth, and I answered, "No thanks. I'm just thinking about Samantha. I wanted to see her after court and I'm eager to get to the hospital."

"Slow down, Gabe. She's fine. The best thing for her is for you to leave her alone so she can get some rest. In the meantime, you haven't even thanked me for getting you off."

Beth was probably right about Samantha, but I was still dubious about her court performance and said, "Getting me off? I had to pay a five hundred dollar fine and was placed on six months probation. You call that, 'getting me off'?"

Beth took the term, attorney-for-the-defense, to the extreme and answered rather defensively, "Look, you big ox, you could still be sitting in a cell awaiting arraignment and trial. I think a moderate fine and a stint of community service is a pretty good deal for commandeering a police vehicle and threatening two cops with their lives, or am I missing something?"

I replied, "I'm sorry, Beth. It's just that I've got a lot of things on my mind, things you might not understand and, well, just let's leave it at that, okay?"

"Look Gabe, I know you've got some issues. I've been with you since nine this morning and you haven't said one salacious or provocative word. If this is a new technique you've developed to get me into bed, I must confess, it's a puzzling one." Biting her lower lip, she added, " I'm willing to help you get through whatever it is that's jamming you up. I remember the man you were and I think I might want him back."

"Thanks, Beth. I promise that when I do get back to being myself you'll be the first woman I provoke. In the meantime, I've got some things to do before I hit the hospital."

My attorney raised her hand to get the check and said, "Look Gabe, it's been a long time since I've rubbed shoulders with you and I've got an open slate this afternoon. What do you say I tag along for a while?"

Recalling that my first stop was the Land Management Office in Town Hall, it occurred to me that having Beth beside me might not be such a bad idea. I wanted to find out more about those transfers of property on Gin Lane that the Kutchakokovs were now calling home and if the bureaucrats working the room were slow at getting me what I needed, then the daugter of Judge Shapiro working by my side might come in handy. Also, The Caddy was no longer viable and I needed wheels.

I said, "Thanks, Beth. If you wouldn't mind, I could use your help. Just remember, this is my show and I call the shots. If and when I tell you to go, you go."

"Whew, that didn't take long. I'm glad to see you're already getting stronger. Let's get going. We'll take my car and you're paying for lunch. It's a small price for my services: legal and automotive. Don't think you're getting off easy, though. If things work out, I'm sure I'll find some other ways for you to pay."

I dropped two twenties on the table, turned to follow my pushy and provocative lawyer out of Barrister's and saw the eyes of nearly every man in the place follow her out the door. Gazing at the same fine ass all those other guys were pondering, I wondered why I hadn't yet made a real move on Beth. After all, she certainly wasn't playing hard to get, and then the thought of Samantha in the hospital and Danny Fisher and Esmie in their graves brought me back to reality. I wasn't sure, but the thought occurred to me that I might be going soft in more ways than one.

15

The Land Management Office is located in Town Hall, a three story red-brick edifice on Hampton Road just outside the town's commercial district. Beth and I entered the small glass-doored office and the two people working the room, a man and a woman both in their fifties, acted like they hadn't dealt with anything but paper for years and were grateful to have something other than filing to do. They were quite helpful, guiding us to the file cabinets where the most recent land transfer records were kept, and it was a good thing Beth tagged along, because being an attorney, she was able to find the things I was looking for in half the time I would have needed.

I discovered that just as Ilya Kutchakokov had told me, the place where he and his sister now called home was once the site of four separate and distinct parcels belonging to owners whose names were once very prestigious in the annuls of American industry. There was the Collingsworth Property, owned by the heirs of a man who had made his turn-of-the-century fortune in the cereal business, The Hubbard Property, an estate owned by the family of an oligopolist railroad tycoon, The Smythe Property, owned by the grandson of a guy who actually had built a better mousetrap in the early 1900's, and the Remington Property, owned by Maximillian Remington, a guy I'd read about in the local papers who'd committed suicide about a year ago, seemingly just after finding out he'd lost his vast fortune to Madoff. The only thing on the documents that I didn't know for sure was a bit of information I'd suspected, but upon seeing in black ink left me with a very uncomfortable feeling; the Southampton lawyer representing the Kutchakokov's on every transaction was Oliver Dines.

Everything Ilya Kutchakokov told me about the land purchases rang true, right down to the amount of money he'd paid for the property, but even though everything seemed kosher on paper, I couldn't dismiss the concerned expression I saw on Beth's face after she saw the last piece of purchased property had belonged to Maximillian Remington.

I said, "What's up, Beth? You look like you've seen a ghost."

Looking up from her chair, she answered, "I'm uncomfortable with something, Gabe. Through my father, I became an acquaintance of Maximillian Remington after I finished law school. I did some legal work for him and got to know him pretty well and it never sat right with me that he was judged to have committed suicide. He was a nice old man who kept to himself, gave anonymously to various charities and lived a small life in a big house. I went to Maximillian's funeral and tried to speak with members of his family about what had happened but none of those who attended his service would speak to me and all of them left before he was even in the ground." Handing me a piece of paper, she added, "From the dates on the deed, it appears that his property was purchased just a couple of days after his death, almost as if the family couldn't wait to get rid of it. Now, why do you think that would be?"

I answered, "I don't know for sure, Beth, but I've got some ideas."

I could see the wheels turning inside her head and she proved to be driving the same road as me when she said, "I do, too. Let's go to the library. There are some things I think we ought to find out."

Beth and I thanked the Land Management office staff for their help, got into her car and drove the few blocks down Hampton Road to the Rogers Memorial Library on Windmill Lane. A state-of-the-art building when it was completed eight years earlier, the twenty-six thousand square foot library had everything a modern library should have, including, Beth told me, digital access to The New York Times and county mortality records.

We hit the computers and after Beth found the home page for Suffolk County Records, she searched for the mortality records and typed in the names Collingsworth, followed by Hubbard and then Smythe. In each case, the head of the family had died within a week of Maximillian Remington's death, and checking the dates of the sale of their estates against their deaths, all sales were completed within seven days of their passings.

From the Times obituary pages, Beth and I discovered that Mr. Collingsworth had suffered a heart attack and died in a car crash on a lonely expanse of Tuckahoe Road, just a half mile north of Shinnecock Golf Course, Mr. Hubbard drowned in a freak accident in his kayak off Clam Island in Noyac Bay and Mr. and Mrs. Smythe succumbed to an abundance of carbon monoxide fumes leaking up to their bedroom from a bad boiler in their basement. None of the deaths were covered in the local papers and nobody, save the family and some close friends, knew of the demise of the rich property owners who kept to themselves and died as quietly as they lived.

Beth asked, "Well, what do you think?"

"I'd say that all these people dying and their heirs selling their properties within a week after their deaths is quite a coincidence. Unfortunately, I don't believe in coincidence, so I've got to say that some pretty bad things must have happened and that there are some pretty bad people who think they got away with murder."

"You and I are thinking the same, Gabe. No wonder we fit so well. What do we do now, tell the police?"

I shook my head and said, "I'm afraid that's the last thing we want to do. Didn't you catch the name of the lawyer working for the Kutchakokovs?"

"Sure I did, but you don't think Oliver and Melanie Dines had anything to do with this?"

"I don't know what to think, but until I do we're not telling anybody anything."

I checked my watch, saw it was three o'clock and asked Beth if I could use her cell phone to call the hospital. She said something about me getting into the twenty-first century, handed me her phone and I punched the number for hospital information.

"Southampton Hospital," came the response.

"Hello. I'm calling to inquire about the condition of a patient. Her name is Samantha Goodbody."

"Just a second, please, while I get that information for you."

I held the phone and watched Beth continue working at the computer, still digging away to find out anything she could about the land sales and the untimely deaths of the previous owners. I thought she was smart, beautiful and devoted, and knew for a fact she was a wonderful lover. I asked myself, what more could a man want, and then, the operator's voice returned.

"Miss Goodbody expired this morning at nine o'clock, sir."

"What?" I cried. "That's impossible."

"I'm sorry, sir, but Ms. Samantha Goodbody expired this morning. Is there anything else?"

I dropped the phone onto the library floor, held tight onto Beth's hand, and when I got my bearings, said, "Samantha died."

Next thing I knew, we were racing down Meetinghouse Lane and headed for Southampton Hospital.

16

We burst into the hospital admissions area and I stormed to the front desk. Beth was only steps behind me, telling me to calm down, actually begging me to, but I was suffering a blind rage and the only thing I heard was the rush of chaos in my ears.

I yelled at the volunteer, "I want to speak with somebody!"

The woman behind the counter looked sorrowfully into my eyes, telling me in her own quiet way that this was not the first time she'd been called upon to help someone in pain, and asked gently, "With whom would you like to speak, young man?"

I gazed around the crowded area, saw distorted and frightened faces staring at me from every part of the vestibule and hollered into space, "I don't know! I just know I want to speak with someone! I need to find out what happened to Samantha! They told me yesterday she was fine and that she'd be leaving today. Now they're telling me she's expired." Reaching across the desk and grabbing the old woman's hands, I cried, "You've got to help me!"

Once again, creeping up behind me like a bad habit, Homeland Security Agent Frank Ledbetter invaded my space and said, "Let her alone, Fortuna. I'm the one you want to see. I'm the one who's going to tell you once and for all to think about something other than your meat. That teenaged libido of yours has gotten you into plenty of trouble, but now it's caused the death of someone who only wanted to help you and her country."

I tried to collect my cool and through gritted teeth hissed a simple question, "Where's Samantha?"

"Right now she's in a chopper about to be dropped off at Fort Dix. Once there, they'll dress her up, pack her in ice and ship her home so that her parent's can give her a decent burial. And it's all because of you and your need to prove how big a man you are."

My cool deserted me far faster than I'd collected it and I charged and slugged that cop with everything I had. The only thing that saved Ledbetter from having a permanent GF stamped on his jaw was that he was faster than I thought he'd be and avoided most of the damage my punch would have done by trying to duck under it. My fist glanced off the top of his forehead with only the two bottom knuckles catching him, but it was still enough to put Ledbetter on the seat of his pants and slide him along the polished floor until he came to a halt against the far wall.

"You finished yet?" he called, placing a hand to the top of his head.

"Not hardly," I panted.

"Well, you'd better be. I've got ten G-Men outside, just waiting for me to give them the order to come in and clean up on you, but that's not something either of us want." Slowly rising to his feet, Ledbetter ran his fingers over the small bruise that was already popping on his forehead and added, "I know this is The Hamptons and property price wars often make people do crazy things, but you keep forgetting that the people we're dealing with are The

Kutchakokovs. They're terrorists, extortionists and murderers and they could care less about beachfront property on The East End. Get it through your head, Fortuna, these are bad people who do bad things. Who do you think blew up your house? Who do you think is responsible for Samantha's death? Do you think it's going to stop there? These people are out to do something big and hurtful. There's no other reason for their presence here. You've met with Ileana Kutchakokov. There's something about you she likes and because of that you may be able to get close enough to find out what they're up to. I hate to say this, but you may be the only one who can stop them. Fortuna, whether you want to believe it or not, there are things bigger than your dick. Now, are you going to help us or not?"

Everything the Fed said was true, including that crack about my johnson, but it wasn't something he had to tell me and I answered, "Alright, Ledbetter, I'll work with you. What are your plans?"

"That's the problem, Fortuna. We haven't got any. We've got nothing on them and can't get a warrant to search their place because we haven't any probable cause and they've still got that damned diplomatic immunity. Even if we had a warrant, I don't know what the hell we'd be looking for. The only thing we do know is that after several months of hearing nothing, our contact finally got in touch with us and told us something big was going to go down this weekend. We don't know what that is because the message we received came to an abrupt halt. We're still in the dark, but I was hoping you'd know something, anything that might give us a lead."

My mind tripped to little Miss Yu and her substantial grip, but shaking off the feeling I got of the bad thing that had probably happened to her, I said "Well, I know a few things, but I don't want you and your men around to complicate matters. Give me tonight and Friday and I'll find out what I can."

"That's cutting it awfully close, Fortuna. Our contact said this weekend was when the fireworks would begin. That could mean as early as Saturday."

"I know the days of the week as well as you, Ledbetter. If you've got a better idea, tell me about it."

Ledbetter bit at the inside of his cheek, grimaced and responded, "Alright, alright, but just what are you going to do?"

"That's my business and something that shouldn't matter to you. If anything bad happens, you can disavow any knowledge of my actions, because truth be told, I won't have told you a fucking thing. Now, give me a number where I can reach you and I'll call as soon as I discover something. If you don't hear from me, don't try and reach me. I'll get back to you when I can and that's all you need to know." Admiring the welt that was forming at the Fed's hairline, I added, "Sorry about the lump, but even you have to admit, you had it coming."

Ledbetter removed a small card from his wallet and said, "Maybe I did and maybe I didn't, but don't you worry about it. Anything a Neanderthal like you can throw, I can take."

"You wouldn't want to make book on that, would you?"

"Not on your life," Ledbetter quipped, and then, holding out his hand as a peace offering, added, "Good luck, Gabe. America is depending on you."

I didn't think I had to give any thanks for the well wishes, not even after he called me by my first name, but I shook his hand just to show we were on the same side. Walking up to Beth, who had remained in a protective kneeling position behind a gurney, I looked down and asked, "Ready to go?"

With eyes as wide as a teenaged girl's who'd just had her ass squeezed for the first time, she asked , "What the hell was all that about?"

I answered, "That, my bodacious attorney, was how Gabriel Fortuna gets the Feds to tell him what's going on."

Rising, she asked, "And what might that be?"

I didn't answer her question, but placed an arm around her waist and drew her tightly to me. Leading her out the hospital doors, I felt the late afternoon breeze caress my face and responded casually, "I'll tell you on the way to Frenchy's Scuba Paradise out on Indian Cove. By the way, think you might be in the mood for a moonlight swim?"

Still a bit shaken by what I'd done to the Fed and unclear about what my firm hand around her waist actually meant, Beth lost all that bravado she'd been throwing at me since we reconnected and reverted to the young woman of five years earlier whom I'd taught so much in a very short time and stammered, "I'm not sure."

"Good," I declared. "Then you can watch the boat and make sure it doesn't float away while I do.

17

Located just past the intersection of Route 27 and North Road in Hampton Bays is a small inlet named Indian Cove. It is the home to a modest marina, a fine waterside restaurant and a broken down old scuba shack, all belonging to a naturalized American citizen named Guillaume LaMonde, whom everyone refers to as, Frenchy.

Beth and I drove across 27 and made a left onto the gravel road leading to Frenchy's place. Turning right just past a tight bend, we came upon him standing on his ramshackle porch, in a sea of empty tanks, sorting out the good from the bad and cursing every time he threw one into the mounting pile of rejects. As usual, whenever he saw me pull up, a smile appeared on his face, one that told me he was recounting our many good times together before he got married and began raising a family. When Beth and I got out of her car, that smile grew larger and brighter, and because his eyes were frozen onto the driver's side, I knew it was not merely the recollection of our mutual memories causing that grin.

"Bonjour, mon ami. Comment ca va?" he called, eyes riveted on the curvaceous Beth.

I answered, "Ca va bien, Frenchy. Now, let's can the Francais and communicate in American. Frenchy LaMonde, meet my good friend and lawyer, Beth Shapiro."

An aristocratic eyebrow rose high into Frenchy's forehead, almost to his rapidly receding hairline, and he asked, "Shapiro? No relation to that *piece de merde,* Judge Shapiro, j'espere."

Beth laughed good naturedly and answered, "Mr. LaMonde, that piece de merde just happens to be my father."

Frenchy slapped an open palm onto his forehead and lamented, "Mon Dieu. That man, all he does is give me a hard time. Do this; do that. He is no more than a *Jacobin.*" Then, after a continental shake of his rather large head, punctuated by a lascivious smile, he added, "Mais, au contraire, mon cherie, you are a perfect piece of puff pastry"

I ordered, "Cut the crap, Frenchy," and looking at Beth, added, "He's just pissed at your father because he ordered Frenchy to clean up his kitchen and hire documented workers. Your dad fined him, too. A thousand dollars, as I recall."

Frenchy broke in and spat, "*Bastard.* Just thinking of him makes my ass *tweetch.* One thousand dollars for nothing. You know, your papa, he is one steenking judge."

I answered for Beth and said, "She knows, but we're not here to talk about him or your legal problems."

Checking out Beth's fine form a la Chevalier, he asked, "Ah, then what can I do for you, mon ami?"

I pulled on his shaggy goatee and turned his head towards me and said, "I'm over here Frenchy and here's what I want. At eight tonight, I need the services of a small boat, a wet suit and a tank with at least two hours of air waiting for me at your dock. I'm going out when it's dark and I'm sure I won't be long. Think you can do that for me?"

"But, of course, Gabe. Pour vous, anything. I'll give you the best rate." Leering at Beth, he added, "Peut etre, you can find a way to pay that does not involve money, eh?"

I barked, "Up yours, Frenchy. This one's on the house. Think about it as payback for living a super-fine life in America."

At the prospect of not being paid, the frenzied Frenchman suddenly forgot about Beth, spun to face me and complained, "But, Gabe, I am a businessman. If word got out I was giving freebies to people, even mes amis, I would wind up in the poorhouse."

Placing a firm hand upon his shoulder, I said, "Frenchy, one call from Ms. Shapiro to her dad and the Southampton Health Department will be all over your restaurant like mold on brie. Now, we wouldn't want that, would we?"

Through a resigned sigh, he said, "You are one hard man, Gabriel Fortuna," but with a slap on my back and a glint in his eye, he added, "What the fuck, eh? You know I was kidding. Vous etes mon ami. Be dockside at eight. I will have the best little boat and the full tank for you." Again, openly leering at Beth, he asked, "Will your friend be with you?"

I answered through tight lips, "Yes, she will."

"Ah, je comprends. Okay, Gabe, on the house, for old times. The boat, she will be here."

Beth and I left Frenchy on his porch, returned to her car and started back to her place. Again she loaned me her phone and I gave a call to Enrique Santiago, who was at home with family and friends mourning the passing of his sister. I told him what I wanted and he said he would do anything to get back at the motherfuckers who'd killed Esmie, but I got a cold chill just hearing him say her name.

Handing the phone back to Beth, I said dispiritedly, "Let's get to your place and get some rest.

It occurred to me that Beth must have thought I was joking about getting some rest because she hit the road and drove home faster than the law permitted. I caught an anticipatory smile wash cross her face and I wondered what was wrong; why wasn't I thinking the way I knew she was?

18

We drove past Southampton Village, the small strip of stores that was Watermill's downtown and turned right off Route 27 onto Mecox Road. Heading south towards the ocean, we made another left and pulled into a driveway off Summerfield Lane, one with electric eye gates that opened widely as Beth nosed her car into the property. Crunching along a short gravel driveway surrounded by late blooming dwarf hydrangea trees, it wasn't long before a beautiful two-story Hampton's style cedar shingled house with a wrap around front porch, breezeway and three-car garage sat before us.

Beth brought her car to a halt in an outdoor spot at the end of the drive, turned off the engine and said, "Here we are, Chez Shapiro."

I said, "This place is beautiful. How long did you say you've been practicing law?"

Beth answered proudly, "Thank you, Gabe, and the answer to your question is three years, the first two in a high-powered New York firm, and the last one out here, working and practicing on my own. Once I realized that putting in eighteen hours a day and making big money wasn't everything I wanted and that a beautiful home in the Hamptons might mean more to me than a two thousand square foot condo on the twentieth floor in a loft building in Tribeca, it wasn't hard for me to sell my Manhattan place at a big profit, buy something out here at a distressed price and still have a nice piece of change left over to buy whatever else I might need. Come on in, I'll show you around."

We left her car and climbed three wooden stairs to a covered front porch filled with comfortable imitation wicker outdoor furniture and an oversized hammock that looked just right for two. Opening the door without use of a key, she led me into a friendly entryway of wood floors, Ralph Lauren wallpapers and Hamptons cottage style furniture. The place felt so warm and cozy that by the time I took two steps into the family room I couldn't help releasing a large yawn.

Beth said, "My, my, maybe you were serious about taking that rest. Here we are, alone in my house, with absolutely no possible intrusion from the outside world and you yawn. This is not the Gabriel Fortuna I used to know."

I said, "Maybe, when all this is over, we can get reacquainted. Right now, I've got Samantha on my mind and Esmie and Oliver and the Russians. Right now, I'm just not ready."

With a soft hand to my cheek, Beth said, "Looks like my Gabe is finally growing up."

"Just like a woman to say something like that," I snapped. "Look, I've always been grown up. It's just that right now I've got some things on my mind besides sex." Checking out the spreading smile on my attorney's face, I added, "Don't you have some legal stuff to do?"

"That's what I mean, Gabe. It used to be that when we were alone you never had anything on your mind but sex." Stepping away from me, she eyed the flat front of my pants and added, "Wow, you really have changed. Come on, I'll take you to your room where you can relax." Once in my room, she pulled down the comforter, shook her head and left me alone with a sarcastic, "Sleep tight."

Lying on the firm mattress, I looked up at the blank white ceiling and wondered what the hell was wrong with me that I'd let her out of the room after she'd just about begged me to make love to her. Balling my fists at the thought I might be losing it, it occurred to me that Beth might be right and that part of me was growing up. I was just pissed that it had to be that part.

19

I made a few phone calls and we left her house at 7:30, driving to Hampton Bays without much conversation. After all, there really wasn't much to talk about. I didn't want her to know about the danger I might be confronting and I certainly didn't want to talk about our lack of progress in bed. Every now and then, I caught her gazing at me through the corner of her eye and smiling. I didn't know if it was in anticipation of things to come or remembrances of things past, but I was uneasy about it, and couldn't wait to get to Frenchy's.

Reaching Indian Cove at eight on the nose, we left the car parked in front of the scuba shack and walked down to the dock, where we found Frenchy leaning against a lightpole. Beth took hold of my hand and gave a squeeze, her way, I guess, of simultaneously telling me she was with me on the mission and to make sure I would protect her from the Huguenot hound.

From the dock railing, Frenchy smiled and called, "Bonjour, mon ami." With a nod and a leer towards Beth, he added, "Mademoiselle."

I said, "What are you doing here, Frenchy? I don't recall

extending an invitation to you and we sure don't have need for a chaperone."

My Provencal pal answered jauntily, "This is my boat and my equipment, Gabriel. I am here only to make sure I get them back in one piece."

Glancing into the rear of the craft, I saw that he'd left the scuba equipment stowed in the corner of the sixteen-foot low-drafting power boat as I'd asked. I signaled to Beth that it was time to board but he got in first, rocked the boat vigorously from side to side, and then extending a hand, laughed at her unease at boarding. I smiled at Frenchy's flirtation, jumped in and headed to the captain's console to make sure everything was ship-shape. When I was sure they were, I took off my shirt and saw Beth's mouth drop at the sight of my pumped pecs and ripped abs. Aware of the memories my broad chest had just stirred, I pretended to ignore her searching eyes, dropped trou and heard a moan.

Pulling on my skin-tight wetsuit, I saw Beth take another hard look before licking at her dry lips. She didn't have to say a word to communicate her feelings, and Frenchy, picking up on what was going on, growled in his little corner of the boat when the realization struck that he was nothing more than a third wheel and was just wasting his time.

He whispered, "Merde," and added with faux regret, "Un moment, mon ami. I have forgotten a very important meeting at the restaurant. I am afraid I will not be able to accompany you on this trip. Go *sans moi,* and good luck with whatever you do. Should anything happen to my boat or my tanks, you will get my bill. Otherwise, it is the last freebie you will ever see." Leaping from the boat, by the time he hit the dock his disappointment must have dissolved, because turning to us, he added through a fabulous French flourish, "Au revoir, mes amis et bon chance. I wish you both un copulation magnifique."

He drove off in his Peugeot and I went about the silent business of preparation. Snapping on my fins and strapping the filled single tank onto my back, I went to the captain's console, turned over the engine, and sending the unusually silent Beth a provocative wink, set out of Indian Cove.

Cruising along at five miles per hour until leaving the small marina, we were nothing more than a tiny dark speck humming away under a bright early September moon. Once into the heart of the bay, we picked up speed, passed numerous moored boats lashed to buoys or bobbing gently on the waves and headed towards the open ocean. White moonlight reflected off the calm bay waters, giving everything on its surface the appearance of being part of some gigantic x-ray, and although the serene light might have been wondrous and beautiful, creating the intoxicating illusion of an evening made for love, it was the only thing that wasn't perfect on our trip to The Kutchakokov Estate, as I would have much preferred the darkness of a new moon to the luminescence of the full one that embraced us.

Hitting the light chop of the ocean, we veered east towards Montauk, traveled six nautical miles and stopped about a half-mile out to sea, at a point exactly opposite the Kutchakokov Mansion. I explained to Beth that her job was to sit in the boat, keep the motor idling in neutral, stay alert and make sure it didn't drift while she waited for me to return. I emphasized that should another boat come her way, she was to forget about me and get away as quickly as possible, staying as close to the shore line as she could and ground our little boat at the Southampton Yacht Club about a half-mile to our west. Upon reaching that enclave of old money and prestige, she was to run into the club's restaurant, where she would be surrounded by a couple of hundred upper-echelon Southamptoners enjoying their pre-Labor Day dinners and presumably be safe, except from Louie, the maitre'd who would probably demand to know her membership number.

A tigress in court, Beth Shapiro was a lamb on the ocean. Astonished that I would even suggest her leaving without me, she asked, "What do you mean? I can't just leave. I'm going to wait for you no matter how long you're gone."

Grabbing her tightly at her shoulders, I responded, "I mean what I say, Beth. If I'm not back in ninety minutes or if another boat comes your way, you get lost and you get lost fast. If you're caught, just say you're out for a solitary night on the ocean under a full and glorious moon. If they don't believe that, well…you might be in trouble. Make them believe it. I guess what I'm saying is, don't get caught." I checked my watch and added, "Okay, it's eight-thirty. I'll try to make it back by ten. If I'm not here by then, you leave without me."

I didn't wait for Beth to argue and checked my mask, cleared my air line and dropped backwards off the boat. Under the waves and away from Beth it was quiet and peaceful and I was more than glad to finally be on my own. The only sound I heard was the hum of our little boat's engine; the only movement, the soft current that tried to take me out to sea. Checking my compass, I started towards the beach.

It took me twelve minutes to reach dry sand. Removing my fins and tank, I stowed them under a kayak that lay waiting on the beach for a paddler. I didn't know exactly what I was looking for, but I knew for whom. Madame Yu was my target. It had to be she who notified Ledbetter about an upcoming event, but she had been prevented from completing her message. My hope was that she had stopped transmitting because someone was coming towards her and not that she'd been caught.

I crossed the narrow beach, hiding in a natural path between two large dunes, and scurried my way to the edge of the field where I'd participated in Buzkashi. Raising my eyes, the hard moonlight illuminated my greatest fear; there was Miss Yu, impaled on a large pole, assuming the role of a tars tarkus. I stooped low and sped across the open landscape, hoping that she'd found a way to secret a message on herself, something that might tip me off to what The Kutchakokovs were up to, but upon reaching her, I was stunned to find her still alive, her glassy eyes staring at me.

"Fortuna," she managed to croak before her head dropped lower into her chest. "You fuck…ing…ass…hole. You've… killed…me."

I wasn't going to argue with the fallen Fed, especially when I saw the pointed end of the wooden shaft emerging from the top of her back, but I felt I needed to defend myself and whispered, "I'm sorry if I've caused you any grief, Miss Yu, but I don't know how any of this can be pinned on me. I was nowhere around when you were impaled."

Her forehead dripping cold sweat, her every word laced with pain, somehow the diminutive agent found the strength to say, "Fortuna…you…are such…an…ass…hole. Let…down…my… guard…be…cause…of…you. The…I… phone…in…your… room…on…SpyApp. Every…word… recorded."

I echoed, "SpyApp," and then asked, "What the fuck is that?"

Miss Yu rasped, "Shut…up…you…id…i…ot…and…listen. This… Sun…day. Hamp…ton…Class…ic. Great…dan…ger."

"What's going to happen, Miss Yu? What's going to happen at The Hampton Classic?"

The impaled one managed to raise her head and looked deeply into my eyes. Through great effort, she uttered one word, "AMERICA," and then Wo Tu Yu shuddered and died.

I murmured reverently, "Sorry, Miss Yu," but there was nothing more I could do because a moment later I became a fly in milk.

The Buzkashi field turned ghostly white from the glare of a hundred high intensity floodlights and through the white night, from dozens of hidden loudspeakers, the rancid voice of Ilya Kutchakokov bellowed, "Good evening, Mr. Fortuna. How fortunate for me to see you again. And yet, how unfortunate for you."

It occurred to me that although the voice coming at me sounded almost exactly like Ilya Kutchakokov's, there was something about it that was different, something that was not quite the same as the voice of the man whom I'd seen get waylaid just yesterday on this Buzkashi field and I called, "What do you want from me, Kutchakokov? Do you expect me to beg for my life?"

Kutchakokov laughed a long, deep, coarse laugh and then answered my question ruthlessly, saying, "Of course not, Mr. Fortuna. We both know that would be beneath you. No, Mr. Fortuna, I do not expect you to beg; I expect you to die."

My predictable Fortunan reply was, "Fuck you, Kutchakokov! Fuck you and your entire clan!"

There came a deeper laugh and then, from behind me, the sound of roaring thunder. Turning to its origin, I saw a phalanx of horsemen and horsewomen galloping from the gates of the stable. Spreading out as they approached, the riders had pit themselves between me and the ocean and were slowly closing in to surround me. Assured by their positioning that the water route was not going to be my means of escape, I reached the point where Plan B would have to be employed.

Opening a zipper on my wetsuit, I pulled a whistle from my breast pocket and blew hard into it. A shrill piercing sound filled the night and very few seconds passed before its call was answered from the other side of the estate's boundary wall. It was a loud and singular wail, one I thought I'd never get accustomed to hearing, but one I'd finally learned to welcome with all my heart.

"Muthafuck!!!!"

A thousand sprinkler heads erupted from all parts of the Kutchakokov lawn, violently spinning and throwing cascades of water in every direction. My assailants' horses, not used to the hissing and spitting of water coming at them from every point of the compass, were startled and spooked and began to rear. No matter how expert the Russian riders were, they could not completely contain their mighty animals, and the horses, blinded by the flailing torrents of H2O, began to scatter across the Buzkashi field. I took this as my opportunity to escape and quickly headed towards the stable, the place from where my enemies had first appeared.

Grabbing a small war club from the ground, I made my way across the open expanse and occasionally took the opportunity to land a body or head shot to a Russian rider who was trying to rally his horse or had spotted me through the splashing sprinklers, doing away with six in such fashion before reaching the stable. Over the sound of a thousand clicking water heads came a series of four nearly simultaneous explosions and I turned from the stable gates to see a throng of Latin Zombies, recruited by Enrique that very evening from satellite Zombie gangs throughout the Hamptons and The North Fork, come charging through the smoky openings they had blasted in the walls and front gate.

Screaming, "Viva Esmie," at the tops of their lungs in that shrill Latin Zombie war cry I once thought was the private property of Enrique, they further spooked the Russians' horses and I rushed into the stable.

Turning to my right, I saw Kimosabee standing patiently in a stall, looking at me as if he'd been waiting all day. I ran to his side but didn't have time to throw a saddle on him because Sergei, sitting atop his mount like some granite monument of a Civil War general, suddenly came charging into the stable. Drawing his hand viciously across his throat as a way of telling me what he had in store for me, he must have thought he was scaring me, but I knew what a punk he was from that time in Danny Fisher's office when he let the Iranian refrigerator catch all the pain. Defiantly throwing him a smile, I jumped on Kimosabee's back and charged through the closed gate of my mount's stall, splintering it into a thousand pieces. Riding directly at Sergei, I was distressed to see him suddenly produce a pistol and aim down its barrel, straight at me.

A shot went off and I cringed thinking that this might be the end of Gabriel Fortuna, but instead of feeling the dull pain of a hollow point bullet, I felt nothing. Focusing on my would-be executioner, I saw the most perplexed look wash over his face and a moment later I noticed the little black dot in the middle of his forehead start to run red with blood. Sergei dropped his gun, tilted to the left and fell in a heap as I simultaneously felt someone jump onto Kimosabee's back directly behind me.

Grabbing me around the waist and holding tight, my savior barked, "Let's get out of here, Fortuna. Move, before one of us gets killed."

I turned, gave Samantha Goodbody a quick kiss on her lips and said, "I was hoping you'd turn up. I just didn't know it would be now."

"Let's get out of here," Samantha repeated as a spinter of wood was blown from a plank beside her head. "They're trying to kill us."

I kicked Kimosabee lightly in the ribs and he sped from the stable faster than an overweight baby sliding down Octomom's cooch. Charging across the open field, I heard and saw Samantha shoot a few Russians who came a little too close for comfort, and through it all, I heard the inimitable Enrique shouting, *"Muthafuck!"* high above the incredible din. What freaked me out most, though, was the sound of Ilya Kutchakokov's warning voice, roaring through the loudspeakers as Samantha, Kimosabee and I made our way out through the blown-out and twisted wrought iron main gate and onto Gin Lane:

"I will get you, Gabriel Fortuna. I will get you!"

20

We galloped wordlessly for a good mile, reached the convergence of Flying Point and Cobb Roads, and turned left to cruise under a shroud of trees until once again hitting ubiquitous Route 27. Satisfied that we had escaped immediate danger, I settled Kimosabee, and finding ourselves surrounded by a fifty mile long parade of cars and vacationers coming out to The East End for their Labor Day Weekend, we cantered easily along The Distressway's shoulder until reaching Mecox Road and made the right towards Beth's house.

As we trotted past The Halsey Farm and its row after row of multi-varietal apple and peach trees and pumpkin and squash patches, Samantha finally broke her silence and said, "Whew, that was a close one."

I replied, "I've been in tighter spots," and then added, "Hey, I thought you were supposed to be dead. At least, that's what Ledbetter told me."

"That's what he wanted you to believe. He was pretty sure that false info would guarantee you paying The Kutchakokovs a return visit. To ensure you found out all you could and not get hurt too badly in the process, I snuck in this morning with the pool crew and waited to help out if you got into trouble." With a perplexed expression, she added, "By the way, you don't seem too surprised at finding me alive."

"That's because I'm not. It's been my personal and professional experience that Federal agents just don't know how to tell the truth. When Ledbetter told me you were dead, I just took it for granted that he thought that would make me angrier and I would do whatever it was he wanted. The guy thought he was playing me, but I knew he was full of it. It's like when you tell me you don't want to go to bed with me. I know that's a bunch of crap. I mean, what healthy woman wouldn't want to spend some quality time with me."

Samantha buttoned her lip for the rest of our ride, at least until I turned onto Summerfield Lane and we saw the tight mass of BMW's and the lone Chevy Caprice filling Beth's small parking lot. Pulling her gun from her waistband, she blurted, "What the hell is going on here?"

I answered calmly, "Put it away, Sam. I recognize most of these cars and they belong to friends. You know what friends are, don't you? They're people who don't work for the Federal Government and actually know how to help."

Sliding from Kimosabee's broad back, I turned to lend a refused hand to help Samantha down and then petted my equine friend who'd helped save our lives.

I said, "Be right back with some sugar, Boy," and turning to Sam, added, "And thanks again for showing up when you did. I owe you one."

Goodbody replied, "You don't owe me anything, Fortuna. I'm just doing my job."

"Yeah, I know, but I still owe you one...but just one. If you want more, you'll have to ask nicely and get on line."

I tied Kimosabee to the porch railing, climbed the steps and opened the door to Beth's place, where inside it appeared a facsimile of a mad tea party was being held. With Beth serving as a dazzling hostess, handing out beverages, cookies and pastries to a mob of multicultural men, the place simultaneously reverberated to the sound of one of The Notorious S.H.I.T.'s latest hits, *This Shit Don't Stank,* and was a maelstrom of urban movement.

"Hello, everyone," I called.

There was a moment of silence, except for Sylvester Hightower's shrill vocal antics and the sound track's accompanying deep base, and then Beth turned and saw me standing at the door.

Hollering, "Gabe," she dropped a tray of sliced cornbread onto Romey's lap and ran towards me, threw her arms around my neck and kissed me hard on the lips. Pulling away and wearing an angry expression, she shouted, "Where have you been? I've been frightened out of my wits."

I answered, "I've been out for a ride with an old friend." Gesturing with my thumb over my shoulder, I added, "Attorney Beth Shapiro, meet Federal Agent Samantha Goodbody." A sudden gurgling sound from deep in my gut reminded me I hadn't eaten in hours and was in need of fuel. Rubbing my hands together, I asked, "Now, what are we serving? I'm starved."

Rising from his easy chair, Romey stopped the music with a flick of a switch on the boombox. He brushed the crumbs from his satin pants, and with eyes as shiny as a polished cue ball, approached me and said, "Mo'fo', why didn't you tell the lady we'd be coming her way to escort her home? She nearly put Cornell and Quantone in the hospital when we tried to board her skiff. Man, if I didn't get her into a bear hug and explain who we were, I might have had to clip the pretty little thing, and you know how I hate to hit good-looking women."

I took a look at Cornell and Quantone standing at either side of their boss' massive shoulders, sporting pained expressions as well as newly applied butterfly band-aids to their eyebrows, and said through a wry smile, "Sorry, fellows. I didn't think you'd have that much trouble escorting the little lady from her boat. Anyway, I wasn't sure I'd need you to pick her up. It was my plan to return and motor off with her; it's just that The Kutchakokovs changed things. Like an insurance policy, you were something I hoped I wouldn't need."

"Well, Mo'fo'," Romey continued, "it's a good thing Frenchy was with us or there might have been real trouble. She recognized him, and when he told her it was cool and that we were your friends, she let her guard down long enough for me to grab her from behind and carry her off the boat. By the way, Frenchy took the boat back to his place and said you owed him for battle pay." After a deep breath, Romey shook his head and concluded, "Mo'fo', I keeps telling you; you gots to keep your women in check before someone gets hurt."

I apologized, "Sorry, Romey, it'll never happen again."

Shaking his head slowly, he replied, "Like shit it won't."

From the kitchen, Agent Ledbetter, followed by four other suits wearing identical aviator sunglasses, was threading his way through Romey's boys and heading towards me. Holding a canoli from La Parmigianna in one hand and a cup of expresso in the other, he squeezed in front of Beth and said, "Glad you made it, Fortuna. What have you learned about The Kutchakokovs?"

Evading his question for the moment, I answered, "I was wondering where you were. With GM's problems, you don't find too many people driving around in Chevy Caprices, so you're car was pretty easy to pick out among the crowd of pink BMWs out there. That thing you're driving hasn't come off an assembly line in ten years. Where do you guys find the fucking parts for it?"

Ledbetter placed his espresso cup on a side table, took a satisfyingly deep bite from his cannoli and said, "Cut the crap, Fortuna. What have you found out?"

I wasn't about to let the guy off so easily and countered, "Don't you think it's time you cut the crap, Ledbetter? You lied to me about Samantha and who knows what else. Why should I tell you anything?"

Dabbing lightly at some of the creamy filling that had caught at the corner of his mouth, Ledbetter answered, "Because we're both playing for the same team, that's why. Sure, I told you Samantha bought it. It got you to play ball, didn't it?"

"You're such a putz, Ledbetter. I knew you were lying to me. The reason I went to The Kutchakokovs is because I know they're a danger, not because of any asshole game you're playing. They've got to pay for what they've already done and stopped from doing what they plan. I don't need you to try and trick me into fighting for my country. You'd do better telling me the truth. Then, I wouldn't have to do this."

This time it wasn't a glancing blow off his forehead. I caught Ledbetter with a solid right to the jaw that sent him and the remainder of his pastry flying across the room. After a full tumblesault that would have garnered him a perfect ten at the Olympic Games, he wound up out cold on the living room floor. The only thing saving him from total annihilation was my remembrance of his catching a bullet for me at The Castle. Because of that, I held back and slugged him with only half my strength.

The four G-men with Ledbetter were slow and didn't go into action until their boss was laid out. Dropping their espressos onto Beth's oak floor, they reached for their shoulder holsters, but were quickly outgunned by the band of Romey's guys who pulled out their previously hidden assortment of AKs, Smith and Wessons, Berettas and Colts. Seeing that a shootout provided them little chance for survival, instead of pulling out their weapons, the Feds' empty hands grabbed at the air above their heads.

"Yo, Mo'fo'," Romey laughed, pointing at Ledbetter. "That is one knocked out cop."

Turning to Samantha, I said, "Hope you don't mind what just went down. I don't like it when people lie to me, especially when they make me feel responsible for the death of people I like."

Samantha's eyes flashed and she answered, "It's okay. I told him it was a bad idea and that I didn't like it, and in a way, I guess he got what he deserved. There will be consequences, though. Frank doesn't like being cold-cocked."

Beth must have seen the twinkle in the agent's eyes because she grabbed my hand with the double-entendre and said, "Are you okay, Gabe? Are you hurt?"

I laughed and answered, "I'm fine, Beth, just hungry. Let's get something to eat." Pointing to Ledbetter, I added, "When he wakes up we'll talk about what I discovered and what we have to do."

"*Muthafuck!!!*"

Enrique, sporting a blood-stained homemade tourniquet around his forehead, came charging through Beth's front door faster than a gringo bolting from a Mexican jail. Running straight at me, he grabbed me around the waist, fell to his knees and cried, "Thanks you, Muthafuck. Thanks you for letting me gets revenge for Esmie. Those patos don't know what hits them. We teach them good how Americans fight, eh, Gabe? We lit that place up and left it on fire with some crazy muthafuck's voice booming over the loudspeakers to save the fucking horses. Fuck them and their fucking horses, eh, Gabe? We do this shit for Esmie."

"Yeah, Enrique," I said, placing an arm around my rescuer's shoulders, "we do it for Esmie."

Dropping into my arms and convulsing with tears, I was sure the emotional, gang-leading entrepreneur would snap out of it in a while, but until he did, I wanted to provide the shoulder onto which he could cry. As he wept, I saw Ledbetter begin to writhe in his private little corner of the room. Pretty soon he'd be up, and after shaking the cobwebs from his head and deciding whether or not he wanted to take me on, we'd have to make our plans for Sunday. I caught Beth and Samantha eyeing each other malevolently, each one sizing up her competition for a piece of Fortuna pie, and then there were Romey's boys, still leveling their pieces on the Feds, standing ready to fill them with holes if given the order. I chuckled at the mélange of contradictions surrounding me and thought I'd been right when I'd entered the house; this really was one mad little tea party.

Beth and Samantha never relaxed their suspicious glares and I recognized how in the past their hot and angry expressions would have been enough for me to try to coax each of them to participate in a magnificent menage in one of Beth's upstairs bedrooms, but that night I felt nothing but a bitter breeze blowing through my billowy briefs. I told myself that I needed to get some rest because tomorrow was Saturday and there was someone with whom I needed to talk. That looming conversation might be dangerous, and even if it wasn't, it was certainly going to be tough. I convinced myself I had more important things to do than to take care of the two gorgeous women who wanted to share my bed. That's right, I had more important things to do. Sure I did.

21

A light-headed Ledbetter, Beth, Samantha, Romey, Enrique and I had our late night meeting, where I made it clear to Ledbetter and Samantha that I was calling the shots in spite of their government credentials. Ledbetter seemed to be too punch drunk to argue about anything and Samantha must have been coming closer to my way of thinking because she kept quiet and listened, something I was not used to and an action that I must admit made me more than a little wary. By midnight the place cleared out: Ledbetter returning to Sag Harbor's American Hotel with his aching jaw, Enrique going home to his little place in Noyac after tearfully promising he would get some of his guys to rebuild and paint my burned out home by the end of the month, and Romey leaving for Sylvester Hightower's manse off Meadow Lane, where he assured me he would house and feed Kimosabee in one of the impresario's carpeted stalls.

Beth, Samantha and I remained at Beth's place, cleaned the house a bit and filled four garbage bags with paper cups, plates and napkins before placing them at the end of the drive for a Norsic pickup. As we worked, I did most of the talking, my two would-be lovers checking each other out, each wondering, I suspected, how she might somehow lose the other and get the upper hand.

Beth surprised me when she let out a sigh, threw down her dust rag and said, "That's it for me, I'm exhausted and going to bed. Gabe, if you like, you can sleep in the upstairs guest bedroom. Ladyfed, you can take the couch or the downstairs bedroom. I suggest the couch because it's central to the house and from there you can protect us more easily from any badguys who might try and enter." Sleepily, she looked at me and added, "I'm going to lock my door from the inside to protect myself from any unwanted intruders." Returning to Samantha, she concluded, "I wish you luck, Ladyfed. Here's hoping you get what you want."

Beth turned and walked slowly up her stairs as I watched and admired the way her full round ass sashayed from left to right with every delightful step she took. Reaching the upstairs landing, she turned left for her bedroom, closed the door behind her, and it was then that I noticed Samantha staring at me with what I could regard only as jealous contempt.

"What?" I asked innocently.

"Fortuna, you are just so god-damned obvious and predictable. I don't think I've ever met any one like you...and I don't mean that in a good way. Look, I'm taking the downstairs bedroom and locking my door, too. I don't know where your friend got the idea I want to spend the night with you and I don't know if that same crazy idea is going through your head, but I'm telling you now, I sleep with a gun under my pillow. If you try to get into my room, I will shoot first and ask questions later. You got that?"

"You don't have to worry about me, Agent Goodbody. I won't come knocking at your door. Just don't go changing your mind and come crawling through mine because I make it a point to give women who threaten me with a pistol twenty-four hours to chill before bestowing any possibility of Fortuna romance upon them." Checking my watch, I concluded, "That gives you until one-fifteen Sunday morning, unless of course we change our minds and decide to get it on right now."

Changing her mind was not something on Sam's evening's agenda, so leaving her standing in the living room to stew, I went upstairs alone. Being too edgy to sleep, I paced circles around my bedroom for an hour until finally deciding I could not wait until tomorrow for what could be done tonight. Leaving a note for Samantha and Beth on my bed, I opened my window and slowly descended the decorative rose covered trellis on the side of the house and silently landed on the soft grass of the backyard, where I crouched behind a cluster of viburnum bushes and took a quick look around to see if Ledbetter or Samantha had stationed anyone outside to guard me. It didn't take long to realize the Feds had dropped the ball again when it came to estimating my talents and I raced to the driveway, reached into Beth's car and dropped its transmission into neutral. Pushing it backwards out of the driveway and onto Summerfield Lane, I reached beneath the dashboard and hotwired the starter until it caught and the motor began purring. Jumping into the driver's seat, I took off down Mecox Road and never looked back. There was no reason to. All the danger was in front of me.

22

Although it was two in the morning, Hamptons' roads were unusually busy because of the holiday weekend and it took me nearly forty minutes to travel the ten miles from Beth's place to Melanie's home in a modest North Sea subdivision named, Hills of the Hamptons. I traveled only a half-mile down the quiet entry road before spying the silhouettes of a couple of parked cars at the end of the cul-de-sac. Shutting my engine and lights, I coasted Beth's car down the quiet street and pulled into the driveway of a residence three houses down whose lights were all shut and whose owners I hoped were either arriving tomorrow or were sound asleep. I crouched low, made my way quickly down the street, and comfortably hidden by the tall hydrangea bushes that were the foundation plantings of their property, settled my eyes just above the flowering shrubs and took a peek inside the front bay window of the Dines' home.

Standing in the living room was a glamorous and statuesque Ileana Kutchakokov. She was holding her little white dog tightly to her breasts and was flanked by two of her larger, more simian bodyguards. In a chair facing her, flanked by two more of her people, was a nervous Oliver Dines. I couldn't hear what Ileana was saying, but the expressions on her and Oliver's faces told me that whatever she was saying was not something he was glad to hear. The additional fact that small rivers of perspiration were flowing down his forehead and dripping onto the front of his already stained pants reinforced my opinion that what was going down had to be some very bad news for the prominent local attorney.

Ileana, after pointing a stiff finger into Oliver's face, delivered what I took to be a final warning. Then, stiffly turning, she left the room followed by her two lackeys. The other two goons remained motionless at Oliver's side until Ileana was gone. Then, the one on the left delivered a wicked slap to my old friend's ear, dropping Oliver from his chair and onto the floor. Each smirked to the other before the one who did the smacking gave Oliver one final kick in the ribs. Then, the two left.

Ileana, her dog and her bodyguards got into their car and waited for the others to leave Oliver's house before starting their engines. The two Bentleys pulled away quietly, so as not to awaken any curious neighbors who might be wondering what an outrageous six-foot-two blonde in high heels and short shorts was doing with four clothed orangutans from the Bronx Zoo inside the police chief's house at two in the morning, but neighbors weren't the only ones who were curious. I waited a few minutes to make sure the Kutchakokovs were well on their way, and after giving one last look through the window to a kneeling Oliver, I walked to the front door, found it unlocked and entered the house.

Reaching the living room, I said, "I can't say I like the friends you're keeping."

Oliver forced his eyes open and seeing me, gasped, "Gabe, what are you doing here?"

"A better question would be, what are Ileana Kutchakokov and four of her henchman doing here?"

Oliver's eyebrows went into a wild dance and he responded, "She's a client."

"Really? A client? I didn't know you met with clients at two in the morning. That's what I call superior dedication to your practice. Better keep it to yourself, though. That kind of professionalism will have the State Bar Association breathing down your neck, trying to revoke your license." Taking a step towards him, I added, "Now, why don't you tell me what really is going on. You see, I've discovered some things about The Kutchakokovs and their organization, some piece of shit outfit called, *TRASH*, and I know they're up to no good. What I don't know is what that no good thing is. Unfortunately, I think you might have some answers."

Oliver stood, pressed his palm to his ear and said, "I don't have anything for you, Gabe, and even if I did, I wouldn't just hand it over. We're talking about The Kutchakokovs. You don't just go against them. Not if you want to survive. Not if you want your family to survive."

I shot back, "That's something you should have thought about earlier. I know you got into bed with these people, but now it's time to straighten things out and do something right."

Oliver eloquently countered, "Fuck you, Gabe. What I'm doing is right. All I did was make some deals that made me a lot of money. There's nothing wrong with that. It's the American way."

"Don't hand me that shit, Oliver. Ileana Kutchakokov and her boys aren't here at two in the morning to talk about property values. Even if she was, would slapping you around improve her bargaining position? And fuck you, too. I know she's planning something bad and I know it's going to take place at The Hampton

Classic. Homeland Security knows it, too. You're in the deep stuff up to your ears, old friend, and now you're going to start climbing out of it by telling me what that bad thing is."

Smiling grimly, Oliver said, "Like hell I am."

I adjusted my ring and replied, "Okay, let's play it your way. Think of what you're about to receive as a down payment for what happened to Danny Fisher."

Assuming a favored martial arts position, he snarled, "Up your's, Gabe. Fisher got what he deserved and now I'm going to give you what you've had coming for a long time. All my married life, Melanie talked about how much fun her years hanging with you were, and every chance you got you rubbed it in my face. Well, don't you forget for a second that I was a Green Beret and can take care of myself. The army taught me how to kick ass, use a knife, shoot a gun, handle a chopper and set demolition charges. Now, you big piece of shit, let's see how you do against someone who can fight back."

I bellowed, "Get ready for some pain, Oliver. You're going to be sorry you ever born."

I got within range and was just about ready to deliver my first blow, a crashing overhand right to the middle of his forehead, when behind me, Police Captain Melanie Dines shouted, "Hold it right there, Gabe. Don't take another step."

I wasn't about to listen, but the sound of a shot going off and spraying plaster and paint off the ceiling served to convince me that kicking Oliver's ass was not advisable, at least not at that moment. With my fists still balled tightly, I turned to my old friend and one-time lover and said, "So, you're with Oliver on this."

Dressed in an ash covered Southampton Town Police uniform, Melanie pointed her weapon at me and said, "I don't know what the hell you're talking about, Gabe, but Oliver is my husband and I'm with him on almost everything, especially against a guy I thought I knew pretty well and who's out to do him harm. Now, come towards me and move slowly. We're going back to town and you've got some charges to face."

I barked, "What charges? I haven't done anything."

"Tell that to The Kutchakokovs. They say you and a bunch of your new friends tried to burn down their place. In fact, I just left their estate and can tell you for a fact that the stables are a shambles and the east wing of their main house has been at least partially destroyed by the fire they say you and your pals set. Fire departments from Hampton Bays and Easthampton had to be called in to help halt the blazes and a couple of our local firemen are down with problems from smoke inhalation. Dozens of Kutchakokov's men and women are in the hospital from bruises received fighting off the arsonists and just about the only words that comes out of any of their non-English speaking mouths are, 'Fortuna' and 'Muthafuck'. A few of them have been shot, some hurt pretty badly and one is dead with a bullet between his eyes. Gabe, you're being charged with assault and arson and about fifteen other felonies and I hope you don't get charged with murder. Now, let's go."

There was no way I was going to let her jail me again, and hoping to find a way to convince her to put down her gun, I ranted, "Are you telling me that you don't know what Oliver is into? Where the hell have you been this past year? How do you think he's made enough money to buy acres of property and build a new house at a time when nearly everyone else is sucking wind? He's been working for The Kutchakokovs and *TRASH*, short for Terror, Revenge, Anarchy, Subversion and Humiliation. Just ask him if you don't believe me."

Melanie's face took on a sour expression and she asked, "Humiliation? What the hell is that? Doesn't sound so dangerous to me."

"You can tell that to the hundreds of international CEOs and politicians who've been brought down or controlled through explicit pictures of them cavorting in extremely compromising positions with TRASH men and women."

With an disbelieving shake of her head, Southampton's top cop said, "Gabe, this is ridiculous. You're coming with me. You can tell your crazy story to the judge." Waving her gun in the direction of the door, she added with finality, "Now, let's go."

Searching for anything to slow things down, I noticed that someone was missing from the usually active Dines household and asked, "Say, where's Gabriella? As I recall, my god-daughter wakes up at the drop of a pin. I can't believe she's still upstairs asleep, especially after you pulled one off and put a hole in your ceiling."

Melanie answered, "I sent her to my sister's place in New York. Her horse came up lame after the dressage preliminaries and all she did for the past two nights was cry herself to sleep about not being able to compete at The Classic. Oliver thought it might be better if she just left town and was spared the frustration of merely sitting in the stands and watching. I agreed and sent her away on this morning's Jitney."

"How convenient!!! Gabriella's horse pulls up lame just before she's scheduled to compete and just before something bad goes down at The Classic." Turning to Oliver, I said, "If there's one surefire way to make sure she's out of harm's way, nothing beats keeping her away from the event, does it? What did you do to Gabby's horse, Oliver? My guess is you snapped its ankle to make sure it couldn't be ridden, or maybe you just halved its hoof so it'll walk around lame for a while. Whatever you did, it worked. Gabriella will be pouting in New York while what would have been her competition will be wondering what the hell hit them, that is, if they can wonder at all. Well, let me tell you something, you big piece of shit. If you think protecting your daughter like that makes you a good father, you're wrong. All it does is make you a murdering son-of-a-bitch."

Oliver hissed, "Fuck you, Gabe. I don't have to listen to anything you say. You're a felon and you're going to jail. That's good enough for me."

"Hear that, Melanie? I don't hear your husband saying he was innocent of any of my accusations. All he does is tell me to fuck myself and say I'm going to jail. Do those sound like the words of an innocent man to you?"

Behind me, Melanie asked weakly, "Oliver, are you up to anything I should know about?"

Oliver bristled and roared, "Still siding with Fortuna, huh, Mel? I guess some things never change, not even after fifteen years of marriage. Tell me, when did worrying about our daughter become a crime?"

Interrupting his lame defense, I said, "There's nothing wrong with protecting Gabriella or making money or building a home. Killing Fisher and Esmie is something else. And then there are those unfortunate people who owned the property on Gin Lane that The Kutchakokovs wanted. My guess is you took care of them, also, and I'm sure I'll be able to prove it, too, once we talk to the families and discover how they were threatened into selling." Looking directly at Melanie, I added, "Your husband is a murderer, Mel. I know it, and if you're paying any attention and being objective, I think you know it, too."

Oliver picked up the brass lamp sitting on a side tabletop and bellowed, "Shut the fuck up already, Fortuna. I've been listening to you spout your shit for almost twenty years. It's time to muzzle it once and for all."

Through an expression of panic, Melanie shouted, "Oliver, don't."

I saw a streak of yellow coming at my head. It caught me above my right ear, bringing a crash of thunder and a bolt of lightning. Then, I didn't see anything except the floor, which came up really, really fast before it disappeared.

23

I came to, my arms and legs tied to a leather chair, surrounded by walls of soft fern and a floor of cream colored carpet. Hearing the chink of ice banging around a glass, I raised my aching head and saw the gauzy form of Oliver Dines standing at a wood-paneled bar, taking a slug of his drink while nodding at something being said by a tall muscular man in a black muscle shirt and black slacks. The guy standing with Oliver wore a small red K tattooed onto his neck, so I knew who he was, and it made sense, because I now knew one hundred percent who Oliver was, too. I had one hell of a headache, especially on my right side where it felt as if my skull had been the final destination of a runaway train. An unfamiliar wave of weakness came over me and I dropped my chin back into my chest and saw some dried blood staining the front of my pants. I didn't need to look into a mirror to know it was mine.

Oliver's voice came from somewhere inside a deep well and said, "Well, looks like my old friend has finally left dreamland. You've been out for a very long time, Big Guy. It's Saturday evening. Seven o'clock to be exact. You would have been out forever if I had my way, but Ileana, for some crazy reason of her own, wants to keep you alive. It looks like she has some unfinished business with you and needs to take care of that before I get the chance to take care of mine."

Raising my head slowly, I said, "Oliver, what about Melanie? What did you do to her?"

Turning to the man in black, Oliver answered, "See what I mean, Josef. This is what I'm up against. Our friend here is a real golden boy, a true blue American hero. He wakes up after taking ten shots from a brass lamp to the head and the first thing he wants to know is how my wife is doing. Doesn't that just make you want to piss your pants? He's about to get iced, and this fucking guy is only worried about my wife. Makes you wonder about what might have been going on between those two, doesn't it?"

Oliver walked over to me, picked my face up by the chin so that our eyes met, and added coolly, "You should be more worried about yourself, Gabe. Melanie's okay. I wouldn't hurt her. I love her and she loves me. Our problem has always been that she still loved you. She says it's not true and that you guys haven't been intimate for years but that's not the way I see it. Her face lights up whenever your around, she still talks about you way too much and I bet you've been poking around where you shouldn't have been all the time we've been married. Now, with you being out of the way and with me rolling in some heavy dough, Mel and I can start fresh. She'll forgive me for the shot I had to put onto her jaw. She'll even come to understand that she had it coming."

I responded woozily, "You're talking crazy, Oliver. Melanie and I didn't have anything going except a long friendship. We haven't been together since before you were married. If you think killing me and bringing home a truckload of money is what it takes to keep her, that's the kind of thinking that lost her. She'll never take you back, not after she learns what you've done."

He laughed and said, "Once again, old buddy, you don't know what you're talking about. Melanie and I are still together. In fact, we've never been apart."

Walking to the corner closet, Oliver opened the door and there sat Melanie Dines, tied up in a chair much as I was but with the addition of a piece of gray duct tape over her mouth. There was a large purple bruise on the side of her swollen left jaw, her eyes were opened wide with fear and the hum of tape-muffled warnings leaked from her mouth. No longer in her ash-covered uniform, she wore a pair of red baby doll pajamas, the top of which had been torn so that both of Melanie's large and lovely pendulous breasts had fallen from the garment and were open to view. Adding to the lurid scene, her pajama bottoms, cut to barely mid-thigh, had ridden up to her waist, exposing her brown-furred love triangle.

Oliver said, "Hi, Honey. Comfortable? I sure hope so. This will be all over soon and we can go back to playing house again, that is if you're smart enough to forget about this prick and do as I say. It's going to be easy pickings for us out here with you serving as the town's Chief of Police. The Kuthchakokovs and I can rule and you can make sure there are no problems. I don't want to tell you what could happen if you don't play ball, but you can bet it won't be pretty, and I don't want our daughter growing up without a mother. I'll speak with you more about it after we've taken care of your boyfriend. Don't worry, Honey, you and I will iron everything out. Life is going to be sweet."

Unable to listen to any more of his crazed warbling, I hollered, "Oliver, you're insane!"

Waving bye-bye to Melanie, Oliver shut her door slowly and

returned to my chair. He reminded me of who was temporarily in charge by slapping the side of my head, bringing an eye-closing pain and beads of cold sweat popping on my forehead.

"You've got to learn to stifle it, Gabe. Melanie will take me back because she loves me and because I'm the father of her daughter. She likes her life in The Hamptons just the way it is and talking about what's gone down between you and me would put an end to that forever. If she's not careful, she knows it could put an end to her, too."

Through gritted teeth, I replied, "Even after all these years you still don't know your wife. She's done with you. She knows what you are and who you are and she won't be able to live with that. It's over, Oliver. Surrender now, before you do anything else you'll be sorry for."

Oliver smirked, and then chuckling at my warning, said, "That's where you've got me wrong, Gabe. I'm not sorry about anything. After all, what have I done? Danny Fisher got whacked because he couldn't be trusted. Ileana knew that when she saw him with you in the office talking up a storm. She'd told him before to keep his trap shut about business and he just couldn't do it. I was aware the two of you knew each other from the old days in Queens and all I had to do was set up a meet and let nature take its course. I didn't like the guy, he was taking my spot, and he had a big mouth. I did what was necessary to get ahead and the world is better without him. As for the others, they were old and it was time for them to move on. I didn't do anything that nature wouldn't have done in a couple of years. All I did was speed things up and make a nice commission in the process."

"What about Esmie? You killed her, didn't you, with a roadside bomb intended for me?"

"That's right, Gabe, but that's not my fault. Like you say, it was intended for you. I can't help it if women you've banged just drop by your place without prior notice. Because of that, I'm afraid you'll have to take some of the fall for the little Hispanic girl. I guess you're just too good a lay." After a nod to his accomplice, Oliver added, "And now, Gabe, it's again time to shut the fuck up. I don't want to hear another sound from you. If I do, it will be another slap to that bloody heady of yours. Maybe I'll let Josef give it to you. He likes you even less than me. You see, Sergei was his brother and he holds you personally responsible for that bullet between his sibling's eyes. He'll hit you a lot harder than I will, so, do as I say and keep your fucking mouth shut." After a shrug, he concluded, "Oh, what the hell, Gabe. You never could take an order. Why wait for the inevitable?"

CRACK!!!

My head spun, my chin dropped and I must have blacked out because the next thing I knew there were three more men in the room, all of them dressed in black and all brandishing red Ks on their necks. Keeping my head down and my mouth shut, I finally recognized the back room of *Tatiana's.* Everything looked the same as it had just two weeks earlier, except that now there was a large wooden crate in the corner, about four feet wide and eight feet long. Through my haze, I read the letters U.S.A.F. stenciled in black along the top, and the word, MOAB, written in larger print below.

I called out, "Don't do it, Oliver. There's going to be a lot of innocent people at The Classic. Don't do it."

Oliver laughed to his cronies and said, "Looks like our boy is up again." Through a sneer, he added, "Fuck you, Gabe. This is The Hamptons. Haven't you learned, yet; nobody's innocent."

The door behind me opened, and along with the driving rhythm of a heavy Motown bass came the exotic scent of a foreign perfume, putting more trepidation into me than a hundred Oliver Dines ever could. The men in the room stiffened in their places and a moment later Ileana Kutchakokov walked around my chair and stood in front of me. Her eyes held a sinister and haughty aspect as she stared into mine and I knew she was wondering just what she wanted to do with me. A beautifully coiffed America was in her arms, and as she stroked the dog at its neck I noticed the light from the overhead lamp reflected only from the one large stone in its pink leather collar. The other six were missing.

Dressed in her rider's habit, Ileana paced languidly in front of me and removed the dark brown riding bonnet from her head, exposing her long golden hair. She was spectacular and erotic, magnificent and exotic, a woman whom no man could resist. That was, apparently, no man except me.

Leering at me dangerously, she fashioned her crooked attempt of a smile and asked the men behind her, "Has Gabriel behaved himself?"

Oliver answered, " He's been a good boy. I brought him here as you ordered. Like I told you, he came to my place last night, right after you left, and told me he knew all about what was going down at The Classic and begged me to help him stop it."

Placing America gingerly on the carpet, Ileana lifted my chin with her beautifully manicured but thick fingers and said, "You are such a good man, Gabriel. Always trying to help others, but you are too late. Everything is in motion; the clock has been set and nothing can prevent my plan from succeeding. And yet, as much as you help others, even others you do not know, you do not help me. You are the only man alive who has ever refused me, and although that is something I cannot forgive, I will give you another chance. Should you perform well, as I know you have performed with others, I may allow you to live. Probably, I shall not, but it is your only chance. What do you say, Gabriel? Shall we make love?"

Oliver, growing red with rage, stormed up behind his boss and said, "Ileana, are you crazy? We've got to get rid of this guy. All he is is trouble."

Ileana turned to Oliver and smacked him hard across his face, sending my ex-friend and army buddy careening over the desktop behind him.

"Don't you ever tell Ileana Kutchakokov what she should do. If you again do such a thing, Oliver, let me assure you, it shall be the last thing you ever do."

Rising to his knees and wiping away a trickle of blood from his chin, Oliver said, "I'm sorry, Ileana. Of course, whatever you want. I only meant to warn you that Fortuna can't be trusted."

Ileana stroked the bloodied and caked hair on the side of my head, ran her fingers through its dried knots and said, "I don't need for you to tell me about Gabriel. I have been alone with him and there is nothing to fear. This man will be mine…just as all the others." Her grim smile broadening, she sickeningly added, "Just as you, Oliver."

Knowing my captor lived on the fear and weakness of others, I got a grip and responded, "I'd like another chance with you, too, Ileana. I don't know what happened the other day. Maybe I was afraid that you were just too much woman for me. All I know is I can't wait to be with you. If this is my last go around, I can't think of a better way to go."

Oliver interrupted again, this time barking into Ileana's back from across the room, "Listen to that bullshit! He'll say anything to stay alive."

Lifting a menacing eyebrow, Ileana asked, "Are you telling me that what he says is not true? Are you saying Gabriel does not desire to be with me?"

"No, Ileana, I'm not saying that at all. I'm just saying you can't trust him."

"All of you out now," she ordered. "I want to be alone with Gabriel. An hour should be enough. Return then and I will judge if Gabriel is to live. It will depend on him, of course. On him and his performance."

"But, Ileana," Oliver protested.

Ileana commanded, "Leave, now. There is no way out of this room save that door. Guard it. Do not enter unless I call and make sure Gabriel does not leave unless he is on my arm. Am I clear?"

Ileana was as clear as a silver bullet and none of the five men said another word. The four in black put their eyes to the floor and scampered from the room, and Oliver, after throwing me a look that could only mean he wished I was already dead, left also, plodding across the thick carpet with heavy feet that didn't want to leave, shutting the door slowly behind him as he did.

Finally alone, Ileana leaned forward and kissed me lightly on my lips, the tip of her cold tongue piercing my mouth to touch the tip of mine. She moaned languorously at that meeting, but for me, that tongue of hers felt more like a steel stiletto being shoved into my back than the sweet kiss she intended, but I played along, and when she moved away, I purred, "That was nice."

Rapturously, Ileana responded, "It was good for me, too, Gabriel. Already I am wet from you." Through heavy breathing, she added, "Before I make you mine, I will excite you to the point that you will cry to be with me."

I said, "I don't think I've ever cried to be with a woman, Ileana. Not real tears anyway. If you can do that, more power to you. What have you got in mind?"

My seductress sidled to the desk, opened a drawer, and pushed a button, filling the room with soft sweet music. Gliding towards me in what had all the markings of a somnambulistic trance, she halted mere feet in front of me and that's when the real show began.

Like a tall golden willow caught by a summer breeze, she swayed gently to the romantic music and undulated her body in a slow and hypnotic rhythm. Passing her hands slowly up and down her curvaceous hips, around and around her full, full breasts and across her unusually protuberant snatch, my voluptuous vixen approached me and brought her cloth-covered furry region near my mouth. Taking a measured step away when she was sure she had awakened my passion, she began slowly unbuttoning her blouse.

Starting at her throat and systematically working her way down to her waist, torturous minutes passed before her shirt was at last discarded and her burgeoning bra revealed. Cupping and massaging her magnificent breasts, she rhythmically swayed to the enchanting music, which, in what I realized was her insane attempt at becoming Americanized, had just changed to a swooning orchestral rendition of *Mantovani Plays The Beatles*. When it seemed she could no longer handle her own intense sensual ministrations, she reached behind herself and unfastened the clasps to her bra, letting her lacy undergarment float freely to the floor.

I gasped at the sight of her glorious orbs and she responded to my momentary breathlessness by bringing that magnificent pair to my face, feeding me first one, and then after many seconds of attentive kisses, the other. I tongued those globes affectionately and took it up a notch by licking at her large aureoles in tighter and tighter concentric circles until I reached my final mammarian target and began swirling my stiffened tongue around one and then the other of her protuberant nipples.

Ileana moaned from my oral attentiveness but I wanted to puke, feeling something unnatural, foreign and distasteful in what I was doing, but somehow I managed to keep on kissing and licking and sucking, knowing very well that my life depended upon it.

Groaning like a woman on the verge of a magnificent orgasm, Ileana began to force her breasts further and further into my mouth, until either because she was on the verge of cumming or because she was afraid I was about to suffocate, she pulled her breasts from me and retreated.

Unsnapping her jodhpurs, she tantalizingly pulled them down from her waist and past her hips, and then, after the top filigree of her lovely, lacy, lavender panties were exposed, she drew them to her ankles and stepped out. Caressing her honey-pot as if she was Madonna on steroids, Ileana grabbed me at the rear of my head with both her large hands and forced my face into her panty-covered snatch.

"Breathe my aroma, Gabriel? Is it not intoxicating?"

My face was so far into her crease that my complaint, "Ileana, I can't breathe," must have sounded like garbled nonsense coming from the inside of a conch shell.

Finally pulling my head away so that I might get a breath of fresh air, she placed her hands against my chest and tore my shirt from my body. Not very careful in her rending, her long and pointed nails behaved as eagle talons and tore at the flesh of my pulsing pecs, leaving four neat bleeding furrows.

I yelped, "Whoa, take it easy, Ileana. I like a little rough sex as much as the next guy, but slow down. I don't want to bleed out before I get my chance at some real action."

My warrior woman panted, "Are you ready for me, Gabriel? Are you ready for a woman such as I?"

I answered between deep gasps, "I don't know, Ileana. Tied up like this, I just don't know."

My Russian roué said, "Then, I will find out."

Placing the tips of two fingers at the zipper of my pants, she slowly opened it and placed her cool hand inside, but instead of pulling out a plumb, Ileana withdrew her empty fist and said through a combination of mystification and anger, "You are still soft. Is this how you insult me? What kind of man are you?"

Not the time for any detailed self-inspection, I volleyed, "Take it easy, Ileana. I'm under a lot of pressure. Just what the hell do you expect?"

Her answer was direct and to the point, "I expected you to fuck, Gabriel, but now I expect you to die."

I wondered, what the hell is with these Kutchakokovs? This was the second time in nearly as many days one of them had told me of their gruesome intentions concerning my life. It occurred to me that someone ought to have taught them earlier in their criminal careers that when you're going to kill someone, you kill them and talk later. It was a lesson I looked forward to teaching her, but at that moment, I had other things to consider, like why was I still packing a limp noodle?

Time was not on my side and I knew I couldn't waste the little I had trying to figure that out, so hoping that Ileana's ego and libido were as strong as mine, I cried, "Slow down, Ileana. I'm just not used to being dominated like this. I've always been the one who controls the action. All this is new to me. You're the most beautiful and sexy woman I've ever seen, but my hands are tied. All I want is to get inside you and do you until we're both spent. I think that maybe then I'd be ready to die, but you've got to give me a chance to prove myself. Untie me. I can't escape. There's nowhere I can go. At least give me the chance to know what it's like to fuck a woman as beautiful as you. Please, I'm begging you. Untie me and give me a chance."

I must have hit all the right notes because Ileana threw me that icy crooked smile of hers and again began swaying to the music, this time to what had to be a digitized recording of an old eight-track of Mitch Miller's chorale pitching a mellow version of, *Born Free.*

She said, "I knew you would beg for me. All men beg for me. I am every man's dream, every man's desire. Yes, I will free you, Gabriel, so that you may experience all that is Ileana Kutchakokov, but I warn you, if I am not pleasured, I will crush your pathetic testicles in a vise before you die at my hands."

WOOF!!!!! Now, that's the kind of talk that'll get me hard!!

Ileana began at my ankles and slowly untied me from the legs of the chair. Then, in the same deleterious manner, as if she thought the slower she worked the hotter I would get, she untied my thighs from the seat and my chest from the chair's back. Before she untied my hands, though, she moved away and wound her wondrous hips in slow close circles in front of my face, brushing her panties across my nose and mouth, bringing me closer and closer to heaving. When she must have mistook my gasping for fresh air as over-excitement at having her hot slot near my perspiring mug, she untied my hands from the chair's arms and at last I was free.

Placing her meaty hands on my shoulders, she leaned into me and stood before me nearly naked, voluptuous and sweating. Her eyes shut expectantly, she eagerly awaited the first touch of Fortuna expertise and whispered, "Well, Gabriel, what part of Ileana Kutchakokov do you wish to taste first?

I brought my freed right foot up as hard and as fast as I could, planted it firmly into her privates and gave her a taste of my big toe. Never before having kicked a woman in that spot, it was curious how little difference I felt from the times I'd had to resort to jamming my foot into a deserving guy's nads and how similar Ileana's response was to those earlier unfortunate fellows: her eyes bugged from her head, her jaw dropped open, her hands cupped her crotch and she doubled over at the waist. I took that as ample opportunity to stand up and land a hard right uppercut to her jaw, straightening her out enough so that the left hook I threw landed perfectly square on her chin, knocking the big blonde bitch out while she was still on her feet. She dropped to the floor like a big bag of recalled silicone implants and I ran to check out the crate in the corner, the one that had MOAB written in big black letters.

The top of the crate was nailed down loosely and it took only seconds for me to pry open its lid using only arm strength and good lifting technique. Placing the lid to the side, I looked inside the crate and what I'd feared stared me in the face. It was a MOAB alright, the Mother Of All Bombs. Packing the equivalent of fifty thousand pounds of dynamite, it was enough to blow the Hampton Classic and everything in a half-mile radius from ground zero back into the Stone Age. Locked inside some kind of titanium cage, at its top was a LED clock, counting down the hours, seconds and hundredths of seconds to what I knew was detonation. It was nine-fifteen now, the clock read 17:45:07 and according to my calculations that meant the MOAB would explode at exactly three o'clock in the afternoon the next day, at precisely the moment when trophies and checks were scheduled to be handed to the winners. When my eyes were able to loose themselves from the pulsing chronometer, I set them on the conspicuous row of glittering clear and colorless stones below it. They numbered six and at their end was a larger space where I assumed a larger stone was to be placed, for what purpose I could not be sure.

Hearing a groan, I turned to find Ileana struggling to her feet. She was on all fours when I raced from the crate and caught her with another hard right, this time a harsh uppercut that landed just above her left ear. It was a beautifully timed and leveraged shot, lifting her off the floor and sending her sprawling across the room until she wound up nestled against the far wall. She was one tough broad and tried to stand again but I stopped that when I rushed to her side and delivered my right foot solidly to the bridge of her nose. There came a sickening snap and I felt the spurt of blood from her broken bridge squirt onto my thigh. Ileana rolled over, turned a blood-covered threatening eye at me and opened her mouth to speak, but before she could, I threw my right fist, with all the weight of my body behind it, smack into that yawning cavern, shattering laminated teeth and tearing puffy collagen-filled lips upon its sudden impact.

Ileana was officially out cold, stretched out on the floor, her arms and legs akimbo, and even though closing her lights felt good, when I looked around and remembered where I was, the more important fact was I was still trapped in the room. Wondering what to do next, I heard a groan from the closet and remembered Melanie.

I flung open the closet door, unceremoniously ripped the duct tape from her mouth and said, "We're trapped, Mel. Just do as I say and keep quiet."

Working as quickly as I could, I finally succeeded in freeing her and helped her rise slowly from her chair. She stood weakly for a moment and then fell into my arms. Shaking her violently by her shoulders in an attempt to bring her around, I watched her eyes open half-way and said, "Get it together, Mel. Our only chance of getting out of here alive is through surprise. When I open the door, start swinging. There's no other way. We'll make for the street as fast as we can and hope to get lost in the crowds. Ready?"

Melanie didn't say a word but responded by nodding her head slowly up and down. On the way to the door, she was somehow able to resurrect that tough Hamptons' girl I'd known and loved for more than twenty years and straightened her spine, shrugged me off, and picked up two unopened quart bottles of booze from Fisher's bar. Holding each tightly by its neck, she looked at me and snarled, "Let's do this."

We reached the door and for the first time since I'd seen her enter with her master, I was reminded of Ileana's little white dog. America's tongue was at my ankles, licking away as if it had found its one true love, and when I looked down at her, she looked up and I could swear it smiled.

I picked up that little pup, and after securing her in the crook of my left arm like she was a treasured football being carried over the goal line on Super Bowl Sunday, I looked at Melanie to see if she was ready and saw the grim expression of determination written on her face. I smiled, gave her a wink meant to build my confidence as well as hers, and unlocked the door. Taking three deep breaths, on the third I threw it open as fast as I could and found, standing with their backs to us, leaning over the bar and watching the growing crowd, a small consort of men in black with Oliver Dines at their center. They turned in unison, and before the look of surprise even had the chance to wash across their faces, I delivered my first kick squarely into Oliver's crotch, placing him on the disabled list, I hoped, for at least a few minutes. Maintaining my slight advantage, I was able to deliver similar blows to three of Kutchakokov's guards, followed by solid right crosses to jaws and chins before I heard the remaining two being take out by the sickening sound of bottles cracking skulls.

Tatiana's was not as crowded as it would be in a couple of hours but the place was still occupied well beyond code. Those in attendance were quick to recognize what was going down, screamed in panic and began running for the exits. Before I knew it the entire place had gone berserk, that ensuing panic providing some sort of weird cover for the bare-chested, fingernail-raked, open-flied, dong-hanging guy lugging the white, pink-collared bichon frise under one arm while dragging the half-naked, red pajama-clad, knockout female with his other.

Fighting through the maddened crowd, I looked over my shoulder and saw that Oliver had gotten to his feet, drawn his pistol and was leading a wobbly crew of K-Men after us. Hitting the sidewalk in a rush, we turned left and slalomed our way through a stunned ensemble of bystanders and celebrity hounds to a top-down baby blue Porsche convertible stopped at the traffic light at Newtown and Main. A couple of shots rang out and that was all the warning I needed to wrench open the driver's side door and pull at the arm of the pretty, mini-skirted and stacked brunette sitting behind its wheel. Dragging her out of her vehicle, I pushed Melanie into the cramped rear seat, tossed America onto the front passenger seat and jumped behind the wheel, slamming the door shut behind me. Another three shots rang out, one of them making a hole in and then shattering the windshield and I turned and yelled at the car's highly attractive but nonplussed owner, "Sorry, lady, but I'm commandeering this car in the defense of America."

She cried, "Oh my God, it's Conan. Honey, my name and address are in the glove compartment. Call me!"

I peeled out and ran a dead red traffic light in the center of town, zigzagged my way through opposing rows of oncoming and outgoing traffic, floored the pedal to the metal, turned right and headed for Route 114 and the forested and twisted back roads branching from it, hoping that traversing those dark and winding roads might somehow help me elude Kutchakokov's henchman and anyone else who might be out looking for a stolen Porsche convertible with a half-naked man behind the wheel.

I prayed out loud that Melanie and I might somehow escape the raging Russian posse but found my prayers unanswered because racing down 114, I had not even reached the turnoff of Goodfriends Road for the Ross School when I saw a line of three sets of dancing headlights in my rear view mirror. They were moving fast, gaining ground and I knew they had to be coming for me.

Glancing into the back seat at a passed out Melanie, I saw blood slowly draining from a hole at the top of her left shoulder, realized she had been hit by one of the bullets intended for me and shouted, "Hold on, Mel. We're not dead yet."

Gritting my teeth, I shifted into overdrive and floored the Porsche, felt the incredible pick up of more than five hundred horses and was duly impressed at what more than a quarter of a million dollars of discretional income could do. Knowing that a trip to the hospital was out of the question (Kutchakokov might already have agents waiting there for us), I also discounted going to any of the local police stations, where walking in and saying hello to the desk sergeant with a near naked and bullet riddled captain of the force slung over my shoulder could prove problematic. I knew there was only one place on The East End where both Melanie and I would be completely safe and I also knew it was a half hours drive to get there on a normal weekend and that getting there faster on the vacation filled roads of a Labor Day Weekend would not be easy, if even possible, but I had no choice.

With the speedometer needle poking at a hundred and

twenty, I hit the outskirts of Sag Harbor, downshifted, and with half the car leaving the ground, screeched a two-wheeled left onto Henry Street. Zooming down more than two-hundred-years-old narrow streets, I sped past horror-stricken customers at the jammed Espresso Kitchen, made a tight right at the duck decoy store and zigzagged my way past the old town cemetery on Jermaine. Leaning on my horn, I blazed through a dead red at Mashashemuett Park, miraculously flew across busy Sagg Turnpike and hit the straightaway of Noyac Road. Glancing in my rear-view mirror, I saw that I'd increased my distance from my would be assassins and had achieved an uncomfortable half-mile lead, but my problem was, *they were still there*!

Beating at the steering wheel with my fists, imploring my vehicle to go even faster, the two lane blacktop turned into Brick Kiln Road and from there it was Scuttlehole Road and Cooper's Lane, Uncle Leo's Path, Little Noyac Path, Deerfield Road, Edge of Woods to Little Fresh Pond and then across North Sea Road to Big Fresh to McGee Street and finally across crowded Route 27 where my sudden and dangerous traverse brought a riot of fender benders to a gaggle of high-end cars crawling along in both directions. I was flying and foolishly thought I had made our escape, but checking the rear view glass, I saw those same three cars had somehow made it across The Distressway and were still behind me and closing. A flash from a gun's barrel sparked on the dark road and I felt a jet of warm air rush past me. Time was running out.

Onto Windmill Lane and then a race up Hill Street, a left onto Halsey Neck Road and a few more blocks and there was Meadow Lane. A screeching right and suddenly more shots rang out. My side mirror was blown away, a tire exploded, a screetch, a rattle, sparks from my undercarriage and the sound of engines flying at my rear and then suddenly, there they were, only a hundred yards ahead of me, the stone columns announcing the place I had only recently left with a good riddance and a never again.

Throwing a hard left, I crashed through a pair of heavy iron gates and the Porsche skidded along coarse gravel, coming to a crunching halt at the base of the large oak tree providing shade for the wraparound terrace of the cedar-shingled guest house. I pushed open the creaking Porsche's door, fell out and saw the smoking car, its once sleek hood crushed back in awkward folds towards its gaping windshield, as antifreeze, brake fluid and engine oil poured from its bottom.

The awful smell of burning rubber was my smelling salts, and coming to, I found myself surrounded by the glare of hundreds of motion-triggered floodlights. Blazing like a thousand suns, illuminating the entrance so brilliantly that not even the smallest of ants could avoid detection, the sensory overload was juxtaposed with the accompanying grunts, war hoops and ululus of a small army of pink suited men clambering out from the guest house to surround me and my stolen vehicle. I heard the distinct clicks of magazines set into automatic rifles, opening rounds set into empty chambers, and the shouting of my name, '*Fortuna! Fortuna*'! echoed by a myriad of high/low urban voices.

A screech at the gate turned my attention and I watched the headlights from Kutchhakokov's cars come barreling past the still solid columns, columns that held at their tops a pair of grotesque statues depicting a bent-at-the-waist, reedy, eye-glassed and caped Hip-Hop music mogul wailing a primitive rhyme. Below the iconic images, the column bases announced the name of the vast estate in which I sought refuge and of which long-term Southampton residents demanded an immediate evacuation.

Playthang!, they read. *Playthang!*

24

Waving a pistol over his head like a wagon master about to circle the Conestogas, Oliver jumped from his vehicle and shouted, "Give us Fortuna. We want him, now."

Lemonjello and Oranjello Hernandez, identical twins from the Fort Apache section of the Bronx recently placed in charge of guarding *Playthang's* Meadow Lane Gate, waved their own Mack Daddy's in the air and shouted back, "Fuck you, man. Who the fuck you be charging in here like this? Fortuna be our friend, Motherfucker. You ain't shit. Now, who the fuck gonna pay for dat gate?"

Looking around and taking an approximate count of the numerous rifle and pistol barrels pointed his way, Oliver bristled and called, "Then, give me my wife. Fortuna kidnapped her and I want her back."

With Lemonjello's help, I stood behind the Porsche's fallen fender and countered forcefully, "You're full of shit, Oliver. You know as well as I that I've never taken a woman anywhere who didn't want to come with me and that goes for Melanie, as well, but even if I'd let her leave, she's in no condition to go with you. You should have been more careful with your aim. Your wife's been shot and she'll be cared for here because you can't be trusted. You're a murderer and a traitor and I won't put Mel in harm's way by allowing her to be anywhere near you. My advice is for you to get your ass out of here while you still can. Pretty soon, Hightower's boys are going to get tired of waiting for you to leave and open up, giving you some of what you've got coming. I'd hate to see that because one of them might get lucky and put one between your eyes, taking away all the plans I've got for you myself."

Outgunned, outmanned and outmaneuvered, Oliver spat, "This isn't over by a long shot, Gabe."

I replied coldly, "You've got that right; it sure as hell isn't. Now, get lost."

Waving his hand to the eight thugs kneeling in a firing line behind him, he and his men quickly dispersed, returned to their cars and backed out of *Playthang's* driveway in a frantic but yet orderly line. Behind the wheel of the lead car, Oliver led his crew west and made the first left that would take them from the oceanfront estates to the relative safety of the elm and oak shrouded residential avenues of the Southampton estate section. Laquantrell Jones, from his bird's eye view atop the guest house widow's walk, signaled that Oliver and his men were gone and that was when I collapsed.

Lying on my back and staring into the floodlights, I fought to keep my eyes open, tried to settle down from the rush of adrenaline coursing through my bloodstream and was glad to see a familiar, if not too friendly face, finally look down into mine.

Its lips moved and said from a faraway place, "Mo'fo', you always bring shit everywhere you go." Inspecting my bruises, Romey D added tenderly, "Shit, Mo'fo', you alright?"

I answered, "It's good to see you, too, Romey." Struggling to my knees, I gave a grunt and added, "I'm alright, but you better get Captain Dines inside. She's been shot and needs treatment. Doctor Happy still working here?"

"Mo'fo', ain't no other place Doctor Happy can work, you know that. Now, come on, let's get inside. We'll take care of your shit and get your lady friend patched up, too."

"Gabe, are you alright!?"

To my great surprise and greater happiness, running madly down the bluestone gravel driveway from the main house was one of the most beautiful women on the planet and a woman with whom I had spent more than one superbly amorous evening. Dressed in white tennis sneakers, tight fitting blue jeans, a loose Southampton sweatshirt to hide her incredible curves and a set of dreadlock extensions flying wildly in the wind, the sight of her immediately caused my posture to improve, my smile to reappear and my fingers to comb through my knotted hair for some fast personal grooming, but where I should have been most alert, I noticed there was still nothing.

I called, "I'm okay, Roxanne, just some minor cuts and bruises. I'll be fine in no time."

Roxanne Rosario, the Reigning Queen of Hip Hop and Sylvester Hightower's featured performer on his latest summer tour, came hurtling into my arms. With tears in her eyes, she looked into mine and asked, "Can't I leave you for even a little while without you getting busted up? Gabe, what is wrong with you?"

I answered, "There's nothing wrong with me that you couldn't cure." But not seeing the look of love I was hoping for, I added defensively, "You're mistaken, Roxanne. I haven't done anything wrong. I'm just trying to protect my town and got mixed up with a bunch of bad people."

Pointing at Melanie Dines being rushed to the operating room on the second floor of *Playthang's* main house, where I assumed Dr. Happy would soon feed her some pills and take care of her wounds, Roxanne asked, "What in the world is that?"

With a chance at vindication, I answered, "That's the new Southampton Chief of Police. I just saved her life."

"Gabe, what have you gotten yourself into this time?"

I was long past giving out reasons to anyone for my actions, and checking out the way her magnificent breasts were filling that baggy sweatshirt, I ignored her question and said, "Say, Roxanne, I'm still feeling kind of weak. Think we can maybe go inside where you could help me out a bit. You know, maybe get my blood flowing a little."

"*OOOOWEEEE*! Mothafucka is up to his old shit again. Why the fuck do it always have to be with me and my girl? Why the fuck do it always have to be with me?"

Uh-Oh!!!

I should have known that if Roxanne was around, then so would her HipHop huckster, Sylvester Hightower, better known throughout the civilized and uncivilized world as The Notorious S.H.I.T., owner of *Playthang!* He was following in Roxanne's path, wearing an electric blue dashiki over a pair of faded blue jeans and moving towards me faster than a tidal wave in a hurricane.

His tongue flapping faster than a shredded window shade caught in that storm, he got into my face and yelped, "OOOOWEEEE! Mothafucka, look what the fuck you did to my fucking gate. I mean, what the fuck? You gots to drive through my gate? That thing was imported from Bretagne in Northern France, Mothafucka. That's France, man, not some shithole in Queens or Hunts Point or wherever you get your shit. You got some balls crashing through my gate like that. You will get my bill, Mothafucka. You can be sure of that. You will get my bill and you will pay. Now, take your hands off Ro. She's my woman and I don't wants you anywhere near her."

I swallowed some bile and said, "Hello, Hightower, it's nice to see you again." Looking at Roxanne, I asked, "Is it true? Are you Hightower's girl?"

Roxanne laughed and answered, "You know how territorial Sylvester is. He thinks that all the girls in the show are his so long as we're touring." Looking at her boss, she shot him a pair of fiery eyes and added, "We're home now, Sylvester. It's time to chill."

"Chill? Did you just say, 'chill'? Mothafucka crashes through my imported gate, brings a troupe of gun-toting Eastern European mothafuckas after him, threatens my place with gunfire, drops off a white woman with a bullet hole in her back and wraps his arms around my girl like he's a toasted bun smothering a corndog with all the fixin's, and you tell me to chill?"

Roxanne sighed, and walking soberly to her mentor, pointed a stiff finger into his curdled face and said, "Sylvester, I don't want to have to tell you this again. I am not your property. I am my own woman. Get that through your head."

His tiny face a wrinkled raisin, Hightower cried, "Man, I'm sorry, Ro, but just seeing Fortuna makes me crazy. I can't stands the man. You know that."

"I do know that, Sylvester, but I like him and in my own way I love him and you will treat him with respect." Placing a long and enticing arm around my waist, Roxanne added, "Now, let's all go into the house and Gabe can tell us about what's going on." Leaning into me, she concluded by whispering into my good ear, the one that wasn't still ringing from its encounter with a brass table lamp, "Including you're unusually humble condition, which I noticed when you drew me close."

"My condition?" I howled.

Taking me by my hand and leading me to the mansion, Roxanne knew what I needed just as well as I did, but there were things that had to be taken care of and I knew we'd just have to wait a while for our reunion. I hoped we wouldn't have to wait too long, though, because even I was starting to have doubts, and for me, that was a first.

25

Nothing like the high strung impresario who owned it, *Playthang!* was all first class. Furnished expensively and extensively with rare French and Italian antiques, its linen white walls were adorned by numerous masterpieces by Picasso, Degas, Cezanne, and Monet, its floors were of the finest imported Travertine marble, and its architecture was Jeffersonian, with enoughs columns, arches and windows to make you feel like you were in Monticello.

Holding Roxanne's hand, I followed Hightower and Romey through the living room, out a set of French doors and onto a bluestone terrace overlooking the Atlantic. We walked to the railing, and although holding Roxanne's hand was mildly recuperative, reaching the marble balustrade at the terrace's end I recognized again how weak I was and took a firm grip of it.

"Muthafucka," Hightower began, "I still get pain from that bullet I got in my ass the last time I helped you. I ain't happy about seeing that ugly face of yours and I want to know what kind of shit you've gotten me into now."

Roxanne interjected, "Sylvester, that time at The Castle you were helping me as much as you were helping Gabe."

Hightower chirped, "Yeah, and you were helping Mothafucka and that's why I was helping you and that's why I got shot. No offense, Ro, but this man is dangerous. Trouble follows him like birdshit on windshields and I don't want either one of us getting hurt."

Breaking into their inane argument, I said, "Nobody has to get shot, Hightower."

The hipster turned to me, and grinning insanely, responded through a golden grill, "Tell that to the Chief of Police, Mothafucka."

Roxanne sighed and said, "Sylvester, let's hear Gabe out. Trouble may follow him wherever he goes, but that's because he won't shy from it. He meets it head on and because of that he sometimes stops a lot of other bad things from happening. Let's listen to what he has to say."

Hightower's shoulders dropped a good four inches, his face became a bowl of chocolate putty, and turning to me, he said, not in that shrieking falsetto he'd made his trademark but in that deep baritone he rarely allowed anyone to hear, "Alright, Fortuna, what's the problem and what do you need. If I can help you, I might. But let's get something straight. I don't like you. Everything I do, I do for Ro."

This was not news, but having learned from previous entanglements that Hightower's word was his bond, I told him and Roxanne all about The Kutchakokov's, what Wo Tu Yu told me, that Homeland Security was involved and what I thought the group from TRASH had planned. Midway through my briefing, I saw Romey's big eyes roll back into his forehead and then I saw Hightower's do the same. Only Roxanne remained steadfast, taking my hand and squeezing it when I recounted my narrow escape from *Tatiana's*.

"Well, there you have it," I said. "I'm going to need your help if I'm going to stop TRASH from destroying The Hamptons."

Hightower looked to the heavens and cried, "All my life, I've been fighting against poor white trash and now Fortuna brings them to me again, this time right to my doorstep." Turning his glassy stare at me, he concluded, "The only difference is, this poor white trash has big money and will kill whatever gets in its way."

I said, "That's right, Hightower. This gang will kill men, women and children, Blacks, Whites, Latinos and Asians. It wants only power and will do anything to get it." Noticing Hightower's unenthusiastic expression, I resorted to Plan B and added, "If The Kutchakokovs get away with their plan, your estate will be worthless. Who'd want to live here, a place run by Russian thugs and mobsters who'll pay pennies on the dollar for any property they desire, even for a piece of property as exclusive as *Playthang!*"

I must have said something right because Hightower's brow furrowed into more rows than a sharecropper's money field, his falsetto returned and he shouted penuriously, "OOOWEEE! Pennies on the dollar? What the fuck you talking about, Mothafucka?"

I answered, "Well, just what do you think your property will be worth if The Kutchakokov's are successful? Who do you think is going to make an offer to buy *Playthang!*? And what do you think those buyers will do should you say 'no' to their offer?"

Hightower thought for a moment and then shrieked, "Mothafucka, we've got to stop them."

"Glad you see it my way, Hightower."

"I ain't seeing shit your way, Fortuna. I'm just preserving what's mine. Now what's your plan?"

Knowing that Hightower, in his own urban way, had become something of a king of The Hamptons, I asked, "Have you got a horse entered in the Hampton Classic?

He screeched, "Does Obama want his hand in my pocket? Of course I've got a horse in The Classic. Black Beauty is my pony's name, she's being ridden by Keishalatoyashantaquantisha Washington, and we're going to win first prize in the $250,000 FTI Grand Prix and World Cup Qualifier. That's the highlight and final event of the tournament. It's supposed to start at one tomorrow afternoon and by three I expect to be on the reviewing stand holding the winner's trophy in my hands. The only reason Ro and I left the tour was to come home and collect that piece of silver. I'm going to be the first Black man to own a horse that wins the FTI. Not bad, eh, Mothafucka?"

I answered, "It's not bad if you collect. The Kutchakokovs have other ideas. Now, here's what I suggest."

I laid out my plans for the event, as haphazard and dependent upon good fortune as they were, and was interrupted only occasionally by a precipitous rolling of Romey's eyes and a thousand pops, squeals, shrieks and squeaks thrown out by Hightower. When finished, I looked at the trio and said, "Well, are you with me?"

Hightower said, "You is one crazy mothafucka, Mothafucka."

Romey moaned, "Fortuna, you is one sick mo'fo'."

Roxanne kissed my cheek, squeezed my hand and said, "We're with you, Gabe. All the way."

Relieved to have someone in my corner, I sighed weakly and took a look over the railing at the moonlit waves. A sudden streak of white left the beach and came hurtling up the stairs to the terrace. Drenched by ocean water and covered with speckled bits of sea weed and diamond white sand, America rushed towards me, hurled herself into my open arms, and licked my face like I was the last piece of carrion on a city sidewalk.

"What the fuck is that, Fortuna?" Hightower cried. "I don't like no dogs in my house. They make mess, Mothafucka. I gots expensive carpeting to consider."

Hugging Ileana's little white dog close, I said, "Hold your horses, Hightower. This little beauty's name is America. She's the thing from which dreams are made, and I think maybe the answer to our prayers.

26

Roxanne and I said good night to Hightower, and with me pulling little America along by her pink leather leash, we climbed the wide radial staircase to my bedroom. We didn't talk as we walked along the deep pile carpeting and I wondered if that was because Roxanne was thinking about making love with me as much as I was thinking about making love with her, but upon reaching my door, she turned, kissed me lightly on my lips, and said good night, sounding and acting more like a long lost sister than the woman I'd had crazy sex with only a few months earlier. Old habits are hard to break, though, and placing my hands around her waist, I pulled her close and gazed longingly into her eyes.

Roxanne leaned away and said, "I told you months ago, Gabe, we are no longer lovers. I do love you, but not in that special way I want to love my man. I am a proud Black woman. I will not cheapen myself by giving my body away, not even to you, and I say that knowing you're the greatest lover I've ever had and probably ever will have. I just won't do it."

I appreciated her desire to share her bed only with a man who was to be her lifetime partner and we both knew, no matter how much we cared for each other, I wasn't that guy, but being in big trouble, I put that ethical matter behind me and said, "Roxanne, I'm really hurting. What do you say, for old times sake, maybe just once, huh?"

Her jaw dropping with surprise, she exclaimed, "My God, Gabe, you are desperate! I never thought I'd ever hear you beg for sex."

Releasing her from my arms, I blurted, "Who's begging. I just thought it would be fun if you and I could get it together one last time before I went up against The Kutchakokovs. I mean, you never know what might happen. This could be our last chance. What do you say?"

Roxanne stepped away, and then because she remembered how great sex with me could be or because she felt my perilous predicament and was being kind, she smiled beguilingly, leaned into me, and brought her lips to mine.

We began a slow and rapturous kiss. Exquisite moments passed and our mutual excitement grew, spreading through our bodies like thick lava flowing from an ancient volcano about to blow but holding back its steam until the moment for eruption peaked. Squeezing her tightly within my arms, Roxanne met my strong embrace with the penetration of her scintillating tongue, generating sparks of electricity wherever it touched, making my head spin with desire. There came a guttural moan (I still don't know if it was hers or mine) and she reached behind my head and pulled my mouth down harder upon hers. Her maddened tongue, darting wildly about, at last entangled itself with mine and the two engaged in a tantalizing tango, blowing my mind and electrifying me to the point of swooning.

I broke away and brought my mouth to Roxanne's long and

lovely neck, flooding that swanlike isthmus with hundreds of hot and sultry kisses as my hands swept her body, traveled inside and up her loose sweatshirt and finally stopped their erogenous search at her magnificent breasts. Cupping each within my strong hands, I squeezed tightly, all the while thumbing her taut dark brown nipples until they became as hard and round as hazelnuts.

Roxanne moaned, her breathing grew deeper and faster, and when her body pressed into mine, she worked her knee between my legs, spreading them and giving her open access to anything of mine she craved. Removing a hand from the back of my neck, she placed it against the front of my pants and pulled down on my zipper. Her long and delicate fingers reached into the darkness and ---

NOTHING!

Roxanne's eyes flew open at her inauspicious discovery, and stepping away from me, panted, "I'm sorry, Gabe, but the problem you have might not be something I can fix. Being near you and remembering what you can do to me got me weak for a moment, but this isn't right. Maybe you should just forget about sex for a while. After all, you've got more important things to think about."

More important things?!

I felt a new kind of fear and said, "I can't figure it out, Rox. This kind of thing happens to other men, not me. What am I going to do when all this shit is over? What if it doesn't go away?"

Roxanne took my hand and said, "We can fix you, Gabe. Go back to when this problem began. We can figure it out together."

The source of my current problem wasn't too difficult to recall and I replied, "It all started when I had a chance to score with

Ileana Kutchakokov out at her place. You've got to understand, Rox, you're one of the most beautiful women of color in the world but this Kutchakokov babe is probably the same thing for Caucasians. I mean, she is just incredible." Noticing the sudden mask of disapproval on Roxanne's face, I tempered my enthusiasm and continued, saying, "Anyway, I had a big chance with her but for some reason I didn't work. Since then, no matter what I think or do, it's always the same. Nothing. There's just no movement on my side of the ball. I'd say I was shooting blanks but I'm not shooting anything. Oh hell, I don't know what to say."

Roxanne said, "Take it easy, Gabe. I don't want to say this happens to all men, because you're right, you're Gabriel Fortuna and unlike any man I've ever known, but I assure you, this too will pass. When it comes to making love, you're the king. Just give it some time. You'll see; when the pressure's off, you'll be king again."

I didn't want to say it, but I thought everything Roxanne said was all a bunch of bullshit. Pressure was not anything that had ever bothered me. I liked pressure. I thrived on pressure. She was right about one thing though, I was Gabriel Fortuna, and being who I am I've lived much of my life under pressure, sometimes under extreme pressure, and I never before had a problem with getting it up when a beautiful woman offered herself. No, it was something other than mere pressure that was defeating me; there was something else working on my libido but I just couldn't figure out what it was.

I thanked Roxanne for her understanding, limited though it had been, and then asked her one last time to reconsider and come to my room to help me out.

My urban goddess smiled, kissed my cheek and told me to get some rest. In other words, No!

I hit the sack and America came out of hiding and scratched at the side of my bed. I leaned over, picked her up and placed her next to me, where, after cuddling beside me for a few moments, she turned onto her back and exposed her belly for me to pet. She really was a sweet dog, and once she sensed I was tiring of fondling her underside, she turned over, climbed my shoulders and began licking at my face. I laughed for the first time in days and begged her to stop when her little tongue entered a nostril and attacked a sinus. Then, when she'd had enough play, she lowered her head onto my shoulder, and after a final lick at my cheek, closed her eyes, gave one deep sigh and fell asleep. I watched her breathe for a while and then fixed my eyes on her collar, the one with the one large stone surrounded by smaller, empty spaces. I had a feeling, just a hunch, really. The problem was, it seemed like I'd been wrong a lot lately, and that wasn't good.

27

I guess that a severe beating, moderate blood loss and near-total exhaustion can overwhelm anyone and I fell into a deep, deep sleep. Freed from the dangers and depression of my reality, my subconscious took over and I dreamed I was on an island populated only by women, all of them nubile, all of them beautiful and all of them desirous of a sexual tryst with their king, who just happened to be me. At one point in my dream, a bevy of beauties launched themselves at my throne and began applying the most salacious and libidinous extravagances upon my body. Women were licking me, kissing me, taking turns fellating me and begging me to penetrate them as I orgasmed streams of never-ending seminal fluid from an eternally hard penis. The entire escapade was nothing short of glorious. And then, just when I'd selected a magnificent female specimen of unknown racial and ethnic origin to be the receiver of my unadulterated and consummate lust, a ray of sunlight peaked through my open curtains and attacked my eyes with early morning Hamptons' brilliance. I awoke, sweating, naked and uncovered, to find America licking me in the most personal of places. To her obvious dismay (I distinctly heard a growl), I pushed her away, and not knowing what to expect after my intensely sexual dream and America's nether-world fawning, instinctively placed my hand onto my privates to see what was happening.

Still Nothing!

I didn't know whether to be happy or sad. Knowing that the dream I had should have been enough to arouse any man, the fact that it was America's tongue possibly initiating that circumstance allowed me to reconsider those facts, enabling me to conclude that although I had been unconscious, my body was still able to discern the touch of a fine looking woman from that of an animal's tongue and had chosen on its own to remain flaccid. I told myself I was Gabriel Fortuna, a woman's man, not a bichon's, and convinced myself that being who I was had miraculously stopped me from achieving pink steel status with the pooch. The problem was I wasn't buying it. My impotence had already lasted nearly a week, seemed to be turning from a bad situation into worse and I still didn't know what to do about it. That primal concern evaporated quickly with the hard knock at my bedroom door.

"Ooooweee! You awake yet, Fortuna? It's after eight and time for you to get ready. If we going to do what we gots planned, we gots to get moving. Mothafucka, I knows Ro's not with you, so hop out of that bed and let's get going."

I called, "Give me five minutes, Hightower. Let me splash some water on my face and put on a robe and I'll be right with you."

"Well, make it fast, Mothafucka. We gots to get to The Classic. I's gots to show my face to my branch of the paying public or they won'ts be happy. No sir, they won'ts be happy at all and I won'ts be responsible for what they do. Ooooweee! There's going to be lots of dignitaries, celebrities and camera hogs out there and I've gots to get my share of face time. Now, moves your ass, Fortuna. The Notorious S.H.I.T. needs to get going."

I left the bed with America still in it, hit the shower and groaned with pleasure as the soothing warm water cascaded down my neck and back. I watched it head down the drain, rust colored at first from the blood that had dried on my hair, and then worked the imported lavender Provencal soap Hightower supplied for his guests into a thick lather, felt the soreness of my muscles relax and thought I had never been so badly beaten in my life.

"People are going to pay for this," I promised out loud. "People are going to pay in spades."

Leaning my forehead against the tile wall, with the calming water beating on my back, I tried to place my discomfort out of mind and turn my thoughts to the The Hampton Classic, an event I'd attended every summer since being a kid.

Once a small horse riding and teaching event run for the benefit of Southampton Hospital, it had grown year by year until it became the five day circus officially named The Hampton Classic. In 1982, with the growing crowds, it moved to a large and accessible location on Snake Hollow Road and in 1993 Calvin Klein introduced the $10,000 CK Equitation Classic, a two-phased competition for riders under twenty-one. In 1994, Newsday introduced Kid's Day, an all weather schooling ring was created and the ground in The Grand Prix Patrons Tent was raised eighteen inches to promote better viewing for the attending elites. Today, The Hampton Classic has morphed into the country's largest hunter/jumper horse show, and with more than 1200 horses exhibited, it has grown to become one of the most extravagant social events of the Hamptons' summer season, as well as one of its great sporting highlights.

Enabled by the Unwritten Code of Hamptons Pretension, the last day of the contests finds a select group of two thousand guests seated or standing in what may be the largest VIP tent of any sporting event in the country. These VIP's include the heads of many of the country's top corporations, as well as celebrity guests from television, the music industry, the fashion world and Hollywood. Lots of high powered local and national politicos attend too, their children often riding in the finals and sitting atop the finest horses money can buy. This mix of writers, artists, entertainers, and political and business people produces some of the most exciting parties of The Hamptons Social Season and pictures of those extravaganzas can often be seen in national and international publications, all of them extolling the virtues of big money and the sheer pleasure of being rich.

I thought that if there was another event in the country where as many millionaires and billionaires were gathered in one place at one time, I'd certainly never heard of it, and I asked myself, what better place could there be to explode a MOAB and turn a country's economy to ruin? The answer was simple…none! In addition to the national economy taking a severe hit, I reasoned Hamptons' real estate prices could only plummet precipitously from such an occurrence, enabling people from TRASH, well-heeled dictators from South America and Africa and maybe even some Taliban mullahs to get a piece of once pricey oceanfront property in Sagaponack.

Leaving the shower, I wrapped myself in the terrycloth robe I'd hung from a hook and was surprised to find Ileana's little white dog sitting quietly in the open doorway to the bathroom. Calling her to my side, she wagged her furry tail and came trotting to me as if I'd been her master since she'd left the litter. I stroked her from neck to tail, found it somehow relaxing and said, "I'll see you later, girl, but right now, all I want from you is that last remaining stone." Pushing my thumb under her collar, I pressed its underside and out it popped. Dropping it into my robe's pocket, I prepared a bowl of water for her and pet her one last time before leaving the bathroom.

Opening my hallway door, instead of a cadre of Hightower disciples, I found only Antione Morales leaning against the jam, picking out dirt from under his fingernails with a toothpick.

"Hello, Antione," I said.

"Morning, Mr. Fortuna," he responded cordially before replacing the pick between his teeth. "Mr. Hightower tells me I gots to escort you to the salon for your makeover."

With a shiver, I replied, "Very well, Antione. Let's just go and get this over with."

I waved good-bye to America, shut the door, and with Antione in the lead, descended the radial staircase. Passing through the Louis Quatorze grand salon, we went down a long gallery of antique American woodcut and print etchings until reaching what looked like a baronial den imported from The Loire Valley. Antione walked over to and punched a few numbers on a small keypad beside the fireplace on the far wall and a tangential bookcase bearing leather bound first editions of Eighteenth Century American Authors levered open, revealing an escalator. We got on board, took a short ride down and entered a section of basement that had been remodeled into a labyrinth of white marble hallways, its walls covered by pieces of Twentieth Century masterpieces of impressionistic and modern art. Taking a corridor to the left, we passed several closed doors before arriving at the last on the right. That portal was wide open, revealing Sylvester Hightower and Roxanne Rosario seated side-by-side in reclining leather chairs and surrounded by a small army of what I assumed were cosmetologists and beauticians.

Roxanne saw me enter in the reflection of her mirror, excused herself from a manicurist who was carefully pasting on a set of jewel encrusted fake nails, and rose from her chair to greet me. Her hair, set in an immaculate tangerine and raspberry Afro, rose a good foot and a half above her head, her café au lait skin, sprinkled sparingly with silver and gold glitter, gave her the appearance of a celestial being sent to Earth, and her always spectacular green/orange eyes, surrounded by painted on tapering red and black stripes, were the kind seen only on tigresses living in the wild. Dressed in burgundy skin-tight leggings, silver and gold Luchese cowboy boots and a skin-tight, scoop-necked turquoise blouse that reached down and ended just below the loop where her voluptuous ass met the rear of her tender-yet-tight thighs, she was a spectacular rainbow coalition of color and sexuality.

Still Nothing!

"Hi Gabe," she called. Reaching me, she alighted my nose tip with a light peck before adding, "I've got to go upstairs and get some personal things before we leave. I'll meet you outside by the cars." After a giggle, she mussed my hair and concluded, "Don't do anything I wouldn't do."

We both knew I wasn't doing anything, and despite her finding my condition amusing, I hoped that without my having to tell her she had kept our conversation from last night confidential.

Heading into the salon, I caught the eyes of a glowering Sylvester Hightower. Sitting tall in his chair, he was dressed in a chartreuse business suit, black shirt, black tie and black cowboy boots. I figured the only reason he wasn't wearing a black cowboy hat was because that might have been a sartorial encumbrance for the two-foot high orange and yellow Afro wig he had planted on top of his head. The way his eyes shot dum-dums in my direction convinced me that he still considered me a risk with his prize performer, and more importantly, assured me that Roxanne had kept our secret.

Good! Fuck you, Hightower!

The impresario was having his eyebrows trimmed by a bodacious half-naked ebon babe, and she must have plucked a beauty because he suddenly winced, jumped in his chair and pushed her away. With his eyebrow twitching madly above his purple contact lenses, he called, "Ooooweee! Mothafucka look like he had a bad night. Get your ass in a chair fast, Fortuna. My people can do miracles and might even be able to make you look decent. It won't be easy, you being so ugly and all, but give them time and they can do almost anything."

I replied, "Fuck you, Hightower. You still look like crap after years of their working on you. And I don't want an Afro or any of the stuff they do for you. All I want is to look inconspicuous enough to get into The Classic without anyone identifying me. If they can do that, fine. That's all I ask."

"Mothafucka, you'll look how they want you to look, or is you forgetting who came to who for help? Now, just shut your big mouth and let my people do their magic." Turning to a soft but extremely large Black fellow busily turning colors on a large wooden palette, he added, "Do what you want, Alphonso, and don't listen to any of his shit. I want Fortuna upstairs and ready to go by nine-thirty." To me, he added, "That gives you less than an hour, Fortuna. You be ready to go by then or we leave without you." Rising from his chair, Hightower checked himself out in the mirror, picked at his Afro and said, "One hour, Mothafucka. That's all you get. I'll see you outside by the cars or I won't see you at all."

Alphonso sighed with his boss' departure, and then smiling broadly at me, said, "Mr. Hightower must really like you. He never calls anyone by their Christian names. To him, most people is just 'Mothafucka.'"

I replied, "Thanks, Alfonso, but I couldn't give a shit what your boss thought of me."

Alphonso laughed and said, "I didn't think so."

With a wave of a large barber's apron, he directed me to a separate chair in the corner of the room. Spinning the chair so that my back was to the mirror, he said, "You may not like what you see, Mr. Fortuna. This is just a precaution so you won't try to leave until we're done."

I agreed to his conditions, closed my eyes and for the next forty minutes was simultaneously worked on by what felt like five different sets of hands. Finally, I felt the chair spin again and Alphonso said, "You may look now, Mr. Fortuna."

In the mirror was a Caucasoid featured Black man, unusually handsome, muscular, a bit toothy perhaps from the golden grill covering his teeth and coiffed in a short neat Afro. And when I say black, I mean black. In fact, the guy in the mirror may have been the blackest person I had ever seen.

I asked, "Is that me?" and watched the guy in the chair opposite me mouth those exact words as I spoke them.

Alphonso answered, "That is you, Mr. Fortuna." Pointing to the other end of the room, he added, "Your pink leisure suit is in the dressing room behind that door."

"Pink leisure suit?" I cried.

"That's right, Mr. Fortuna. That's what everyone in Mr. Hightower's entourage, except Romey D, is wearing. If you want to appear part of the troupe, it's what you'll have to wear, too."

I didn't like taking orders from Hightower, but enthralled by the man in the mirror, I swallowed my anger, placed my hand

to my Afro and patted it and knew there could be no doubt...
Gabriel Fortuna had become a brother.

I said, "Thanks, Alphonso. If this doesn't fool The
Kutchakokovs, nothing will."

"Kutchawhatsis?"

I laughed, found myself a bit surprised by the high-pitched
cackle in which it was delivered, and went to the dressing room,
where I changed into the pink jumpsuit. I was amazed at its
tailoring, how well it fit and how comfortable the cotton felt
against my skin. Checking myself in the mirror, I thought I
looked pretty good in the outfit, right down to the patent leather
pink running shoes adorning my feet. Dropping America's collar-
stone in my tight front pocket, it lodged itself deep inside that
tight space and I felt confident it would remain there until I
needed it. I rode the elevator up and reached the den, finding a
pink clad Antione waiting when I got there.

My bodyguard removed his toothpick from between two
widely spaced front teeth, pointed it at me and said, "Nice fit,
Mr. Fortuna. You looks like you gots some soul in you. Sure you
don'ts have family in Africa?"

I responded, "Fuck you, Antione. Just take me to Hightower's
convoy."

He laughed, and then realizing from my icy stare that his
laughter could prove dangerous to his health, shut his trap and led
me outside. Escorting me to the second car of a line of pink BMW
630i convertibles, he opened the door and I stooped low to get in.
Squeezing into the tight rear seat, I found Romey D sitting in the
front, displaying the widest shitfaced grin I'd ever seen.

"Mo'fo'," he said, "does I know you?"

"Funny man," I replied and stared out the window.

It wasn't long before Hightower and Roxanne appeared.

Heading for the car directly in front of ours, he raced into the front passenger seat, and Roxanne, carrying an unusually quiescent America, moved slowly and sat in the back. She turned in her seat and waved to me, and then picked up America's little paw to wave also.

Checking out the surrounding cars, I noticed that all the aligned Beemers had their tops down, while ours had its conspicuously closed to the elements. I asked Romey, "What's with the closed top? I thought Hightower liked all the cars in his caravan to be open to the air."

Romey answered, "It's yo make-up, Mo'fo'. It's still wet and could pick up dust from the road. A Black man likes you don'ts needs no road dirt on his face. You too pretty."

I replied tersely, "Up yours, Romey," and patted my Afro. Settling into my seat when our driver entered the car, I turned to Romey and asked, "Is my friend ready?"

"Shit, Mo'fo', course he is. We sent him up ahead a couple hours ago. He's waiting for you if you needs him, tied up behind the Horse Haven Tack Shop's tent, but man what makes you think you'll need him?"

I felt a crick in my neck, adjusted it with a sharp movement to the right and answered, "Anything could happen when you're dealing with The Kutchakokovs, Mo'fo'. Any fucking thing at all. My friend is just a little insurance. Let's just hope I don't need him."

A few seconds later, a dozen pink BMW convertibles started their engines, and with The Notorious S.H.I.T.'s latest rap smash single, *Yo Momma Is My Ho!*, blasting from each vehicle's octophenia stereo system, we slowly made our way down The Sunrise Highway to The Hampton Classic.

28

It was a perfect day for the finale of The Hampton Classic. It was a perfect day for a bomb blast, too. Hightower's convoy trundled east along sun-drenched Route 27 for seven miles, hung a left onto Snake Hollow Road and about a half mile up on the left came upon the car-crowded dirt-road entrance to the big show.

Those in charge at the barricaded entry were young people paying their Hamptons' dues. Simulating airport runway controllers, they waved small green and red flags, directing passenger filled cars to the dirt and often muddy fields surrounding the tents and jumping rings. Once there, other young people bearing identical flags directed ticket holders to open parking spots on the various grassy fields set aside for the tournament. That was the way vehicular parking was accomplished, unless, of course, you were part of the entourage belonging to The Notorious S.H.I.T.

With Sylvester Hightower standing and barking orders from the front seat of his hot pink BMW convertible, our caravan was waved to a dry VIP Lot where only late-model and high-end vehicles belonging to celebrity guests, horse owners and riders were parked. That lot was guarded by a few officers of The Southampton Police Department and a larger number of men from a private security task force. Most of them, I noticed, had their short hair parted on the left, sported aviator style sunglasses and wore polished black wing tips in spite of the mud that rose over their thick leather soles.

Of the forty or so men who accompanied Hightower, half of them remained with the cars, each wearing an earpiece and under orders to follow whatever directives Romey piped to them during the meet. The rest of us followed Roxanne and Hightower out of the lot and into the flow of merging people who had parked their cars in other areas of the large pastures off Scuttlehole Road and who were then noisily and eagerly making their ways to the array of ticket takers at the end of the many converging dirt paths. I followed the Hip-Hop stars and appreciated how gently Roxanne held America in her arms, keeping the white little fur ball from dirtying herself on the path. I also admired her outrageous ass and got caught up longingly recalling some of the Fortuna magic I had recently worked back there.

AGAIN, NOTHING!!!!!

Reaching the one and only ticket-holders entry gate, Sylvester and Roxanne passed through like they were invisible before a trailing Romey offered a handful of tickets and VIP passes to what I knew was another group of Ledbetter's men and women working the turnstiles. We entered the fairgrounds, hit bright sunshine and found ourselves in the midst of a joyous mob of Hampton vacationers, many of them already holding filled shopping bags garnered at the open merchandising area outside the VIP tent and grandstand.

Comprised of a large circle of many canvas tents, this was the section of the festival where merchants catering to the high-end horsy trade sold their pricey wares and where many long-booted, beautiful and blonde equestrians stopped to chat and be admired. Alessandro Albanese, Antares, Cavalor and Der Dau were running a brisk business with those who wanted to buy imported goods from European and South American vendors, while Equifit, Calvin Klein, The Horse Haven Tack Shop and The Wolffer Estate supplied goods to those who wanted to support our national businesses. Of course, there was the usual multitude of jewelers and champagne sellers, clothiers and car sellers and a bushel of local businesses also trying to cash in on the enormous success of The Classic, and judging from the long lines at their counters and the broad smiles on the faces of the clerks, they too seemed to be doing a brisk trade.

Food vendors were busy selling hot dogs and chicken, ka-bobs and arepas, corn on the cob, French fries, pizza, cotton candy and smoothies at the dozens of small stands and carts peppering the area, giving the trendy showplace an air of a country fair. Those salespeople were almost always Latino, and although I did not see Enrique, I recognized a few of the vendors as being members of the local chapter of The Latin Zombies. The large picnic tent stood just beyond the marketplace and held enough long metal tables and benches to sit a few hundred people. Laughing loudly and busily chatting with their family and friends, the hungry crowd chowed down on the gourmet lunches they'd either brought from home or purchased at Citerella's and chomped down on the tasty but greasy stuff sold behind the picnic area's food counters. Waiting for the announcement that the jumping finals were about to begin, they would then discard whatever food they hadn't eaten and make their way to the grandstand.

Once surrounded by the public, Romey and I took the lead and became a pair of Nubian bodyguards spearheading our way through the milling throng towards The VIP tent. Reaching the entrance to that heady area, we separated our shoulders enough to allow the sudden appearance of The Hip Hop King and Roxanne to the star-struck crowd.

Like a black hole sucking in all the minor stars, planets and asteroids in its system, Hightower took a deep breath and announced through an irritating shriek, "OOOOWEEEE!!!! Fear not, good people of The Hamptons. The Notorious S.H.I.T. and Roxanne Rosario are here. Feel lonely no more and let the party begin!"

A loud *whoop* erupted inside the tent, and if the ground could have tilted I was sure it most certainly would have as most of the ritzy crowd inside rushed to greet the raisin-skinned impresario. At the head of the parade, as if he'd been waiting all morning for this one particular photo-op, came the Mayor of New York City, glad handing the toothy rapper as if they were old classmates from a Harlem Sixties Head-Start Program. Following came an avalanche of Hampton celebrities: there was Lou Dobbs and Larry King, Mort Zuckerman, Chelsea Clinton and George Stephanopoulus, the four Baldwin Brothers, Chevy Chase, Paul Simon, Russell Simmons, P-Diddy, Jay Z and Beyonce, Renee Zellweger, Howard Stern, the chicks from *Sex and the City,* Bill and Hilary, Bobby Flay and Molto Mario, George, Brad, Matt, Ben and Jennifer (two of them, I think), the rest of the middle aged crew from *Friends,* all of the chicks from The View except the really good-looking blonde one, a hassle of nameless supermodels vapidly sucking in their bloodless cheeks and what looked like hundreds of other mini and maxi celebrities I'd seen in newspapers, movies, magazines, and television but could not name, all of them making like starstruck kids chasing a matinee idol.

It would have been awe-inspiring if I could have tolerated

the guy they were feting or if I hadn't spotted the marauding groups of Eastern European men and women at the far end of the tent, trying to figure out, as I was, just what the hell all the fuss was about. Numbering about forty, they were dressed in black, and when a few couldn't contain their curiosity and broke away to get a closer look at what was going on, I noticed the small red Ks tattoed on the sides of their necks. Ilya and Ileana Kutchakokov were not around, though. She was competing in The Finals and was probably preparing herself and her horse for the contest scheduled to begin at noon. Recalling the Buzkashi match and that helicopter dropping something large and dark a mile out into the ocean, I harbored strong doubts about brother Ilya's attendance at The Classic, or at any other future Hamptons' event for that matter.

Leaving the comfortable shade of the air-conditioned tent, I made for the sunbaked grandstand and examined the gathering crowd. The trucked-in metal bleachers surrounding the western and northern wings of the jumping ring were packed with every strata of Hamptons' life. Crowded together under a brilliant late summer sun were weekenders, summer renters, two-week vacationers, locals and city folk who had come out for just this one day, just to be a part of the show. A multicultural crowd if there ever was one, there were throngs of Whites, Blacks, Latinos, American Indians of the Shinnecock Tribe and more than a smattering of newcomer Asians filling every hot and sun-drenched seat in the place. To the south, on the ocean side of the ring, sat the VIP tent. Shadowy, cool, unattainable and rich, it echoed with the clinks of toasting champagne glasses and the hollow smacks of double-kissed cheeks belonging to the people whose famous or infamous faces adorned the covers of hundreds of issues of Hamptons' magazines. To the north was the preparation area where horses and riders warmed up before entering the jumping grounds, and between the riders' entry gate and the VIP tent, far enough away from the course so as not to be an intrusion to the contestants, was the judges' reviewing stand. Draped in red, white and blue ribbons, it sat against the rear fence on a large flatbed which would be rolled to the center of the ring at the end of the contest so that awards and checks could be handed out to the winners amidst the glare of camera flashes and top of the line dental work.

The grassy infield was a jumble of carefully positioned jumping gates numbering twenty in all. Beginning with the simplest, a four-foot tall obstacle of two poles named Easy-Does-It, the course grew more and more difficult as horse and rider progressed. Jumps over horizontal poles six to eight feet in height, jumps over water, jumps over ivy covered walls, and combinations of water and wall jumps faced every horse and rider until the final obstacle was reached, an eight foot high, ten-foot wide jump over water. Appropriately named Last Gasp, for many of the horses and riders in the field, it would be.

Forty horses were scheduled to compete, all beneath a rider who was savvy and experienced in Grand Prix horsemanship. Many were former Olympians, some were from foreign lands, and a good number were the children of Hampton celebrity millionaires or billionaires, but no matter who they were, all wanted a taste of first prize glory, not to mention first prize money. The trick was to negotiate the circuit with the fewest number of faults within the allotted time of three minutes. If there was a tie, there would be an additional round called the jump-off, the winner being the horse and rider to finish the course with the least number of faults, and in case of a tie, in the fastest time.

Feeling a light tap on my shoulder, I turned to find the taciturn face of Samantha Goodbody. Dressed appropriately for the equine event in skin-tight jeans, brown cowboy boots, wide-brimmed hat, and a snug chambray shirt cinched at her svelte waist by a large silver buckled belt, she looked more like a Hollywood movie star than a Federal agent.

"Hello, Samantha," I said through a wide golden smile. "It's been a while."

"Keep quiet, jerk-off," was her icy response. "Do you have any idea how much trouble you got me into by sneaking off the other night?"

"That's not my fault, Agent Goodbody. As I recall, I invited you into my room and was rebuffed. Knowing how difficult it would have been for me to climb down the trellis while inside you, your boss may have a point in giving you a personal reprimand. You've got to be a bit more flexible in how you go about your job, Samantha. There are times you've got to forget about yourself and just do whatever it takes to get it done. I mean, just take a look at me. Do you think appearing in public like this was easy for me? If I can make this kind of sacrifice, I would think that sharing an evening of conjugal bliss with me should not be too much to ask."

Nostrils flaring, my feisty federal filly fired, "Up yours, Fortuna."

"No, Samantha." I corrected with a shake of my newly Afro-topped head. "Wrong again. You see, the whole idea is up yours."

Her eyes flashed furiously and I knew the only thing that saved me from a harsh retaliation was the Grand Prix public address announcer's mellifluous voice proclaiming, "Ladies and gentlemen and children of all ages, we are proud to announce the $250,000 FTI Grand Prix and World Cup Qualifier is ready to begin. Please take your seats."

I left Samantha to stew at the fence and took a position in front of the grandstand, hugging a rail at the right end of the circle to make sure I had a full view of the equestrian field, while trying not to block the view of anyone behind me. Samantha, and then Ledbetter, not having the same respect for the paying public as I apparently did, closed in on either of my shoulders, flanking and surrounding me.

The top Fed shoved his face into mine, cracked a stupid smile and asked, "Well, Fortuna, or should I say Leroy, what can you tell me about The Kutchakokovs?"

Displaying my golden grill, I answered through an uncomfortably high voice, "Fuck you, Ledbetter. I ain't no Leroy, but if yo' ask yo' momma, she may tell you who I really is." Dropping my ghetto falsetto, I added in my normal voice, "Sorry about that, Ledbetter. I promised your mom I wouldn't mention her. Now, about The Kutchakokovs. Things look bad but they aren't bleak. They've got a MOAB planted somewhere on the grounds and I'm sure their idea is for The Classic to finish with a bang."

The mere mention of that device wiped the superior smile from the Fed's face, and after looking around to see if anyone could hear, he stammered through a dry whisper, "A Moab? Here? Are you kidding? There are thousands of people here. They're all endangered. We've got to clear this place now."

Placing my hand securely on his shoulder, I applied enough pressure to hold him down and said, "Do that and we won't know what will happen until it happens. These Russians have itchy trigger fingers, Ledbetter. If they catch on that you're going to stop this affair, something might go *BOOM* before we get the chance to prevent it and nobody wants that little scenario from occurring except maybe The Kutchakokovs. According to the program,

Ileana is scheduled to be the thirty-second rider. Let's at least wait until then before stepping in. If she's ahead in the contest, you can be sure she won't blow the device until she gets her share of good old American recognition. It's noon now. I saw The Moab last night and three o'clock is go-time. There's no reason for us to panic until we get close to that."

"You saw it? You saw it and didn't notify me?"

"At the moment I was too busy worrying about staying alive than to think much about giving you a call, but don't worry, nothing's going to happen until three." As much to convince myself as him, I added, "You've got my word on it."

A bead of sweat trickled from Ledbetter's forehead and down his nose before he said, "Great, I've got Gabriel Fortuna's word that a major explosive device will not detonate until three this afternoon. On that word alone, I'm placing the lives of thousands of Americans in jeopardy. Well, you'd better be right, Fortuna, because if you're not, a lot of people are going to die."

Getting hot under my pink collar, I barked, "You don't have to remind me; I'll be one of them." Regaining my cool, I added, "What you might want your agents to do is begin searching the grounds. The MOAB could be anywhere: in a crate, a stall, a merchandiser's tent, a food vendor's vehicle, or under a pile of straw. Tell your people to be discreet, though. We don't want anyone getting nervous and pressing a button or pulling a trigger. Think you can do that?"

"I can do that, but what are you going to be doing while we search?"

"Me? Why, Agent Goodbody and I are going to stand here and watch the contest. I haven't given up on this young lady yet. I'm still hoping she'll come around and share a good long ride with me."

Ledbetter threw me a dirty look, and averting my eyes said to my federal tail, "Stick with him. This time try not to let him go anywhere without you." Then, after a quick up and down appraisal of my bright pink outfit and newly acquired skin tone, he added, "You look like a cheap Times Square pimp," and scampered away.

You've got to take things from where they come and Ledbetter's insult had already rolled off my back before the first horse, Lou's Girl, was announced. The horse, a magnificent chestnut eight year old female and the rider, a previous Classic winner and the ex-newsman's twenty-something forever little girl, came out of the gate to begin a two-minute warm-up around the course and its obstacles. When the team was ready, the rider set her mount in front of the first gate, kicked it solidly on the sides and the finals were on.

Floating over most of the obstacles with apparent ease, horse and rider traversed the field gracefully in a poetic slow motion. With the crowd oohing and ahing with every successful jump and moaning or groaning with every vibrating or fallen gate, attendees were transported to a simpler and tranquil time, one of bucolic beauty and innocence. Lou's Girl splashed some water at Last Gasp for her fourth fault point and the run was over. The time was one minute and forty-seven seconds, and although the time did not count in the first trial, it was good to know, another timely fact to go along with the one that said at three o'clock everyone within a half-mile radius of The Hampton Classic would be dead unless I found and defused a MOAB originally meant for Osama Bin Laden.

One team of horse and rider after another came out to try their luck with the course and one team after another was defeated at No Turning Back, the six-foot ivy covered wall, and Last Gasp.

With no team scoring fewer than four fault points, and there were four of those in that category, Ileana Kutchakokov, riding Rasputin, was announced.

Sitting tall in her saddle, she rode into the ring, sped around the circuit twice and waved to the cheering throng. Her face, covered by her bonnet's low brim and a large pair of thickly framed black sunglasses, hid the beating she had received at my hands, but with her long, long legs encircling her mount and her magnificent breasts pushing hard at the buttons of her tight riding jacket, she was still so alluring that when she prodded her horse and began her jumps the crowd grew more quiet than it had been for any previous contestant.

Over the first obstacle and then the second and then the third, Ileana and her mount trotted around the course with such obvious ease and speed it seemed that those who came before her were mere charlatans posing as equestrians. From one successful pass to the next, the crowd grew more responsive to the magnificent ride they were witnessing and by the time Last Gasp came, every person in the stadium was on his or her feet, screaming the names Kutchakokov and Rasputin. Ileana stopped her mount for a moment, whispered into its ear and then with a kick and a tug at the reins, began her ride towards the feared obstacle. Rasputin charged and left its feet, floated high and far beyond the poles and water, and with Ileana still perched perfectly in the saddle, brought its hooves thudding safely into the ground. The crowd went wild, witnessing the first, and perhaps last, perfect ride of the afternoon, accomplished in a time of one minute and forty-two seconds.

Checking my watch, I saw it was two o'clock, only one hour to uh-oh and asked Samantha, "Have you heard anything from Ledbetter?"

She played with her earpiece and answered, "Only that they're still searching."

I replied, "That's not good enough."

The next seven contestants scored faults ranging from four to sixteen, leaving Ileana with the only perfect score in the contest, and with only one team left to try their luck, it was up to Sylvester Hightower's Black Beauty, ridden by Keishalatoyashantaquantisha Washington, to defeat the Russian.

Horse and rider were announced, the rear gate flew open and out trotted a vision of bright pink latex seated atop the darkest horse I'd ever seen. Its skin, pure ebony, had been cleaned and brushed so thoroughly it had an iridescent finish akin to a crow caught in a rainstorm. Its hooves were bright pink, its braided ears bright pink, its cropped tail bright pink and the saddle holding its rider bright pink. Keishalatoyashantaquantisha, wearing no rider's bonnet atop her head, wore instead a two foot tall brilliant pink Afro, so densely woven it certainly would have cushioned a fall far better than any cloth, leather or plastic riding helmet ever could. In this manner, Hightower's entry sped about the circle to the cheers of the approving crowd.

The warning buzzer sounded and ten seconds later Black Beauty began her ride. Clearing fence after fence, moat after moat and wall after wall with apparent ease, the silent crowd watched with muted appreciation, the only distinct cheer from the sun-protected tent after Black Beauty had successfully negotiated No Turning Back was an ear-piercing "Go Muthafucka, go! Keishalatoyashantaquantisha, you is one hot shit mothafucka! You go, girl!"

The last obstacle loomed before Hightower's riding team and Black Beauty did not hesitate for even a moment. With rare gusto seen in an equestrian ring, horse and rider galloped towards the final obstacle and took off. Melded into one, they floated over the eight-foot high barrier, traversed the ten foot wide moat and landed easily onto the grassy infield. With an upraised fist reminiscent of those raised in the 1968 Mexico City Olympics, Black Beauty and Keishalatoyashantaquantisha circled the field as the celebrating crowd cheered, shouted and rose to its feet. For any who cared to look at the official clock, the time for the ride was the same as Ileana Kutchakokov's, one minute and forty-two seconds.

The announcer informed the crowd there would be a ten minute break before the jump-off and urged further purchases at the merchandising tents and food carts until the contest resumed. Most people sat around or stretched at their seats, remarking to their neighbors how surprised they had been to actually find the event thrilling, but I could not relax. The time was two-twenty. If everything went to schedule, the jump-off would take place at two-thirty and would end by two-forty, not giving me much time to find and disarm the MOAB.

Turning to Samantha, I ordered, "Come on. Let's get to the preparaton area. Maybe seeing me can get Ileana to make a mistake. Staying here isn't doing us any good. We've got to make some kind of move or Hampton property values are going to drop through the basement."

It wasn't hard to reach the rear fence to the preparation area. I didn't have to slug anyone because it seemed that all Samantha had to do was show her badge and say Homeland Security and we could have gone to Hell and back, and although the contest was over for most of the contestants, there was still a lot going on in the staging area: losing horses being taken by their handlers and trainers to empty trailers, dozens of big and little girls crying in their daddy's arms, and bucket loads of manure being hauled away by truck to be bagged and sold at premium prices at Marders Plant Nursery.

At the rear of the area, beside an improvised stall and inside a protective ring of six burly men, Ileana stood. With one hand on the flank of Rasputin, she used the other to point a stiff digit at a tall, light-skinned, dark-haired, mustachioed man in a black suit. Talking rapidly, she removed her hat, loosened her hair and let her long blonde tresses cascade past her shoulders, reminding me of the bodacious Breck Girls that helped me realize way back in my youth just who I was and what I wanted. She kept her shades on, though. No need to show off those shiners.

Nodding to Samantha that it was time to move, we crossed the small space to join them and I called, "Hello, Ileana. I wasn't sure you'd be able to jump today, not after the ass-kicking I gave you last night." Pointing to the man in the suit, I added, "I don't know who this asshole is, but I assume he's a representative from TRASH. He probably wants to know what time the bomb is set to explode so that he can get his ass out of here before it turns him into Hamptons' compost. I know it's set for three, but what I don't know is where you stashed it. What do you say, Ileana? Want to help me out? Want to tell me where you hid the MOAB?"

Being addressed in such a personal manner by a Black man in a pink leisure suit was something Ileana could never have expected. I sensed the incredulity lurking behind her sunglass-covered eyes as she gave me a quick and disbelieving once over. After checking out Samantha, I saw a flicker of memory cross her brow, and then returning to me, she dropped her jaw and said in an unusually husky voice, "Fortuna?"

Mustache Pete pointed at me and asked in broken English, "Ileana, you know this *schwartzeh?*"

Trash was an international terror organization, so I took it for granted that not all its members came from the good old USSR. This one's speech held a strong German accent, so I answered, "That's right, Sigfried. She knows this brother pretty well. I'm the one who taught her some respect last night, right after she shoved her pretty lace panties into my face. Isn't that right, Ileana?"

Ileana repeated my name, "Fortuna," but this time she did not say it in the form of a question; this time it was a throaty and gutteral exhortation of a name she would have liked to have never heard again.

Snapping her fingers, she gave a simple order to the six bodyguards surrounding her, "Take him."

With Rasputin's large body blocking the view of the crowd in the staging area, I cracked the guy closest to me on the tip of his jaw before he even broke ranks and then took two quick strides towards Mr. Gestapo before laying him out with a solid punch above his right eye. Hearing a tussle behind me, I turned and found Samantha fighting off two of the Russians with the buckle of her silver belt as two more came at me, leaving only the one largest of the guards standing beside Ileana. As I was decking the nearest of my Trash attackers, I saw him leave his boss' side, grab Samantha from behind and put a knife to her neck.

Ileana called, "Does Ivan have to kill your friend, Fortuna, or will you stand down?"

It was my fault. I should have told Samantha to remain outside the fence where she would not have gotten in my way. Now she was a hostage and I wasn't about to have her death on my hands. Dropping the last of the Russians near me with a crisp left cross, I looked at Ileana and said, "I'll stop. Just let Samantha go."

Ileana laughed demonically and replied, "The only thing stopping me from killing her now is that I want both of you alive to witness my victory."

A wad of angry bile climbed my esophagus and I shouted, "You're sick, Ileana. You want to win The Classic and don't give a damn about killing thousands of innocent people in the process. What kind of person does that?"

"A very rich and powerful one, Gabriel. Now, remain still and be quiet or your girlfriend dies."

It was impossible for me to make a move with Samantha's life on the line, so I stood still as ordered, listened and waited for an opening as the public address announcer declared, "Ladies and gentlemen, our first rider in the jump-off will be Ileana Kutchakokov, riding Rasputin."

Ileana threw me one last sneer, mounted her horse and trotted onto the field, leaving us alone with her men. Situated as we were behind the fence, I couldn't see her ride but I could tell from the crowd that it was one of mounting success. The crescendo of cheers suddenly erupted into one long deafening ovation and I knew Ileana had completed her run. Moments later, the announcer crowed over the wild shouts of Hamptons' admirers, "Ileana Kutchakokov, atop Rasputin, has no faults and has completed the course in a record time of one minute and thirty-two seconds. Next to ride will be Keishalatoyashantaquantisha Washington, atop Black Beauty."

Ileana rode her horse into the staging area and flew from its saddle onto the ground beside me. Two of her men were still holding me by my arms, two others were holding Samantha by hers, while the last two flanked Ileana, gripping cattle prods in their hands in case I found a way to make a sudden move.

Placing her face near mine, she said, "No one can beat me, Gabriel. I have won The Classic and very soon I will have accomplished my second mission. My superiors at Trash will have the destruction and economic downturn of America they desire and I will be free to buy land in The Hamptons at firesale prices. You see, Gabriel, I am not all lies. I do believe in America and I do want to live here, but why shouldn't it be on my terms? When your country gets back on its feet, the rich will return to The East End of Long Island. I will welcome them to my fiefdom, and no matter how much money they have, they will be my serfs. It is fitting, for is it not the way of your country that only the strong survive?"

I told my temporary captor, "You are one sick bitch, Ileana, but you're right about one thing; this is America. Just listen to that crowd. Black Beauty is circling the course as we speak and until she finishes her run you haven't won anything."

"It is impossible, Gabriel. Even should she repeat her faultless run, she can never beat my time."

I sneered at her hubris and said, "Fuck you, Ileana…time is the one thing you haven't got."

Outside my makeshift prison, the crowd noise was deafening. Louder and louder it escalated until finally erupting into a volcano so overwhelming the announcer's electrically enhanced voice could barely be heard when he said, "Keishalatoyashantaquantisha, atop Black Beauty, has completed her run with no faults. The time is one minute and thirty-one seconds. Another course record. Black Beauty has won The Hampton Classic Grand Prix by one second."

Ileana hissed, "It shall not matter. No one will remember who won this event…all they will remember is the death and destruction that followed. When that rider and the horse's owner climb the reviewing stand to get their trophy, they will receive much more than they bargained for. All in The Hamptons will receive more than they bargained for."

The loudspeaker came to life again, and this time the

announcer's voice was not nearly so mellifluous as earlier. His higher range, filled with a tremolo not heard since Rudy Vallee sang, *My Time Is Your Time,* said, "Ladies and gentlemen, there will be no closing ceremonies. Please, get to your vehicles and leave the grounds. There is nothing to fear and no reason to rush, but we have been ordered to clear the area. Please move slowly and be careful of your neighbors."

Mounting Rasputin, Ileana cast an evil eye my way and said, "So, they know. It will do them no good. In less than twelve minutes, all will be over."

I strained against my captors' grips and hollered, "Don't do it, Ileana. This is no way to start the citizenship process. If you want to be an American you can't begin by killing thousands of them. You'll never get your Green Card. That's not the way it works here."

Turning to Ivan, she said coldly, "I am leaving. Kill them and return to the mansion."

Convinced her command would be followed, Ileana used one arm to pick up the mustachioed stranger whom I'd slugged and galloped away with the man from Trash doubling up on the rear of her saddle.

A mass of maddened people suddenly stormed through the small opening of the prep area. A few seconds later, its prefab walls came tumbling down and hundreds of shrieking fanatics clambered over the toppled walls, and sometimes over each other, to escape. I craned my neck to see if I could find Ileana in the panic, but she'd already become lost in the waves of fleeing crowds.

Ivan pulled a gun from his jacket and aimed it at me. Being one of the guys I'd dropped into Hop Sing's dumpster a couple of weeks back in Sag Harbor and the Buzkashi rider whom Wo

To Yu had dumped on the field, I said, "You again. I would have thought you'd learned your lesson and had enough of me by now."

Bringing his pistol close to my face, he said, "I owe you lot of pain, Mr. Fortuna. You responsible for deaths of some of my friends and embarrassment of others, but I am fair man. I give you choice. Do you want me kill you now, or watch me first kill your lovely girlfriend?"

Barely had he finished his last word when a full brown bottle of *Dos Equis* beer came hurtling through the air, passed my head by less than an inch and cracked into the left eyebrow of my gun wielding antagonist. The bottle caromed high after impact, a torrent of red blood arching behind it, and the bleeding Russian, who would have killed me in just a few moments, had his eyes roll backwards in their sockets before he crumbled helplessly to the ground.

I took that moment of utter surprise to take advantage of about ten-million heavy-weight repetitions at the pec-deck by violently bringing my arms together like a set of giant nutcrackers. The nuts they cracked that day were the heads of the two Russian thugs holding me by my arms. Their faces collided in a colossal splash of flesh, the teeth of the taller one tearing into the eye of the other, opening a gigantic gash above his lid, but I didn't have time to admire my handiwork.

Kicking the one grasping his eye in his nads, I sent him howling to the ground in a fulltime fetal position, and then put the other out of commission by judo chopping him across his open throat. He fell to his knees gasping for air and I reached down to retrieve Ivan's gun and pistol-whipped him across the back of his head, putting an end to the miscreant's suffering, at least for the time being. Finished with the Russians who'd held me, I raised and pointed the pistol at the two goons standing beside a barely conscious Samantha. They showed me how much they didn't want to die by releasing her arms and raising theirs high above their heads. Samantha dropped like a bag of flour, but at least she was alive.

Enrique and his merry band of food vendors suddenly came charging into the area. With Beth Shapiro in the vanguard, there were about twenty amigos in all, coming from lands as far south as Argentina and as far north as Mexico, all of them wanting to take part in the American dream, all of them planning on saving The Hamptons for their children and their children's children and all of them screaming various forms of "Aiyeeee!!" while waving their makeshift ammunition, two full brown bottles of Dos Equis beer.

I grabbed Enrique by his shoulders and barked, "What took you so long? You were supposed to be right behind me."

He answered hysterically, "Muthafuck!! It is nots so easy for us to get backs here. The police keeps stopping us and asking where we goes. They say, 'Where are your badges?' I say, 'Badges? We don't need no stinking badges.' How many we have to knocks out, I don't knows, but there were many. I hopes we don't gets into trouble and loses our contracts."

I said hurriedly, "Don't worry, Enrique. You won't lose shit after I tell them what you did. I wouldn't worry about it, though. The way you can hurl a beer bottle, you could probably get a job pitching for the Mets any time you want."

I had to get moving, but feeling a tug at the rear of my patent leather pink belt, I turned and found Beth Shapiro staring into my eyes. She was wearing a tight cotton shirt and anyone with eyes could see that she was braless and her headlights were on. I gasped at the sight of those mighty twins, but remembering that time was of the essence, quickly came to my senses and said breathlessly, "Beth, what the hell are you doing here?"

Pushing her mighty chest into me for emphasis, she answered, "Are you forgetting you're still my client?" Licking her lips approvingly, she continued, "My reputation is invested in you, Gabe, and I'm not about to let that get tarnished by any two hundred twenty-pound Black man in a pink latex suit who looks sexy as hell and just happens to be out to save America."

I'd forgotten what a great liberal Beth was, and her implied message that my sudden incarnation as a brother was sending shock waves to her vulva sent me back into our lively conjugal bed with memories of Sly and The Family Stone blasting *Dance To The Music* from her stereo.

I panted, "Not now, Beth," and holding her at arm's length and turning to Enrique, shouted, "What time is it?"

Enrique checked his watch and said, "It's two fifty-five. Muthafuck, how much time have we got?"

"Not much," I hollered. "I've got to get going. Hold on to these guys and don't let one of them go. The cops or the Feds will be here soon to pick them up."

I pushed Beth into Enrique's open arms, rushed out of the enclosure and found myself battling my way through a crazed throng of people who knew something dangerous was going down and were running for the Noyac Hills. Pushing my way against the human stream, it took me valuable lost minutes to reach the one place I didn't think had been thoroughly searched, the reviewing stand in plain sight of the audience the entire day.

Climbing onto it, I scoured its surface and found nothing dangerous save the podium where the ubiquitous Alec Baldwin had been scheduled to deliver the winner's check after a few glib comments promoting something with which he was involved.

Jumping to the ground, I lifted the red, white and blue streamers covering the stand's base, crawled beneath the flatbed, and in the shadows saw a familiar large brown crate lurking ominously below the middle of the stage. Scrambling forward on hands and knees, I reached the crate, stood as tall as I could, looked inside and there it was, The MOAB, its LED counting down, showing 00:52.11 and falling.

Hoping my hunch was right, I reached into my front hip pocket and removed the large stone that had once decorated America's leash. Finding the row of smaller ones to the left of the display, I worked my fingers along the line and found the large vacant opening. Except for the dim light cast from the flashing LED indicator, there was only darkness, so I was forced to depend upon my acute sense of touch to place the stone into its final resting place. Anxiously, I spun it around that opening several times before it finally caught the grooves and fell into place. The red flashing stopped and I looked at the LED, frozen at 00:00.69.

Crawling out from under the reviewing stand, I found Ledbetter waiting and asked, "Well, where the hell have you been?"

Over the clamoring herd still seeking escape, he shouted, "My team and I have been collecting Kutchakokov's people and there were more of them than we thought. Did you find it?"

I answered coolly, "Check your watch. If I hadn't, by now we'd all be toast."

Releasing a sigh of deep relief, he queried, "Well, where was it?"

"It's under the reviewing stand. You can send some of your bomb experts to get it out of here when you get the chance. It's over though. Just tell them to be careful with the diamonds."

Ledbetter's face turned quizzical at my mention of the valuable stones but his expression quickly morphed into one that showed he'd been more impressed by my work and he asked, "How in the world were you able to stop it from going off?"

"I learned from guys in the NYC Bomb Squad that there's always got to be a way to stop these things from exploding, just in case something goes wrong and the person setting it doesn't feel like turning to dust. When I saw the bomb at *Tatiana's,* I noticed a row of small glimmering stones inserted into the bomb's casing. There was only one opening left, and that was for a different sized stone than the others, a much larger one. That led me to believe that particular space was meant to detonate an immediate explosion, or more likely, a stoppage of the countdown. I was lucky; I guessed right."

Ledbetter actually smiled and said, "We're all lucky."

I almost felt good, but then it occurred to me that my work was not yet complete and I asked, "Where's Ileana? Have you caught her?"

"Not yet. With the crowd flying everywhere to find safety and the place being in total pandemonium we weren't able to reach her. Last she was seen, she had thrown some guy from the rear of her horse and was making her way west along Montauk Highway. We picked him up hiding behind a hydrangea bush outside Warren's Nursery, but he hasn't said anything."

"Well, hold on to him. Once you get the chance to check him out, I think you'll find him to be a pretty bad man with a long record. As for Ileana, I've got a pretty good idea where she's going."

"Where? I'll get a crew over there pronto and we'll catch her."

"Sorry, Ledbetter. I've saved The Hamptons. The rest of this is personal. Something between me and the lady."

"Are you crazy, Fortuna? The Kutchakokovs are international terrorists. They must be stopped. Now, tell me where they're going. That's an order."

An order??? Is he fucking kidding me???

Remembering the Fed's glass jaw, I popped a light right onto Ledbetter's chin as much for his being a jerk as for being in my way. After laying him out neatly beside the stand, I turned and made my way to the merchandising area. Fighting my way behind the canvas tent of the Horse Haven Tack Shop, I found Kimosabee tied to a post just as Romey had told me he would be.

I may have been a conspicuously dressed Black man to the sea of frenzied people racing past me, but Kimosabee picked up my scent immediately. Hammering his hooves on the dirt excitedly, his nostrils flared, his mouth broke into a bright horsy smile and his eyes gleamed in recognition.

I petted his long neck and said, "Hiya, boy. We've got one more trip to take before we get some rest. Are you ready to go?"

That beautiful horse whinnied loudly and shook his head, 'yes', five times before I untied him from the post and hopped onto his bare back. With a snort, he burst though a seam in the canvas, put down his head and charged through the scattering people. Holding tightly onto the mane of my gallant steed, I shouted encouragement into his ears and we rushed from the fairgrounds.

29

There was only one place Ileana Kutchakokov could be going, and that was to her estate on the ocean, where she would probably find her helicopter ready for takeoff at the pad on the beach. She had at least eight minutes on me, and no matter how strong a horse Kimosabee was and how weak Rasputin had to have been after its trials at The Classic, there was no way I was going to catch the lady if I followed Route 27 all the way through The Village of Southampton. My only hopes of success rested that in her haste to escape the law she would race Rasputin too fast, forcing the already fatigued horse to break down, or more likely, she did not know the Hampton back roads as well as I, and that by using them I might overtake her.

Saving Kimosabee, we trotted along Sunrise Highway to Watermill and that was where I made my first big move, veering hard left just past the town's only traffic light, a block past the old gray windmill. We clippity-clopped our way down tree shrouded Cobb Road at a comfortable canter, keeping our strength for what I prayed would be a final push at Ileana's estate, and turning right at Flying Point Road, picked up our pace and after another mile made a left and quickly found ourselves at the beginning of Gin Lane, just a short distance from our goal.

Holding tightly onto the base of Kimosabee's neck, I leaned forward and whispered into his ear, "If you've got anything left, boy, give it to me now."

You would have thought the horse knew English by the way it kicked up its hooves, reared on its hind legs and took off down the road. Galloping past one stately mansion after another, I finally spotted Ileana Kutchakokov not a half-mile in front of us. Glancing over her shoulder, she witnessed my relentless pursuit and took to beating her riding crop at the flank of the listless Rasputin before turning into her front gate. I knew that half-mile could be covered in little more than a minute if only Kimosabee could keep up his pace but he did even better. At my command, his ears pulled back and his body moved into a gear I'd never felt. Tearing along Gin Lane at break neck speed, we got to the Kutchakokov gates fast enough to see Rasputin grazing alone on the front lawn as Ileana made a bee line around the right side of her mansion.

Kimosabee and I flew down the gravel lane, raced across the lawn and sped behind the house onto the sandy beach. There, less than two hundred yards from me, was Ileana racing to an already whirling chopper.

The helicopter waiting for Ileana was no whirlybird. A transformed Huey Cobra from the 1960's, it was obvious from the scars on its armored shell that the old gunship had seen more than its share of action, during and probably after The Vietnam War, but there was no machine gunner at its open side, no one to man a gatling gun to protect Ileana from my hot pursuit. There was only a pilot, and in his glass enclosed cockpit, he appeared too busy checking his dials and gauges to notice the bareback riding brother closing in on the heels of his boss.

Ileana reached the chopper and climbed on board just as Kimosabee and I reached her. The craft immediately began to lift and Ileana turned to flash a hideous grin of victory at me. There being no time for me to get off my horse and climb into the open chopper, I stood on Kimosabee's back and leaped into the open side door of the listing vessel.

Ileana kicked at me as I rolled aboard. I took one to the face and another just above my nads before I grabbed her foot and threw her backwards against the wall. The rear of her head hit hard against a row of metal rivets keeping the chopper together, and with a wail of pain she slid down to the seat of her jodhpurs and looked up at me with fearsome eyes.

The ball was finally in my court. As she tried to rise, I took full advantage of my sudden good fortune by sending a barrage of blows into the face and body of my terrorist temptress. After a twist of my ring to assure a proper stamping, I was just about to land the finishing blow to Ileana's murderous career when the pilot's door flew open and caught me on my side, forcing me to lose my balance and crash headlong into the ship's hull. Regaining my balance, I straightened myself and found a pistol toting Oliver Dines throwing a packet of smelling salts onto Ileana's lap before turning his hate-filled eyes towards me.

He calmly said, "You are one tough son-of-a-bitch, Gabe. Looks like if I want you dead I've just got to take care of it myself. I've set the chopper to auto-pilot on a due east reading. That ought to allow me to finish something I should have taken care of years ago and then dump you into the ocean. Now, say good-by, Gabe. This is something you've had coming for a long time."

Oliver hadn't counted on the strength of his smelling salts or the desire of Ileana Kutchakokov to get to her feet. One hit of the ammonia-laced salts exploding in her brain was enough to make her lurch violently backwards into Oliver's thigh, throwing off his kill-shot enough to make it pass my ear and penetrate through the ship's hull, hitting the rotor blades at the rear of the craft.

With the destruction of its rudder, the Huey Cobra began a whirling ride. Ileana, Oliver and I crashed about the open cabin, smashing into each other and its walls as Oliver continued firing. Ricocheting as we were off the metal hull, the bullets meant for me flew off course, clanged about the cabin or made small holes where they penetrated the craft's shell. Falling into Oliver after one particularly powerful lurch, I was able to grab him by his gun-hand and twisted with all I had. The weapon fell from his grasp, slid along the floor and towards the open door as Ileana slid after it. In her haste to retrieve the weapon, she followed it out the door, falling what had to be a good one hundred feet into the Atlantic. Oliver and I continued grappling inside the careening aircraft, and only when we heard the ship sputter and felt ourselves whirling even more terrifyingly through space did I see a look of fear flash in his eyes.

Punching him squarely on his nose, he fell away from me and I called, "See you, Oliver. I'll tell Melanie you'll be late for dinner."

I dove and realized immediately that the drop from the chopper to the sea was not as far as I thought. Plunging headfirst into the waves, I knew it would soon be following me, and frantically gripping water and pulling it behind me, I dove deep and reached the sandy bottom, hoping that eighteen feet of water would put enough of a barrier between me and the chopper to escape the shrapnel that was bound to come searching once the craft crashed.

The muffled sound of the large machine driving into the ocean filled my ears. Strong shock waves hit me and then the missiles from its disintegrating body flew about me, some hitting my legs with a sharp pins and needles kind of feeling. The water became a canvas for meandering trails of red escaping from my legs but I kicked them easily and knew I'd been lucky to have suffered only small wounds. Springing to the surface, I gulped in some life sustaining air and made for the beach.

Emerging from the waves, I saw Ileana clawing her way along the wet sand. Badly stooped over and bleeding from numerous cuts, her high fall from the chopper must have been forceful enough to strip her clothes from her body because all that remained of her costume was a lovely pair of red panties. Her long and luscious legs glistened in the afternoon sun and her breasts were still round and full and superbly nippled, but all I wanted was to get my hands on those panties, and I wanted to do it fast.

My legs stung from the tiny pieces of shrapnel lodged in them but hate and revenge are strong enough allies to overcome such things, and picking up steam, I ran at my escaping foe. She had the beached kayak in her arms and was carrying it to the sea as I dove into her, tackling her at her ankles and dragging her down into the surf with me. The kayak floated away on a wave, and as she screamed at its lonely departure I clocked her a good solid one on her jaw. She went down like a cement bag in the briny sea and I grabbed the tops of her scarlet panties in my two groping hands. With a mighty pull, I tore the fabric from her body, and holding its remnants in my hands, watched Ileana Kutchakokov bobbing below me, the bubbly surf framing and turning her magnificent body in its white froth.

She certainly wasn't beautiful any longer, but what was most interesting was the large penis that suddenly sprung from between her legs. That warty purple-hued shlong, a good ten inches on the dead hang, had to have been taped backwards along the inside of her ass crack to prevent anyone from ever noticing any telltale bulge while its owner paraded about in the tightest of outfits. I winced at the discomfort her charade must have caused her, but dropping the shredded panties into an ebbing wave, I cocked my fists over the fallen fiend and demanded, "Who the fuck are you?"

Breathlessly, she answered, "I am Ileana Kutchakokov."

I kicked her another good one in the face and asked again, "Who the fuck are you?"

Spitting blood, she gasped, "I am Ilya Kutchakokov."

One more taste of an instep sandwich to her drowning mug and I asked again, "For the last time, who are you?"

Spewing capped, crowned and laminated teeth into boiling seawater, Kutchakokov babbled, "I am Ilya Kutchakokov and Ileana Kutchakokov. I am both. I have been trapped in the body of a man all my life. I killed my twin brother when we were young, ran away from my parents and became Ileana. Since then, there have been many Ilyas. You could be the last one. Ever since I saw you, it has been my dream to have you by my side and in my bed. It is not too late. Please, Gabriel, come with me. We can rule the world."

Coming with this thing was the last thing I wanted, and lifting the mixed-up character by its long blonde hair, I stretched out its frame to its full length before landing a thunderous right to the jaw that would have been enough to knock out Andre The Giant.

I was weak and stumbled out of the surf, pulling Kutchakokov's body by her hair behind me. Falling and then lying on my back in the wet sand, I watched the seabirds fly through the late summer sky, heard their calls and felt more at peace than I had in weeks. Finally, it all made sense. Ileana was Ilya. She was a guy in drag, not a beautiful piece of ass. I didn't know it when I first saw her, but my body did. Unconsciously, it refused to allow me to get excited when Ileana wanted to make love with me. Sure, I got confused, and that confusion carried over into possible sexcapades with other women, but at least now I knew why. I had been saved by my body, not betrayed by it.

My sense of victory was short-lived. A shadow passed in front of my eyes, blocking the birds and the sun, and Oliver's familiar voice said, "You almost got away from me, Gabe. You know, it's amazing what hate can do. Most men would have been killed when the chopper crashed, but I pulled a piece of propeller out of my arm and a chunk of glass from my bleeding gut and here I am, half-dead but still standing over you with the derringer I always carry in my waistband. It's a small pistol, Gabe. Fires only two bullets, but they're both .36 caliber and they ought to make big holes in you. I think the first one should be in your balls, don't you? They've always been too big for you, anyway."

Too exhausted to make a move, I said, "Go ahead, asshole. Do what you've got to do, but you've been all wrong. Melanie and I had nothing going ever since you two met. We were just good friends."

"Sure," Oliver coughed through a river of blood, "just good friends. That's what she said whenever we made love and she called your name. It didn't happen often, maybe just a couple of times over the years, but how much of that do you think a man can take?" Pointing his pistol at my friends, he gurgled a bit, spat out some blood and said, "Well, enough small talk. Say good-by to the boys, Gabe. They're history."

"Drop it, Oliver! Don't make me do it!"

Standing barely twenty feet from us, Melanie Dines stood with her service piece drawn and tears in her eyes. Having heard everything that had gone down between her husband and me, she added through a trembling voice, "You are such a fool, Oliver. We had everything: a good marriage, a wonderful child, a place in the community. Why did you have to throw it all away?"

Through a mask of anguish, Oliver shot back, "What good marriage? How do you think I felt knowing it was Gabe you thought about whenever we made love? All those years. I couldn't live with it anymore. What man could?"

Melanie begged, "Drop your gun, Oliver. Drop it into the sand and step away from Gabe. Please, do it now."

"Sure," her husband answered through a sick smile. "Just let me take care of business. Then, I'm all yours."

The shot that rang out was not from the derringer. It was the report from Melanie's service revolver that filled the air and sent the birds to screaming. Standing above me, Oliver's expression questioned what had just happened. When he looked down, he saw the hole in his chest pumping dark red blood, making it clear to both of us that I needed to change out of my pink jumpsuit.

Oliver wavered and squeezed off a shot. It wasn't anywhere near my boys, but it did crease the side of my head, sending sparks of pain through my skull while making an unusual and unpleasant part in my temporary Afro. His second shot creased the other side of my head, in perfect symmetry with the first, just as the next bullet from Melanie's service revolver crashed into his chest and sent him falling backwards into wet sand.

I lost consciousness and the next thing I knew I was being thrown into a meat wagon, its heavy doors thudding shut behind me. My thoughts were whirling, but I became aware of a bevy of female voices surrounding me and for the first time in days felt a familiar kind of comfort seep into me.

Samantha was crying, "I'm sorry, Gabe. I didn't know what to do. I hadn't been trained in how to deal with wanting a man I'd been ordered to protect. Hold on. It isn't too late for us. Forgive me."

Roxanne, holding one of my hands sensuously within hers, kissed its fingertips and whispered, "I'm so sorry I left you, Baby. Roxie will stay with you this time, Sugar. You're my man. We'll make it. You'll see. We're gonna make it."

Beth, not to be outdone by a superstar Hip-Hop rocker, held my other hand, and in between slurps at a provocative digit, said, "I'm not done with you yet, Gabe. You're still my client and we've got five years to make up for. These other ladies will just have to wait their turns.

And then, there was my newest female friend, America, Ileana's little white dog and the unknowing savior of The Hamptons. She was licking my toes, one after the other, rolling her tiny pink tongue around each toetip and then between each sea-cleansed digit, sending a guilty chill up my spine when I realized how much I was enjoying my first canine toe job.

I opened my eyes, and in my delirium saw Ileana Kutchakokov's beautiful but indecipherable face, and it came to me again, loud and clear, liberating me with trumpets blaring, its truth shining like a brilliant comet in a clear night sky:

SHE WAS A GUY!!!! ILEANA WAS A GUY!!!!

It was in that ambulance, bleeding from scores of different wounds and surrounded by a trio of incredibly beautiful women, that there came a sudden and vigorous movement under my shrapnel-shredded pants. And as I closed my eyes to welcome oblivion, I was not afraid. Everything was going to be alright.

THE END